WINGS AND FANGS

WINGS AND FANGS

SUPERNATURAL LEGACIES #1

T.J. DESCHAMPS

All pirates will be sent to Oberon's faerie where Carmen will interrogate you.

This book is dedicated to the black sheep, the rebels, and the misfits, who, despite what the world has thrown at them, have the best hearts and most loyal of spirits.

FOREWORD

I found myself staring at the blank page and thinking, what does a fifty years old know about being a young woman in her twenties? Then, the scrappy young woman I used to be screamed, "Did you forget about me and the women that shaped you? I should kick your ass for that!"

Since I'm kinda scared of her, I wrote this book.

Roxanne "Roxy" Crowfoot, the main character, is the ultimate softy with a hard shell. Once you're inside her armor, you'll see her love and loyalty are things well worth having.

CHAPTER ONE

My job at the International Supernatural Enforcement Agency was never dull but always bordered on the ludicrous. Some days annoyed me. Today was one of those days. Not bordering on ludicrous—we were smack dab in the middle of ridiculous. However, if I'd known I'd soon be longing for the absurd whimsical days, I'd have appreciated them more.

Whimsy certainly did not fill my heart as my partner and I approached a pile of rabbit pellets that littered a trail along the Sammamish River. Alone, rabbit leavings wouldn't be a bizarre occurrence. However, each of the pellets was the size of an adult human head.

"Here comes Peter Cottontail, hopping down the bunny trail." Jada wasted her gorgeous singing voice on the dumb song. She was disarming like that.

Everything about my stepsister and work partner belied her powerful nature. Her sweet face with apple cheeks and dimples. Jada's big brown eyes with thick, long lashes could be described as doe-like and innocent. Even her vibrant green ringlets bounced with her walk. Unlike supernaturals with natural green hair, Jada's natural hair was dark brown.

Other than our required suits, our job allowed nonconformities: our hair and our own bodies remained ours. We could dye, tattoo, and pierce ourselves as much as we wanted. So, ever the rebel, my naturally white blonde hair was back to the electric blue I'd worn in my high school emo era.

The dress code applied to all International Supernatural Enforcement Agents on duty, unless working an undercover case. Jada and I wore the same black suit, black shirt, and black tie. She wore black, sensible shoes. I wore black Doc Martens that were barely under dress code restrictions. The suits weren't just suits. They had a lot of magical extras from the days before our parents revealed to the world that supernaturals were real. Only mundanes worked for the agency then and needed magical protection from us monsters. The world and the agency changed. Now the monsters were protecting the world from our own kind.

...or playing shepherd to a giant space rabbit.

I grunted and shook my head, condemning her song. As far as our friendship went, I was the grumpy one and Jada was the sunshine. At least on the surface.

She wrapped a casual arm around my shoulder. "Come on, Roxy. It's funny."

This would mark the fourth year the giant, planeswalking rabbit appeared near Easter. The fourth year since we'd released its more diminutive form from the Vault, a former supernatural prison for supernatural criminals...or giant, sentient lagomorphs that liked to hop from world to world throughout the multiverse, destroying cities and devastating crops. The rabbit wasn't evil. It was simply a pest of mass proportions.

"Do you have short-term memory loss? There's never *one* of these guys."

Every year when the giant lagomorph showed up, it laid massive eggs. Objectively, the eggs were beautiful with their shimmering pastel shells, and the bunnies that hatched from the eggs were adorable...at first. These creatures were born ravenous. The offspring ate all the foliage within sight like a cutesy swarm of furry locusts.

"Also, the pellets are a real health problem."

Jada pulled out her phone. "I'll text the MFD for a cleanup crew."

Biological materials from supernatural beings couldn't be left lying about. Even before mundanes knew magic and magical creatures existed, I.S.E.A. had a team of druids who performed magical hazardous materials cleanup. Back then, Magical Forensic Department's job had been to ensure that the mundane public didn't know how big the multiverse was or that the things that went bump in the night were real. There was another even more important step besides clearing biological materials that shouldn't exist. Light, or the magical power source of supernatural beings, lay in their biological materials. Light tended to stick to objects, imbuing them with supernatural properties. That's when things got weird.

"Good choice. No one wants a planeswalking, sentient sidewalk."

Jada didn't laugh. She swallowed hard as she read something on her phone screen. "Oh, crud."

Alarm ran through me. "What is it?"

"They asked me to collect Maria and her brother Hugo."

"Are things awkward now?"

Jada and Maria had been partners, but I.S.E.A. moved the witch from the field as an agent to a division called Magical Forensics Department. MFD not only came and did magical cleanup, but they also analyzed and studied magic. Jada had been tight-lipped about it. So, it was my guess that Maria, a homeschooled witch, had cracked under the pressure of the field. She'd be more comfortable in a laboratory or poop scooping than wrangling, and sometimes fighting, monsters.

Unlike Maria, I was comfortable with the violence and the scary creatures. Why be afraid of the monsters when you were one of them with wings and fangs to prove it.

Goody-two-shoes as she might seem, so was Jada.

"Did I tell you that they didn't make her switch? She *requested* the transfer." Her voice broke on the word requested.

"Did she do it to hurt you?" Even I could hear the growl in my voice. My wolf was extra protective of Jada. She might not be a shifter, but as my oldest friend, stepsister, and work partner, she was pack. No one messed with pack.

"No. I did the hurting." Her voice was so soft that I wouldn't be able to hear her if I weren't a shifter.

Since we were toddlers, Miss Sunshine and Rainbows hadn't ever hurt anyone—well, no one who hadn't deserved it. Instinctively, I rallied to her defense. "Look, if Maria wasn't cut out for the field and you told her, so what?"

Jada grimaced and wove her fingers together, hunching her shoulders as she did. "I had a crush on her, but we were partners, and I didn't want to make work weird, so I set it aside. Then I started dating Sarah and *really* set it aside. Maria asked for a transfer after I introduced them." She looked at her hands. "I didn't know my feelings were reciprocated. Now I don't know what to do or say to her to make it right."

I felt sorry for them both and a bit guilty for my harsh judgment of Maria. If anything, I could relate. In high school, I'd had a crush on Jada. There were times that it seemed like she liked me that way too. It sucked big time because I never knew when to tell her. *If* I should tell her.

When our parents started dating, and it was clear my dad wanted Miriam as his mate, I gave up. Stepsiblings dating would have been too incestuous for both of us. Contrarily, Maria and Jada were only work partners. One of them should've asked for a transfer and then asked the other out. Maybe that had been Maria's plan? Too little, too late, I guessed.

"Ugh. The Seattle dating pool is too small." I threw up my hands. "Add being queer and a supernatural, and it's miniscule. Do you know what I think? Everyone should just make out. Come here. Let me jam my tongue down your throat and make it better." I stuck out my tongue.

It wasn't comforting. I didn't do comforting. If she wanted a shoulder to lean on, she needed another friend for that.

Fortunately, Jada guffawed and waved her hands in front of her face. "You're unhinged, Roxy."

Quirking an eyebrow, I gave her a wry grin. "Are you saying you don't want to make out with me?"

Pretending to be exasperated, she groaned and rolled her eyes. Then she straightened her shoulders and lifted her chin. Jada might look nothing like her literal fairy princess mother, but in this moment, she certainly presented herself as regally as Miriam. "Alright. I'd better do this."

I made a shooing gesture. "The sooner the better. The turd pile is the least of our problems. We have a giant, magical space rabbit to catch and release."

Jada lifted her arm and sliced downward with her hand. The air rippled in waves. She stepped into the ripples and vanished. Moments later, she returned with two people. One, a petite brunette in her late twenties with eyes so dark they were almost black, wearing lipstick that almost matched the shade of her irises. Equally dark eyeliner rimmed her eyes with sharp wings. Her nose was pierced and so was her septum. Earrings climbed up each of her lobes. All studs. No danglies allowed for agents of I.S.E.A. Anita Maria Gonzalez's crown stood equal level with my chin, but the witch was towered over by her brother.

Hugo Gonzalez wore his wavy black hair pulled back in a ponytail. Black-framed glasses sat upon a prominent nose. Both were dressed in white magi-hazmat coveralls with black symbols painted on, adding a layer of magical protection on top of the material. Both assessed the scene, taking everything in without comment.

Getting straight to work, Maria produced some chalk and started drawing a circle around the giant pile. The witch was on her hands and knees, doing the grunt work of what looked like a containment spell. Even though she was the youngest of five, Maria didn't act like the youngest. Her brother, in no hurry to help, didn't act like the eldest.

Hugo sidled up to Jada, smirking at the pile of giant pellets. "That wascally wabbit is at it again."

I snorted. I didn't like a lot of people outside of my pack, but the Gonzalez family had so many siblings, they were like a pack of their own. They made work lighter. It was too bad that Jada and Maria had a rift. Hopefully, the little witch would get over her crush on Jada, and they'd be bosom buddies again soon.

Since Jada was ignoring him and watching the witchcraft taking place, Hugo made his way to me. "I see you field agents did nothing to start the cleanup."

Rolling my eyes at his teasing, I replied, "Um, not our job. Besides, what were we supposed to use?" I spread my hands, indicating the lack of tools and magic.

"You're part angel. Can't nephilim smite the poo away?"

"We're trying to capture and release the alien presence. Do you think razing everything in sight might alert the space rabbit that we're on its trail? Not to mention the Supe Council and our superiors chewing my ass out."

"True." He glanced around as if looking for something. "But you could have done *something*. Don't they provide doggy doo-doo bags along the trail, Jada?"

Worrying her lip, Jada didn't respond. Hugo's gaze bounced between her and his sister. He looked like he was about to make a comment.

I stepped into his field of vision, blocking his view of her. "Hey! We tried." I pointed at the pellets. "See that dent? We filled fifty bags and called it a day."

Distracted, Hugo laughed and mock-looked around. "Where are the bags?"

"That knowledge is above your pay grade." I crossed my arms, daring him to challenge me. Perhaps I also might have flashed a little fang with a grin.

He swallowed hard, the tinge of primal fear changing his scent. Hugo was a powerful witch, but I could tear him to pieces before he had a chance to conjure a protection spell.

Yes, witch lab rat. I'm the big bad wolf.

Not that I would harm him, but he needed to lay off Jada. Whatever was going on between her and Maria wouldn't be fixed by smart-ass commentary. You couldn't tease them back into being friends again.

"As riveting as I find your back and forth," Maria began in a dry tone, "I'd like to get this waste collected to study. We can learn a lot about the Easter Bunny's migration patterns and predict where and when it will show up on Earth next time around. We might even be able to redirect it to another planet with a lower risk of upsetting the natural balance."

Hugo grinned. "Like a planet with giant sequoia-sized carrots?"

"It's possible." She gestured at the containment spell. "Start helping."

The older witch patted me on the shoulder. "Watch this."

The two drew the spell together, chanting in a combination of Spanish, English, and Kairska. The last language was older than every mundane language on Earth. Kairska came from the world the witches had left. The world they'd also destroyed.

The language spoken out loud made my skin itch and tickled my ears, and thanks to a gift inherited from my grandfather, I could understand what they were saying.

The witch siblings were calling upon the magic of the land and the sky—the Mother and the Father, loosely translated from Kairska—to help them deliver the giant pile of poop to a place where they could study it.

The entire pile disappeared. The witches performed one more spell and the chalk markings swirled, rose in a cloud, and then also disappeared. Poof! Gone.

Witches freaked me out.

When the two were done, Hugo grinned. "Poop scooped."

Jada took them back to the lab and then rejoined me.

"Did she even speak to you?"

She wiggled her flat hand and shrugged. "Only regarding the case."

"Well, that's better than icing you out completely." I slung an arm around her shoulder. "Let's go hunting wabbits."

IT WAS GOLDEN HOUR, which meant sunset was approaching. We hadn't found the "wabbit" in question. I'd get the scent and then lose it. We did, however, find several drying wet patches and puddles on the trail. Deducing from that evidence, we figured the wayward bunny was taking dips in the Sammamish River.

Jada had offered to use a small piece of one of the rabbit's pellets she'd saved to create a link to the space bunny and just track him through her planeswalker gift. We decided against it. Experience had taught us that if we just popped up on Peter, the bunny would get spooked and disappear. It took a lot more time and magical energy to track him hopping from one universe to another and back to this one than to track him on Earth.

My dad was nephilim and so was I. Instead of an angelic father and a human mother, Gran had been a wolf-shifter of the Salish coastal descent. Kirsten, my mother, was a wolf-shifter of the Nordic variety. In this case, my ancestors mattered. Different belief systems created different shapeshifters. Different magics and *curses* had been passed down to lil ol' me.

I'd pushed out of my head how Kirsten's ancestors had gained the power of shapeshifting into wolves and the price I was destined to pay for that. Besides, I'd shifted a billion times over my lifespan and Fenrir had never come calling for his due.

The old gods hadn't had as much power before the Mythic Games, a niggling voice reminded me. I told that voice to shut up. There were treaties to observe, and the Supernatural Council of the Americas had my dad and stepmom on it.

Normally, on duty, it was required of agents to wear their suits, but I was sick of tracking in my human form regardless of the risk.

"I need to be a wolf."

Jada grimaced then nodded her agreement. If something happened to me out of my suit, we would both be at fault. I would get written up for taking it off. She'd get written up for not reporting it. I didn't give a crap about I.S.E.A.'s rules, but Jada did. I smiled in appreciation that she let me do my job my way.

I stripped off my clothes and handed them to her. While I shifted from one form to another, my mind and senses were blind. Coming into the other form always felt akin to waking from a nap and not knowing how much time had passed. All senses went askew until your mind settled into your new form. At the very least, shifting could make you feel slightly disoriented like that. At worst, you could not come back and be stuck an animal forever. It was rare to lose your human half, but it had happened. Shifters never spoke of the rare occurrences to outsiders—even if we loved and married them. It was our greatest secret and biggest fear.

Another secret shifters carried. What happened during the shift. My mind, or spirit self, touched Heaven—as in the realm or world of Heaven. I didn't know if it was because I really wasn't human at all or that the angelic part of me returned home. It happened to my dad, too. My mother said she touched Asgard when she shifted. What I experienced sounded a lot like when witches used astral projection —but I couldn't control it. No shifter could.

As all of my muscles screamed in agony and my bones popped and cracked, I left my changing body behind.

Before me vast plains of ice and snow stretched. Blue, snow-capped mountains bordered the plains in the far distance, and a pitch-black sky dotted with constellations that I didn't recognize hung above. The wind howled and bitter cold enveloped me.

This was not Heaven.

As soon as the realization hit, I was several feet shorter and could feel cool pavement under my paws. It smelled of fresh grass and running water. No ice. No frozen plains. My tongue lolled as I panted in relief. I shook my furry head, as if I could shake off what I'd seen.

It hadn't been Heaven or Asgard. I'd been to both. I'd been to where I'd seen before, too, but it didn't make sense. I didn't have a drop of Frost Giant blood in my heritage—did I? I shook my muzzle, banishing the thought. No way. If not that, what had drawn my mind there?

"Are you ready?" Jada asked.

Wolves didn't bark, but I huffed in answer and then began sniffing the ground. Not only could I use my extra-sensitive, complex sense of smell, but in wolf form I could also see residual magic so faint even other supes couldn't pick it up. The scent was there, but more clearly, smatterings of magenta light spotted the trail and marked low points of the river. I took off, following the magical trail. The scent and magic grew stronger. A huge magenta splotch colored a copse of trees close ahead.

Gotcha.

I stopped to shift back to human form, hesitating before inciting the magic for the transformation to take place. What if I ended up in that place again? I shook the fear off like water on my fur. It didn't matter. I wasn't materially there. I kept an image of my grandfather's palace in my head as I shifted, hoping that would help my mind manifest there. No such luck...

The icy plain stretched before me. The howling wind didn't mute the howl that shuddered through my astral form. A call home. The pull was stronger than any alpha call I'd ever heard.

Then I was back in my body with Jada shoving my clothes into my newly reformed hands. Past her green curls, something shimmered in the golden sunlight. Knowing what lurked amidst a copse of trees, my heart leapt into my throat at the sight.

I cursed softly under my breath, stuffing my legs into my pants.

"What?"

I cringed, forgetting Jada had fae hearing. I swore it was as good as the hearing my wolf form possessed. Maybe better, because fae could read minds if you didn't keep your guard up. Being of mixed magical heritage like me, Jada had a fae grandfather and that ability. I did *not* want her digging in there, even on accident, so I fortified my mental defenses.

"That."

Her gaze followed where I pointed between evergreens.

Together, we approached slowly, discovering a pale blue egg. Silver swirled and eddied on the surface of the shell That wasn't the only remarkable thing about the egg either—it stood about ten feet high and six feet in diameter across the widest horizontal point.

I finished dressing while Jada examined the egg.

"Look at those markings. They move," she gushed. "The real thing is much prettier than the dyed ones."

"So pretty until it cracks." Finished dressing, I nodded to the egg. "That thing is a ticking time bomb. We need to get it to the safe world before we've got a ravenous litter to hunt down and relocate."

"If we move it, we could lose the trail of the rabbit."

"Magical Forensics again?" I asked.

"If I time it right, we can come in right as we're carrying it into the safe world."

Not only could Jada walk the planes to anywhere she wanted, but she could also walk to *when* she wanted. I didn't like time travel.

"You'll need our help," I said, except my voice didn't come from my mouth. I hadn't spoken or thought the words. My voice had come from behind me.

We turned to see ourselves. Time travel paradoxes in science fiction movies weren't true, but it felt really freaking weird to look at yourself.

A version of me spoke. "You two decided—well, a version of you two decided that you'd go ahead and pursue the rabbit and go back in time before that egg erupts into a hundred space bunny babies and devour half of Woodinville. So, we'll handle it."

"The rabbit isn't too far ahead, but that egg is about to burst," Other Jada said, adding, "This isn't our first try."

Thank whatever god would listen that this event wasn't a pivotal moment in time and that we'd had plenty of do-overs.

Future me scowled. "What are you waiting for?"

My Jada and I exchanged a look. We'd established a safe phrase so that we knew something that looked like us was actually *us*—or us from another point in time—and not a skinwalker or some other nasty. We'd learned to confirm the hard way our rookie year.

"Oh, for Heaven's sake!" Future me griped. "You really don't think we're you? Fine. Strawberry scones and tea. Now go!"

Having what I needed, I saluted past me and let them get to it.

We tracked the rabbit from the paved trail into a wooded area. Crashing noises and thumping confirmed that the space bunny was nearby. The bunny wasn't running away after sensing our presence, like he normally did. Judging by the steadily increasing volume of the crashing sounds, he was heading straight for us.

"Ready?" After hunting this thing all day, I couldn't keep the excitement out of my tone.

"Getting there." Her hands sliced through the air. She'd open a Nowhere door, a.k.a. a portal to mundanes or a wormhole to I.S.E.A. agents, to a world ready for something this rabbit's size. We had to trust our future selves were doing the same thing for the egg.

Trees came crashing down in our direction. Jada pulled me behind where she'd created a path through time and space. Ahead, the massive white bunny the size of a ranch home hopped out of the woods straight at us. It had done this maneuver before last year in an attempt to scare us away from her eggs. It had worked before, but we were on to her tactics now.

I crossed my arms over my chest. Beside me, Jada whispered, "One Mississippi...two Mississippi..."

The rabbit leapt...

The rebel in me wanted to keep my eyes open out of spite, but when a rabbit the size of a house jumps at you, there is no amount of spite that will keep you from flinching and shutting your eyes. When I didn't get crushed by a ton or two of bunny, I opened them.

Scanning the copse afterward, the giant rabbit had wreaked havoc on the trees and brush. This wouldn't be my problem. I.S.E.A.'s Mage Unit, Agent Doyle and his Not Druids, were all about making trees grow.

"Ready to go move the egg?" she asked, slicing her hand through the air.

"Ugh. Not particularly."

Jada's responding grin lit up her pretty face. "At least we're not in the timeline where we have to chase the babies."

"Ugh. Don't jinx it." I threw up my arms in mock exasperation and then shared in her grin.

She laughed. "I'm part fae, remember? I wouldn't ever manifest something. At least Director Tan would love that report."

"She does love when our jobs are miserable," I agreed. "She must miss field work."

"That's why Roanhorse, her partner, retired. He missed all this giant space rabbit chasing glory."

CHAPTER
TWO

After work, I always breathed a little easier when we reached the aluminum gates of the pack property. The land and the sprawling farmhouse atop a hill. Evergreens hid most of the house from the road, but I caught glimpses of it in the dying light as I drove up a winding driveway.

Seattle was an expensive city and so were the suburbs. Jada and I lived rent-free on a self-sustaining farm with hunting grounds and among shifters, a couple of witches, and a few fae. It wasn't always a haven, especially after my parents split, but Miriam and Phyr and their people moving in changed the dynamic.

We pulled into a garage with tons of cars, jeeps, and SUVs. I saw my aunt's motorcycle and a few that belonged to other shifters. A few brooms and cauldrons hung on the wall. Exiting the car, tiny creatures that could be mistaken for lightning bugs—if the Pacific Northwest had lightning bugs—flew in our direction. Pixies, or as Miriam called them, light sprites, lived in her witch garden and loved Jada. No. Love would be too weak a word.

Jada was fae royalty. Her grandfather was High King Oberon of the Unseelie Court. The pixies were cute and sweet, but they were not to be underestimated. They could wield magic and flit between worlds as easily as a planeswalker, even if they could only carry themselves across the multiverse. This made them excellent couriers and spies. Which worked for us—as long as Jada stayed in favor of the king. Their loyalty to Oberon was unwavering.

A few landed in her hair, playing in the bright green curly locks. Some sat on Jada's shoulders, reclining much like the way one would sit on a shore of a creek—if that shore moved. Others did an aerial dance around Jada, rejoicing that their princess returned to the castle. A typical welcome home for my friend.

There was no fanfare for me. The sprites gave me the distance I established as a moody teen, which was fine by me. I would get annoyed with their preening and singing.

On a path not far from the driveway, Miriam approached. Her white antlers gleamed in the lighted pathway. Her skirts floated around her thick frame like a dream. A wicker basket hung from her arm. Miriam was ethereally beautiful even in small tasks. What was even better than how gorgeous my stepmother was is that she loved us unconditionally. Sometimes that meant firmness but always care.

Once, in a fit of jealousy, my mother Kirsten had thrown my stuff all over the front yard of Miriam's old house. I was embarrassed and angry. Without considering my feelings, my father accused me of saying something to piss Kirsten off, which honestly was accurate. I'd told her he was dating Miriam just to get a rise out of her. Back then, I'd liked making my mother as miserable as she'd made me for cheating on my dad. Was it toxic? Oh, hells yeah. Was I just a hurt kid with no therapist, especially one capable of dealing with the supernatural politics that had made my life a hell worse than actual Hell? Also, yes.

That day, Miriam had seen past the tough smartass act and had hugged me. She'd made tea and snacks and resolved the issue. Though I'd never admit it, not even now, that day I'd begun secretly wishing she was my mom for real.

Presently, her smile felt like a warm hug. The stress of the day melted in her calming presence. I didn't care if it was her magic. Even if her fae light acted a little like a drug that made you want to adore her, Miriam had proven time and again that she actually gave a shit about me. "Did you two get that wascally rabbit?"

We filled her in on our day as we walked together to the main entrance to the multi-story farmhouse. Inside, Jada broke away.

"I have a dinner date with Sarah, Mami," she announced, kissing Miriam on the cheek.

"You should bring her by the house. We have coven business to discuss at some point. Ostara is nigh," her mother suggested over her shoulder as she and I made our way from the foyer down the hall that led to a massive kitchen.

Jada's voice traveled from the stairs. "Sure."

Miriam muttered something about vague answers in High Fae, but her annoyance faded as we entered the kitchen. I was in elementary school when I realized that most kids didn't live in a household of more than twenty people who weren't related. I'd only known how shifters lived before that, and it was shocking to me that only parents and their kids lived together, or on rare occasions, a grandparent or aunt lived with them.

The kitchen was a great room of sorts with a couple of six-burner stovetops, multiple ovens, a restaurant-grade fridge, and a pantry that rivaled doomsday preppers' storerooms. The table seated thirty people and it could extend magically, thanks to Miriam.

There, a tall, horned fae with skin like a bronze statue, ladled something out of a large pot. Phyr, my stepdad, gave my dad—an equally tall but broader and hulky man—a taste. Gabriel nodded and hummed his approval. It had taken the pack, who had a strict sort of monogamy mate-for-life culture, time to get used to my parents, but the three of them together always felt natural to me. Maybe because I'd been sixteen when it all started, and I'd felt like an outsider in my own home until Phyr and Miriam became a part of it.

My dads grinned in my direction. Correction, they grinned at Miriam. I got noticed after they each kissed her.

Gabriel grinned my way. "Oh hey, Box O Rox! Didn't see you there. How was work?"

Feeling surly because he didn't even pretend to have noticed I'd come in with his wife, I replied, "I had group sex with a bunch of Valkyries. Before you judge, my actions saved the planet. All in a day's work at I.S.E.A." I slumped into a chair at the table. Yes, I could've been more mature, but my dad could've been a lot of things over the course of my life. He should've said hello to his kid first, or at least noticed I'd walked in the room, but I never came first to him. It made me feel fifteen years old all over again despite inching toward thirty.

Gabriel scowled his disapproval but didn't vocalize his thoughts.

I didn't begrudge Miriam or Phyr, but before they came along, he put the pack first, doing damage repair after my mom was abjured. Then, when he started dating them, his priorities shifted. Saving the world and being the hero to supes became Gabriel's modus operandi. He almost screwed up his relationship with Miriam multiple times due to his ego. I hoped he didn't mess up their relationship now that he was a state senator. My dad liked power. Heck, all my parents, except Kirsten, did.

A grin touched the corner of Phyr's mouth as he approached with a ladle. Amber eyes assessed me for injuries. Phyr played it off, but he worried about Jada and me much more than our biological parents did. Well, that wasn't true. Miriam loved us but...she wasn't always in this world, so to speak, and literally. She spent half her time at Eastside Charm School in her faerie and the rest of her time was divided between her duties to the Rosemary and Oleander coven and her spouses.

"If that's how you save the world, there was a time that I would've applied for the job."

I wasn't into males of any variety, and it was not okay to think of your stepdad as anything but a handsome older fae, but when Phyr said things like that, it was not hard to imagine he'd cause a multiverse-wide competition or two to gain his employment in that capacity.

"You'd cause a riot, Papa." I chuckled softly as I kissed his offered cheek and then took a sip of the sauce from the ladle he offered next. "Mmm...red coconut curry. Nice."

"It will have an even better flavor when the Thai basil from my garden is added upon serving," Miriam assured.

"I have no doubt." I meant it. If it were up to the shifter cooks of the pack, we'd eat grilled meat and basic sides forever.

Fortunately, Phyr and Miriam took turns on the cooking roster, which explained why all my parents were home. Phyr ran several bakeries in the area and made magically enhanced treats. His groom's cake had looked and acted like a real dragon before it burst into pieces of cake that floated to the guests. Not only had the cake been magical, but it had also tasted delicious.

More of the pack started filing into the kitchen, and a witch with brown curly hair and sharp eyes that took everything in—that is, until she noticed you noticing things. Then her eyes would dull, and her mouth would run, speaking nonsense. I caught on to Rhiannon's ways a long time ago. She stopped pretending with me about the same time that I'd caught on.

Most of the pack ignored my presence as everyone had come to set the table for dinner or do some other task—it wasn't my turn for kitchen duty, so I offered no help. Miriam gave out orders. While everyone else treated me like another object in the kitchen, Rhiannon's gaze met mine. A grin touched the corner of her mouth.

The witch smelled of wild fae magic, as much as Miriam but not as much as Phyr. Witchcraft and potions, earth and wet stone clung to the older witch as well. She claimed to be one-sixteenth brownie, but low fae didn't reek of faerie the way high fae did. The witch had secrets, but I didn't mind. She never treated me poorly and always had the pack's best interest at heart. That was enough for me to let sleeping dogs lie.

"Something is different about you," she remarked in the Unseelie tongue, sitting herself next to me. "Frozen landscape and biting wind cling to you." She tilted her head to the side, examining me with eyes that saw more than just this plane of existence and were more than shrewd. Ancient wisdom lived within them. Her voice was not exactly her own when she asked, "Where have you been, little wolf?"

Miriam turned from her duties and stared.

My stomach dropped. The Mórrígan lived within Miriam, Jada, and Rhiannon as they were avatars of the triple aspect goddess...Yes. The people I lived with were extremely complicated in nature and in their relationships. Welcome to the supernatural world, where everything was messy, sometimes bizarre, and sometimes scary as heck.

"I'm not sure."

Her stare intensified. Miriam drew near. This was getting creepy. To make matters worse, something scratched at the mental shields Phyr had taught me to put up to protect my thoughts against fae and other creatures that could sift through them. I fortified the barriers.

"I think you do," Miriam said in the same voice, also in Unseelie.

"I'm an agent of I.S.E.A. You aren't supposed to go digging around my head."

"We don't have to. He has marked you," the two women said in unison.

The shifters looked between me, Miriam, and Rhiannon, confused. "Everyone, give us a moment," Gabriel ordered.

The room cleared almost immediately. All that remained were my stepparents, my father, Rhiannon, and I.

Dad put a hand on my shoulder. "What's this about, Roxy?"

I blew out my breath. "Remember how you sent me to seek out the Aesir for the council a few years ago?" I was referring to the Supernatural Council of the Americas. Supernatural leaders had reps on the council to make sure that their group was being taken care of. My dad was the leader of the group and took those concerns to the state senate to put into mundane laws.

Tension eased in his shoulders as he nodded. "Yeah. Lady Sif occasionally joins council meetings when she's not being a social media influencer." He chuckled softly at the face I pulled. Lady Sif was more of a nuisance than a true representative. She liked "Midgard" and how much her beauty and style were appreciated here. His amusement was short-lived. Sobering, he asked, "Why did the Mórrígan think you're marked?"

How could he forget what Jada and I went through to get her on the council? "I don't know if I am, but I did go to Jotunheim and dealt with a frost giant there." I swallowed hard. "I think I ended up in that place the last time I shifted."

His whole body stiffened and his voice gentled when he asked, "Has this happened before?"

My father never coddled me a day in my life. Yeah, he'd been a caring dad, but babying wasn't in a nephilim. We held too much power for that. Uncomfortable with the gentleness in his tone, I shifted in my seat. Considering his question, I raked a hand over my face. "No. It's always been Heaven." I met my father's gaze. "I think this has to do with the bargain Kirsten's ancestors made."

He grimaced slightly as he always did when I called my mother Kirsten, but the look of disapproval passed. "It makes no sense that he'd come for one of you now."

I spread my hands. "Who knows the thoughts of gods?"

Normally, this is when Gabriel would disagree. He would say an event of those proportions wouldn't happen. That the Aesir, Vanir, and old gods the Norse worshipped had so little power, but times were changing. Even before supernaturals revealed that gods and mythological beings were real, there was a rise in mundanes interested in polytheistic and non-Abrahamic monotheistic religions that Christianity had once systematically snuffed out.

After the inaugural Mythic Games, the old gods and monsters had made an even stronger comeback. I didn't think this was entirely a bad thing, but some gods didn't play nice. Some prophecies needed to stay myths. Some debts were being called.

With this knowledge weighing on him, Gabriel blew out his breath and looked at his hands. He was used to being in charge and defending his pack. Dad might not notice me walk into a room, but he'd feel compelled to protect me out of his sense of duty.

I lifted my chin, threw back my shoulders, and straightened my spine. Mustering more courage than I felt, I promised, "I will handle this."

"Remember, it's not on your shoulders to pay the debt, and if he comes after you, he comes after all of us." My father swung his long arm. His gesture included everyone in the room, the pack, and supes in general, I supposed.

Right. If I got everyone involved, we'd have an incident that might just be as bad as the near clash of the Olympians and Titans that had brought on the Mythic Games. I didn't want the kind of collateral damage that transpired before the games were invented. An Aesir couldn't care less about games to distract them.

"Bargain or no, this pissy little god may be calling his due, but he's going after an agent of I.S.E.A. There are consequences to that."

This seemed to mollify my family. The Mórrígan called me on it by narrowing Rhiannon and Miriam's eyes at me. I stared back unflinchingly. She seemed to let it be, freeing the hold she had on the others to look at themselves again.

We moved on. The pack filed in. Dinner went on as usual without further discussion of what I saw.

After dinner, someone knocked on my door. While we were eating, Jada had texted me to meet her and Sarah at a bar in Capitol Hill. It was a work night, but it was still early, and grabbing a couple of drinks was better than mulling over what happened for the thousandth time. So, I was mid getting ready when I heard the knock.

I pulled on a robe over my bra and underwear and answered. Shifters didn't care about nudity, but the witches and fae of the household minded, and I had no idea who was knocking.

My father waited there with a sword in a sheath in his hands as if he was about to bestow it in a ceremony. His jaw was set, and his lips were pinched tight. "Can I come in?"

I gestured for him to enter. My eyes never left the shining golden metalwork of the T-shaped hilt. Right above the leather hand hold at the T, there was a shining ruby. Identifying the sword by the hilt, I was speechless.

He waited until I closed the door behind him to speak. "I have to go to D.C. for a few weeks."

Gabriel then paused as if waiting for me to say something about that, but he traveled often since being elected to state senate. He was gunning for a federal senate seat after he served his term and had to schmooze in the capitol all the time. I didn't understand what his travel plans had to do with the sword in his hands, so I said, "Safe travels?"

With a small chuckle, he shook his head. "Small talk isn't us, is it?"

"Not with that in your hands." I pointed to the sword.

"I can't be here to protect you." He looked down at the weapon. "I never thought I'd do this, but I want you to not be defenseless against a deity."

"I could always smite them."

A flippant answer—smiting was like detonating a bomb, destroying more in the wake than the intended target.

He lifted his gaze to meet mine. Determination set in his jaw. "If you're off this world, I want you to do it anyway."

My stomach dipped. He was serious.

"On this world, I want you to have Igni." He stretched his arms out, offering my grandfather's sword. The archangel Gabriel's sword.

Rearing back with my hand on my chest instead of taking the offered weapon, I asked, "You want me to wield Grandfather's flaming sword?"

He lifted his eyebrows...surprised I didn't take Igni?

I held up my hand. "They give us guns loaded with bespelled

bullets. Gods who aren't ascended feel bullets and these ones can take one out long enough to get them to Oberon's faerie."

He gave me a long, assessing look. "That might be true, but you're not always going to be able to depend on Jada and Phyr, or some Nowhere door for access to faerie. I don't even know if the fae are more powerful than the Asgardians and their ilk."

I laughed. "Yeah. The Mórrígan freaked out a bit."

His eyebrows knitted together, and his nostrils flared. "That should concern you."

It did. A lot. However, I didn't want to make a big deal about it in front of him. This was my case and my problem. If my father was giving me this sword, he was letting me handle it. I had to accept it.

I held out my hands, taking the weapon. Igni felt heavy in my hands. The Grace, or angels' magic, within it hummed against my skin. The sword didn't smell like fire and brimstone. The weapon carried the scent of the crisp clean air and dense clouds that floated around Heaven's grand cities that sat upon floating islands.

"Igni is yours now. Use her wisely." Gabriel kissed me on the forehead, and he was gone.

I looked down at the sword. "You're going in my closet. I have plans."

After putting Igni away and getting dressed, I drove into the city and found parking in a garage not far from the bar. Capitol Hill had the best nightlife on the weekends, but on a weeknight, it was mostly quiet—as quiet as a district in a city as big as Seattle could be. It wouldn't be like the pack compound or my father's cabin north toward the Canadian border. There, at night, the near silence of the forest was as peaceful as my childhood had been turbulent.

The bar Jada chose was LGBTQ, emphasis on the L. There were a few scattered tables and a lot of flannel, t-shirts, and baseball caps, mostly older women. Jada and I were femme, meaning we dressed in skirts and what society deemed as feminine—girly girls. The queer community was layered and not everyone ascribed to these notions.

Jada waved me to a booth she shared with Sarah. She had on her blouse from work but wasn't wearing her tie or jacket. The open collar exposed a choker with spikes. She'd lined her amber eyes and had on more mascara than she'd wear at home or work. Black lipstick as dark as the liner on her eyes. She'd freed her moss-green curls from the ponytail.

Sarah kept her black, straight hair cropped short. It spiked a little in the front. She wore a green Seattle Storm hoodie and some oversized jeans. When she stood to let me in, I noticed that her Nikes were immaculate as usual.

"Try to convince this woman to join my soccer team, will ya?" Sarah begged. She had a high, dulcet voice that contrasted with her clothing. Her very presence exuded warmth, and I saw what Jada saw in her. Sarah was pretty with dark eyes and a wide, sensual mouth. She had the kind of complexion skincare companies would love to pretend their products created. She also had the annoyingly endearing habit of being perpetually cheerful.

I arched an eyebrow and indicated my own clothes. I'd changed into a hot pink sports bra under a black mesh, long-sleeve fitted top paired with a mini-skirt and some fishnet tights. My boots laced up to my knees and had about three inches of sole. My ears were laden with clip-on jewelry and a clip-on nose ring. The thing about being a shifter and jewelry: we wore no silver, because it burned, and we couldn't be pierced or tattooed. Shifting from animal to human healed wounds.

"What about me says I've ever been any sort of person who would encourage my friend to play sports?"

Sarah chuckled and lifted her hands as if in surrender. "It's a good stress reliever. Maybe you both should try it."

I slid into the booth, hailed the server, and then slanted a dubious glance in Sarah's direction. "No."

"No, thank you," Jada corrected, pulling her girlfriend back into the booth on her side.

"Sorry, Mom."

Sarah opened her mouth as if she was winding up for a second round of why we should compete against mundanes. A redhead with streaks of gray winding through her cropped curls approached the table, thankfully interceding. She had a voluptuous figure no amount of flannel and jeans could hide. She grinned as her eyes gave me a quick once-over. I couldn't tell if she was checking me out or if she was eyeing me to see if I'd be trouble.

I was definitely the latter in my younger days, but not anymore.

"What can I get you?"

"Got any Tank?"

The waitress smiled, her eyes crinkling in the corners. "Do you howl at the moon?"

"Only when I have big eyes and teeth." I gave her my best wolfish grin. A sheen rolled over my eyes, giving me away as a shifter and someone who could handle Tank.

"I'll get you a bottle, Big Bad." She winked. The waitress had given me the test no fake ID could pass. Shapeshifters' eyes could gleam like any predator. Sometimes when we were in high emotional states, we did it involuntarily, but we also could control it. Bartenders, wait staff, and clerks at stores that sold it were trained to ask in a casual way.

When the waitress left, Sarah leaned forward and asked in a conspiratorial tone, "What's Tank? Is it any good?"

"Don't even think about it," Jada replied for me. "Even I can't handle Tank, babe."

Jada was right to put Sarah off from trying the drink. Tank was a drink that was made for shifter metabolisms, but supernaturals, especially those with demigod blood like Jada, could certainly handle at least a bottle. One bottle of Tank would inebriate a mundane for hours. Sometimes they'd vomit from alcohol poisoning before they finished the bottle. Two bottles of Tank would kill a mundane. Two bottles would make me feel slightly drunk and wear off in an hour. It had been an underground drink for years, brewed by shifters who'd been taught by an elder of the pack. After the supernatural council revealed that supes were real, the shifters who'd run underground distilleries banded together and formed a company that began supplying Tank to mundane bars a few years ago.

Sarah grunted and waved her hand dismissively. "Babe, I can drink grown men under the table. I think I can handle a sip." Her eyes tracked the server as she returned. She licked her lips as the redhead sat the lime-green bottle with an illustrated tank on the label on the table.

I thanked the server, but my gaze remained on the near-salivating Sarah. Next to her, Jada's attention was on her girlfriend, too. We couldn't help it. It wasn't often you'd see someone so focused. The look in her eyes triggered something instinctual in me that made me want to growl and say "mine" because I'd seen that look before. Predatory shifters who hadn't released their animal in a long time would eye rabbits and birds that way. Vampires eyed mundanes with the same level of thirst and desire. I held in my hands what addicts would ruin their whole lives for—a forbidden fruit that promised something to the beholder that only they could see.

"Not from my bottle, you can't," I argued, swiping the bottle of Tank from the table preternaturally fast. "This isn't about what a mundane man can handle. Supernatural bodies are..." I almost said "superior," but Jada flashed me a warning look, stopping me. "Adapted to consume higher concentrations of poison—which is what alcohol essentially does to the brain, especially Tank."

Sarah sat back, shoulders slumping. "That's why you don't want to play soccer. You don't want to outperform the weak, magicless humans like me. That's why you call us mundanes. That's all you think of outsiders."

I almost affirmed her fears out loud, but Jada cut me a sharp glance. Her face softened as she regarded Sarah and cupped her girlfriend's chin to look at her. "Hey. I'm with you because I think you're special. I'm pretty human when it comes to athleticism. Roxy and I were on the cheer squad in high school and college."

Jada didn't mention that I probably could have lifted most of the cheer squad. I wasn't "pretty human" when it came to strength and speed. Shifters held back until recently. However, this information wasn't going to help Sarah's self-esteem. Hurting her girlfriend would upset Jada, too.

"There was a mu—magicless human who made it through the Mythic Games," I said. "Nike Nora Jones."

"She became a supernatural, didn't she?" Sarah said, her face lighting up.

Not the point, but I nodded. Jada and I exchanged a brief glance. The goddess Athena had had a hand in helping her priestess with a magical boost, but belief had grown a spark into a bonfire. Her smell was different, too. She wasn't born with gods' magic like Jada. I.S.E.A. and the Supernatural Council of the Americas couldn't quite grasp what kind of supernatural Nora was, but her gifts seemed dang close to a demigod. That had made I.S.E.A. and a lot of supernaturals nervous. We were fine with monsters that already existed, but something new never sat well.

It was all about knowing strengths and weaknesses. A wild card in the supernatural world was dangerous.

Nora, however, was a good person. A devout priestess of Athena, she helped women across the country get out of domestic violence situations. I liked when supernaturals used their powers and fame for good. Still... I.S.E.A. likely had watchers keeping tabs on her. We've had good gods go bad before.

The way Sarah eyed my bottle of Tank, she could not handle the power.

Moving the bottle of Tank below the table, I willed Sarah to meet my gaze and said in a flat tone, "Nora is an anomaly."

Jada nodded profusely. "Yes. An anomaly. Nora is one in a trillion."

That was an absolute lie, and only I saw Jada's fae heritage exacting the price of it in her slight flinch from pain. The falsehood was necessary. Power corrupted. Not all could handle it. Besides, belief wasn't all that was necessary. Some never developed their light beyond their initial small magic.

"The thing is," Sarah began, her focus somewhere distant and her tone taking on a dreamy quality, "if even only one magicless human can become a supernatural, it's still a possibility."

We were saved from further awkward conversation by the DJ playing a danceable song in the space adjacent to the bar, where her booth and the dance floor resided. The late-night crowd started pouring in. I polished off my bottle of Tank and hit the dance floor. Jada and Sarah joined.

I got lost in the music, dancing and singing my cares away, feeling slightly buzzed from the Tank. A cool breeze wafted in, likely from the door where patrons entered. Overheated from the crowd, I found myself drawn to it.

I almost face-planted into a woman taller than me. Taller than most of the people there. Unlike everyone in the club with one style or another, she wore her long chestnut hair in loose waves as if just unbound from braids. Under a set of fluttering lashes, twin pools of a blue so deep they could be black twinkled with mirth. Her lips, a swath of red, quirked in an amused grin. Freckles sprinkled her nose. Her clothes were simple: jeans and a long sleeve, fitted top. A silver link chain choker adorned her neck.

"Care to dance?"

No one really asked to dance on the dance floor anymore. We danced close and then together if we wanted, so I was struck by the formality of it. She seemed familiar, too. Like I'd seen her somewhere before and couldn't place where.

"Sure."

I took her calloused hand in mine. Everything about her was a contrast of yielding softness and hard muscle. The fragrances of honeysuckle, chill mountain air, and a spark of magic gave her away as a supe.

"New in town?" I asked, knowing full well she was.

She grinned. "Does my accent make it that obvious?"

I hadn't noticed an accent, but I didn't register such things. The way someone smelled. The way they moved. Those were important things to a wolf shifter.

"The fact that you don't recognize me, or my sister, means that you're not local." I gestured in Jada's and Sarah's direction.

They both waved. Then whispered back and forth, giggling. Very mature.

I turned my gaze back to the supe I was dancing with. Confusion marked her features as she glanced at Jada and then me. Maybe she was confused because Jada and I didn't look alike. Plenty of sisters didn't, but we also had very different magic. Since magic was mostly inherited through curse or blessing, that would be more puzzling to a supe than our looks being different.

"We're stepsisters," I explained.

She nodded slowly as if I'd answered a question brewing in her mind, and then she answered mine. "Passing through for work, but I'll be back."

We danced and danced, not speaking in words, but our bodies held a conversation that had passed between strangers dancing since fires blazed in the center of an open space under the stars.

She leaned in so that our faces were a breath apart. I assumed so I could hear her on the loud, crowded dance floor, but I placed my hands on either side of her face, silencing whatever she was about to say. It felt like goodbye, and I wasn't ready yet for that.

Looking into those cerulean depths, I said, "I'm going to kiss you."

Surprise flashed in her eyes, but then she was the one that breached the distance between us. Her lips were petal-soft against mine. The kiss was gentle, a simple press of lips, but a fire blazed beneath—at least inside me. I wanted this stranger like I hadn't ever wanted anyone before. I wasn't alone in my desire. The kiss deepened. Her long-fingered hands gripped my waist, branding my flesh with her gentle but firm touch.

All too soon, she broke the kiss. Both of us panted. Her eyes had darkened with desire, but her words contradicted her look. "Not yet. You don't know who I am."

I laughed. "That's simple to remedy. I'm Roxanne. Who are you?"

She shook her head, distancing herself from me. Touching her necklace, she said, "I must go."

Wisps of white smoke surrounded her, and then she was just that. Gone.

I howled my frustration. A few people around me jumped at the eerie wolfish sound. Jada and Sarah surrounded me with worried looks on their faces. "What happened?"

I scrubbed my face with my hands. "I just made out with a fucking goddess or something, and she disappeared back into her realm. That's what happened."

Sarah gaped. "Whoa! For real? An actual goddess?"

That I doubted, but I wasn't going to get into it with a mundane right now. Ignoring Sarah, I directed at Jada, "I'm going home. See you in the morning."

Jada nodded, pulling her still-stupefied girlfriend to the side. I guess they hadn't had the talk that Jada's biological dad was an ascended god. Not my problem.

CHAPTER THREE

Located in the Fremont neighborhood in Seattle, the International Supernatural Enforcement Agency Pacific Northwest branch sat between an organic supermarket and an insurance agency. The unimposing building opened to a pocket universe on the inside, so that it seemed to be small, but it was the largest building in square footage on the west coast—if it were actually there. Quantum physics and magic made my head hurt, so I didn't think about it too much. Only agents knew how big the building really was, and we didn't really give away the location. This was one of the many secrets Jada and I kept from our family.

Blocks away from the facility, we pulled up to a gate for an underground garage. A man in a black jacket and hat sat in a guard booth outside the gate. He pulled down his sunglasses, revealing eyes with flames for irises and pupils. Djinn gave me the creeps, but this one had made a legitimate deal for his body in this world. Two people existed in there. Both recognized us and the gate opened.

Jada pulled in, releasing a shudder as the gate closed behind us and our vehicle glided down the twisting ramp. My stomach flipped and my head swam as we crossed from Earth to the other world.

Exiting the car, we got on an elevator, coffees in hand. Just another day at my weird job. The elevator dinged.

"Time to report to the boss," Jada sighed as we exited.

Director Emily Tan, a woman in her late forties, possessed shoulder-length black hair, neatly pulled back at the nape of her neck. She kept her makeup to a precise minimum as if she followed a rule book on how to keep herself as unremarkable as possible. I knew she was in her late forties from her files, but the Director hadn't changed since I met her when I was a teenager. It's like elder millennials and some Gen X decided to stop aging at thirty-eight until they hit their later years. Add damned near immortal like my stepmom Miriam, and it made placing an age on them even harder. Tan was human, though. Most agents weren't supernaturals until it became apparent that I.S.E.A. needed us.

We don't count the druids who call themselves mages, because they don't count themselves as like us.

Pssst...they're supes.

Even though she didn't go out in the field often anymore, Director Tan still wore a black, I.S.E.A.-issued suit and tie. Not a single wrinkle, let alone a piece of lint, marred her ensemble. She sat behind a modern desk. A mug of coffee paled by an exorbitant amount of creamer and a laptop were the only two items on said desk. Most agents had pictures of their family or friends. Agent Tan had none of this. Her shelves and walls were covered in pictures of her three cats: a British Shorthair named Lady Di, a Himalayan named Everest, and a Scottish Fold named Bonnie Prince Charlie.

Jada found the cats' names and photos cute. The excessive number of pictures and the content disturbed me. The three dressed up as cowboys, in seasonal "gear," holiday pictures, and matching pjs contrasted Tan's no-nonsense professional personality. She would mention them by name like most people her age mentioned their family members, but I'd never heard her once mention a domestic partner, human children, siblings, or even her parents. To each their own, I guess.

Director Tan hadn't always been a director. She'd been a field agent like Jada and I when we'd agreed to join I.S.E.A. Rumor had it that former Agent Roanhorse, her old field partner, had been the only person she'd let know her well. He was an empty nester who had retired to travel with his wife. I'd liked Roanhorse. He wasn't a rule follower, and neither was Tan.

These meetings were usually pleasant exchanges where we'd give her a briefing and move on to the next assignment. There was always a next assignment. Supernaturals had always made a lot of work for I.S.E.A., but after an event called the Mythic Games, where power through believers was up for grabs, became a yearly event, we had a LOT more work than our I.S.E.A. agent predecessors.

The Director usually greeted us with a warm smile and loved hearing about our quirkier cases. Nothing was pleasant about Tan's expression today. Her mouth was set in a grim, flat line. Her gaze focused on a monitor, not even a hint came from her to acknowledge our presence.

My partner and I exchanged glances. Worry limned her big brown eyes. She didn't like when we had to investigate anything dark. She'd do it, but Jada was raised on sunshine and lollipops. Miriam sheltered her as much as possible. I didn't blame my step-mom. She'd had a totally messed up childhood. For example, Jada's grandmother had stolen Miriam from faerie, blocked her memory of being a fae princess, and then had offered Miriam to the King of Hell as a weapon and a lover. That kind of brutal childhood made her the best mom despite her trauma. Mostly.

Pretending everything was fine while she hid deadly secret wasn't the same as what Miriam's mother did. However, at sixteen, Jada had a sharp wake-up call when she'd learned just how deep the rabbit hole of deception went. It made a person worry.

My gem of a mother was unstable as heck, so our boss acting out of character made me nervous, too. The tension built as Tan clicked her mouse a few times, grimacing even deeper.

Finally, Tan looked up. She blinked as if just realizing we were there. Odd. The Director had called us to her office. I'd assumed she wanted a briefing.

Jada nodded to me. She'd already typed up our full report. We'd gone over the highlights that I'd present to Tan. I opened my mouth to start giving the report on our successful extrication of the giant Easter bunny and its egg filled with more vermin, but Tan held up a hand.

I shut my mouth with a snap. She never interrupted, so I knew she had good reason and wasn't just being rude. The way my stomach knotted, so did my instincts.

"Is the case closed, Agents Crowfoot and Diaz?"

"Yes," Jada and I answered in unison. Our voices held a higher than usual octave, like nervous new recruits, even to me.

My hand itched to reach under my collar and finger the protective talisman Miriam had given me. It was ridiculous and superstitious to do here, but it had been a comfort.

"I'll look at your official report later. Right now, I have something for you two to start investigating ASAP." She frowned, her gaze darting to the screen. "I don't like giving murder cases to rookie-ish agents. Given your previous experience as enforcers, I think you two would be the best to handle it."

Previously, only mundane humans and human mages were allowed to be I.S.E.A. agents. Mundane and mage agents usually served in law enforcement or the military prior to applying to the academy. Jada and I had served as enforcers for the Supernatural Council of the Americas. After a seaworm the size of a kaiju had attacked the shores of Washington's coast, federal and international laws changed. I.S.E.A. swallowed up the council's enforcer duties and brought supernaturals on board as agents.

I swallowed hard. As enforcers, we'd only worked on one truly heinous, multi-victim murder and kidnapping. The case was our hazing into becoming I.S.E.A. agents. We hadn't worked anything like it as agents. Most of the time we were supernatural babysitters at best, not violent crimes investigators.

"At first, the police thought that they had isolated murder cases. Then they believed they had a serial killer on their hands and didn't alert I.S.E.A.," Tan continued. She shook her head and blew out her breath. Frustration was clear on her face. "The deaths were spread apart by several months, occurring in different locations across the country—mostly in the Midwest and more recently in the Pacific Northwest."

"Is that how we became involved?" Jada's whole countenance changed from nervous to that preternatural stillness that only the fae exhibited when they were faced with a challenge. She hadn't grown up with the fae, but she'd spent a lot more time in her grandfather Oberon's faerie than I thought was healthy. It didn't matter how far back your fae ancestors were. Faeries took on the personality of their ruler and changed anyone with fae blood in a way that was at once subtle and insidious.

"That would have been optimal, but no." Tan's tone and accompanying sigh expressed more heaviness than usual. As junior enforcers, Jada and I had worked a violent case with her before. She stayed professional throughout. This, this seemed to affect her in a way that I'd never seen, furthering my discomfort. "They're trying to make a federal version of our organization, so they haven't been as forthright with giving us information. It wasn't until a neopagan officer in Vancouver spotted the signs that the victims there were allegedly sacrificed that we got the call."

Shocked, I reared my head back. This was disturbing news twofold. Sacrifices in our modern era were rare. Also, I.S.E.A. wasn't part of any singular government organization, hence neutral. That was the beauty of the organization. No politics got in our way, and we weren't really law enforcement. We represented and protected Earth.

Jada tilted her head to the side, brow furrowed. "Vancouver, Washington?"

"No. Up north in British Columbia. The murders are now an international supernatural crime and our jurisdiction." Tan's derisive tone and her expression revealed just how much she didn't like that I.S.E.A. wasn't involved until now. She glanced at me with apologetic eyes. "Also, the victim was mid-shift when they died."

A frisson of fear danced an arctic waltz, chilling my flesh to the bone. Killing someone in that vulnerable state between human and animal was every shifter's nightmare. Instead of sounding afraid, my tone came across as sardonic. "Lemme guess. Internet pagans decided a lamb shifter would make the land fertile?"

Despite my tone, the thought terrified me. How many of the docile shifters would fall victim?

The Director frowned her disappointment in my reaction but didn't lecture about being flippant like she typically would. "Perhaps. But the victim wasn't a docile lamb shifter." Her gaze met mine, apology in her eyes as she said, "He was a wolf."

My mouth went dry, yet somehow I managed to form the desperate question, "Which line?"

Shifters all had a root source of why we were sometimes human and sometimes animal. In general, we didn't talk about shifter lines coming from curses, deals with powerful entities, personifications of deities, and other supernatural means. We'd like everyone to think it's genetic and our animal was always part of our ancestry, but it wasn't true. We were once human as any mundane. This was information most of the magicless weren't privy to, and not many supernaturals knew either. However, all I.S.E.A. agents learned everything about supernaturals in academy. Therefore, Tan knew exactly what I meant by which line.

"The victim's family didn't share. Based on the officer being a Norse neopagan, he was of Fenrir's line."

Jada made a small, choked sound. Or was that me? I couldn't tell. Usually, I could keep my cool, but not about this. Never this.

Tan lifted her eyebrows at me. "Will this be a problem?"

It most definitely would be a problem, but I wasn't going to back down from an assignment. I threw back my shoulders and lifted my chin. "No. Of course not."

She observed me through narrowed eyes, and then straightened. "Alright, I need you two to get to Vancouver by the quickest means possible to check out the crime scene. The murder was committed somewhere between midnight and four in the morning, and the first forty-eight hours are the most important. The Canadian authorities know you'll be arriving by unconventional means."

Not much later, we stood outside the I.S.E.A. building in downtown Redmond, Washington. The quiet suburb of Seattle that we'd grown up in was now a small city. High-rise apartment buildings and condos, footed with shops, trendy restaurants, and nightlife activities, replaced the old one- and two-story buildings that had closed by nine every night. It still had a lot of that suburban family soft feel for the most part, but a city's harder edges came with the bigger buildings.

Jada peered down at her phone, fixated on a picture of the rose garden of Stanley Park. "Planeswalking is so misunderstood. Everyone thinks I can just magically poof us to wherever I want, but it's a science and magic wrapped into one."

"You can go anywhere in the multiverse whenever you want. How terrible for you." A grin tugged at the corner of my mouth, perhaps for the first time this morning—definitely since we'd walked into Director Tan's office.

My best friend and partner cut me a look that could wilt flowers and strike fear in the hearts of men. Lucky for me, I was neither a flower nor a man.

"You have so much empathy. It astounds me you can function with all your feelings."

"I manage." I bowed with a flourish of my hand.

Jada rolled her eyes and then her features settled into a look of determined concentration. She sliced her hand through the fabric of reality and then walked through, disappearing entirely. Only a disembodied hand returned, beckoning me to pass through.

CHAPTER FOUR

On the other side, the air was brisker than in Seattle. The garden and arbor we found ourselves under was still barren of flowers this time of year. From my experience with my stepmother's gardens, the roses would bloom in early May. Funny these were the things I noticed. It was as if my brain didn't want to see what had happened here.

Someone cursed softly. The blue-uniformed officer stood at about five foot ten, had a short, dark beard, and a blue turban that matched his uniform. Shock widened his eyes.

"Where did you two come from?"

"International Supernatural Enforcement Agency," I replied, flashing my badge. Jada did the same. "I'm Agent Crowfoot and this is Agent Diaz."

Assessing eyes took in our badges, our faces, and our black suits. His Canadian accent colored his words. "The supe cops, eh? I thought the monster hunters were a myth. Hate to say it, but I think this was committed by a human. No need for you."

I narrowed my eyes. At the same time, I pushed down the growl bubbling up in my throat. Until not too long ago, the agency that I begrudgingly worked for was called the United Nations Monster Unit. U.N.M.U. dropped the name when supernaturals revealed to the world that they were real and wanted to be recognized as part of communities and society at large. Calling us monsters wasn't good optics for anyone.

His scent told me he was some sort of big cat shifter. This guy wanted us out when we had every right to be here. Was he covering something or was he just being a weird cat?

"That's not true. We're investigative agents of supernatural activity that may or may not be a threat to the world," Jada replied, grin wide. "We also investigate any acts against supernaturals that could lead to potential global consequences, but we're not law enforcement. We work together with law enforcement, so that might be the cause of your confusion."

"We also prefer not to call supernaturals monsters," I added in a lot less friendly tone.

He shrugged. "Some of them are."

I made a show of sniffing the air, but no wolf needed to be far from another supe to smell their magic or a shifter's animal. "Are you calling yourself a monster?"

His eyes narrowed. "It's not polite to out someone without their consent."

He was right. A lot of supes didn't like their magical nature known, especially if they held a public position. I couldn't care less. He was rude for no reason. I held up my hands in mock surrender. "Sorry." Narrowing my eyes, I added, "I get defensive when people call me a monster."

"We're only such if we act as such," he replied, his tone softening despite my obvious sarcasm. He blew out his breath. "I apologize, too. It's been a rough day."

I tilted my head in acknowledgment. We were here to investigate a murder, not to fight.

Jada turned on her heart-warming smile. "Now that's settled, can you show us to the crime scene—" Pausing, she eyed his name badge. "Officer Singh?"

A kind grin lit his face, making him appear less of an arrogant ass and more of a gregarious sort. I was immune, but I'd bet that smile won women over all the time. He waved for us to follow. "Sure."

Jada had that effect on people, making friends out of potential enemies.

Distrusting anyone who wasn't pack, I only knew how to piss everyone off. We didn't mean to play bad cop, good cop. It was how we always were. Everyone loved Jada and begrudgingly accepted me —or at least tolerated me for her. I didn't mind it.

"A little warning, what I'm about to show you is gruesome. First violent crime of this sort for me." He amended, "Well, I've seen shootings and stabbings, but this." He sighed, much in the way Director Tan had sighed, and waved his hand as if waving off a foul odor. "This is different. My partner vomited. No shame in it."

My hackles raised as we followed him. The way he spoke felt dismissive of our professional ability to take in a crime scene. I was about to tell him off but noticed Jada glancing in my direction with a warning look. She whispered in Kairska, the language of witches, "He's giving us a warning, not calling us weak. Besides, there's puke over there. That's the direction he came from. *He* is the one who vomited."

Smelling and noticing the sick for the first time, I shook off the desire to set things straight. Instead, I agreed, "Yep. No shame in it."

Singh nodded his appreciation.

Despite the officer's warning, I was not prepared for what I saw. A wolf shifter with his limbs still in animal form and his torso, part of his hips, and genitals in human form, and face mid-shift hung from a tree just below his hind paws. That wasn't the worst part. A howl of agony remained frozen on his emaciated features. Dried blood coated his skin and fur that had spilled from what looked like gashes at every major artery. Magic was summoned here, old and powerful. It smelled of harsh landscapes and cold, crisp air. There was something else mingled in it. I should have smelled that much blood and magic, even from the arbor. However, even with the dried blood coating as evidence, there didn't seem to be any present. The magic was muted, as if it appeared and disappeared, fading like smoke.

An officer with a blacklight crawled around the ground of the taped-off area. Another officer took notes. More police were gathered outside the tape, talking.

"These two are from I.S.E.A.," Singh explained to an officer in his late fifties in uniform, wearing a blue cap with a shield on it.

We pulled our badges for brief inspection. "Agent Diaz." "Agent Crowfoot."

The senior officer reared his head back as if shocked. "I just made the call to I.S.E.A. less than an hour ago. Your nearest office is in Seattle. I checked."

"We got here through agency means," Jada replied with a brief flash of her teeth in not quite a smile. She'd learned that less friendly way of greeting from me and perfected it while living with the pack. I didn't play good cop. My stony face read that it was none of his business how we got here so fast.

He lifted his cap, wiped his brow with the back of his hand, and blew out his breath. His gaze lifted to the shifter victim. "Our guess is that they exsanguinated the victim. Might be some ritualistic magic involved. Helena—Officer Aune—is a Norse pagan." He spread his hands. "It's all over my head. She can explain what she thinks," the superior officer explained. His Vancouver accent even heavier than Officer Singh's. Then he looked to the group of officers all staring at us. "Helena, we got the agents here."

A petite, uniformed redhead with her hair pulled back in a tight bun approached. I could smell the sunscreen on Helena's pale, freckled skin. It was as overcast in Vancouver as it had been two hours south in Seattle, but a lot of people wore sunscreen year-round as moisturizer. Many neo-pagans wore Mjölnir, Thor's hammer, as a symbol of their faith. At the base of her throat hung a heart-shaped amethyst pendant wrapped with silver wire in the shape of Yggdrasil, the tree of wisdom.

"Agents," Helena said by way of greeting. "At first, I thought they went Old Norse pagan, and this was a blót. We're not in a time of famine, per se, but the way inflation is going—" She lifted her hands palms up. "Some desperate folks might have decided to appeal to the gods in a big way for abundance."

Jada frowned but said nothing. We exchanged a look. The pagan's explanation didn't sit right with either of us.

"I don't think this was desperation. In the Norse tradition, human sacrifice was rare, and the person willingly sacrificed themselves for the good of the community during lean times. It was usually the elderly or the infirm," I said, gesturing to the face of the shifter. "That's not the face of a willing sacrifice. Also, if it were a true blót to the gods, the perpetrators would have exsanguinated a willing sacrificial victim, collected the blood in bowls, and then spread the blood on an altar to their deity with a sacred branch. The only blood I see is on the victim."

"So, you don't think any magic was performed here?" Officer Singh asked, one of his dark eyebrows slanted upward at a dubious angle.

He smelled what I had. Despite the pungent odor of the victim's fear and blood, the unmistakable peppery scent of supernatural power, religious in nature but not of a deity, remained on the scene. Supernaturals called this kind of magic "small magic" because people who weren't born supernatural could obtain it. Most of us didn't think much of it. I.S.E.A. barely registered small magics as something we needed to look out for.

Jada and I exchanged another glance. When we were in high school, we had come across a pastor with that so-called *small* magic. His magic might have been weak, but he wielded it in a way to create a cult. He could have grown with belief if he'd directed it at himself and not to the Christian god.

However, I didn't want to discuss that with Singh, and even less so with the mundane cops. So, instead of replying, I gave Singh a hard stare. He looked right back at me, pressing a bit of alpha magic for me to submit and obey. That power resided in that stare.

Which startled me. Not because I couldn't handle an alpha or that he was one. I didn't know Singh, and I knew the names of *all* the pack alphas in the Pacific Northwest. What was more important is that he didn't know who I was by my name. That was fine for a pack member, but not an alpha. He'd know where I stood in the pack food chain and, more importantly, who my father was. That meant that he was without a pack, or worse, a new pack had shown up in the Pacific Northwest without anyone notifying my father.

I wasn't an alpha of any pack, nor did I ever want to be, so I usually repressed that part of myself. My father, an actual alpha, wasn't here to make this shifter back down. So, I pushed a bit of my usually checked magic back at Singh, showing him that he was clawing up the wrong tree.

He didn't back down.

Now we were locked in this power struggle, and I couldn't do a damned thing but keep it up, or I'd be admitting submission. I'd rather drop dead than submit to some shifter I didn't know.

The senior officer to Singh and the pagan officer cleared his throat. "I notice your badges don't have a specialty. Doesn't I.S.E.A. have a unit of mage agents who could do a spell that would find the murderers? Maybe you could call them in for a consultation."

"You're looking at those agents. Director Tan assigned us to this case because we're the best for it," Jada said.

"We'll investigate how we see fit," I replied, eyes still locked with Singh.

"Do we turn this case over to you then?" The older officer asked, his voice wavering a little. A mundane couldn't feel the magic sparks flying between me and Singh the way shifters would, but it would make them extremely uncomfortable.

"Yes," Jada and I replied at the same time.

"I'd like to request to be I.S.E.A.'s local liaison officer." Singh's tone came off as polite, but his voice had lowered an octave.

"Granted," the older officer said, somewhat relieved. He seemed too willing to give up this case. Given the murderers killed someone as powerful as a wolf shifter, I would be crapping my pants and wanting to walk away if I were a mundane, too.

I nodded at the neo-pagan, my eyes still on Singh. "Helena knows the local pagan groups. We'd rather work with her."

"True, but I know..." Singh swallowed, the only sign of doubt. His eyes broke contact to flick to the victim. Technically, he conceded, but in a way that signified he was a good alpha, looking out for pack over power. "The criminal underbelly of this city that will know more about where the blood went. You'll need us both."

Shit. This was a move that made me look like I cared more about the latter. Technical submission for the good of the pack made him the better leader. These political maneuvers were why I hoped my father lived forever, or that my Aunt Princess claimed the position if he didn't. I didn't ever want to be alpha. Ever.

"He's right, Roxy," Jada said in the Unseelie tongue, her tone gentle. "Singh knows the shifters and the supernatural community. That's where we'll get more cooperation."

Singh couldn't understand us, but judging by the way he crinkled his nose, he smelled the wild fae magic of the language.

They were both right. Neo-pagans were not a monolith. Despite having groups, they were not at all organized. I relented. "Alright. Both of you will be our point of contact here in Vancouver."

"The rest of you are dismissed," Jada said, a little persuasion magic she inherited from both of her parents in her voice. She could have used it on Singh, but I was glad she didn't. It would've put me lower in the pack pecking order than her instead of having him think of us as equals. He'd listen to her and give me shit at every turn.

"I need you to contact your elders, everyone in the Norse pagan community, and see if there are any priests or priestesses who are gaining a following. Try to get an in," I told Helena, and added a warning, "Be discreet. Under no circumstances should you mention sacrifice."

Once Helena left, I returned my attention to Singh. "Now that the mundanes are gone, do you really not know who I am?" I motioned between Jada and me. "Who we are?"

"Of course. You're I.S.E.A. agents."

I exchanged a glance with my partner. We were used to everyone in the supernatural community knowing who we were. We'd been internationally famous through our parents when the now Supernatural Council of the Americas had been the smaller Supernatural Council of the Pacific Northwest. Our parents had outed the existence of supernaturals and saved the world several times.

"I've applied to the academy four times." The officer rolled his shoulders. "You must be someone special to get in, but I don't know a thing about you. My family kept what they were, my second nature, to themselves, and we've never been part of a pack. So, if you're some pack princess or alpha, it makes no difference to me."

A lot about Singh started to make sense. Most shifters belonged to packs, but some loners were out there. He didn't know the rules, pack culture, and wouldn't know who my dad was other than a guy on television now and then. He wouldn't know me, because I stayed off TV completely after becoming an agent.

I glanced at the wolf shifter, pity for the victim welling up like a rising tide that would burst from my eyes if I let it. I swallowed it down and sneered instead. "He had a pack."

Singh angled his head. "How do you know he wasn't a lone wolf?"

"Because I'm a pack princess. Wolves are rarely loners. It's not in us." I walked over to the victim. The backs of my eyes pricked with the sting of unshed tears. I'd seen worse, much worse, but that had been in battle. This shifter was killed in cold blood. He suffered for this. Someone wanted power or they wanted...I shook my head, unwilling to even consider what they might be asking for by sacrificing one of Fenrir's ilk.

"Do we call MFD to take him for research, or the Mage Division to take care of the body?" Jada asked.

I turned to face her. "Why would we even consider the mages?"

Jada furrowed her eyebrows and grimaced. "If this was a sacrifice to the land, they'd be able to contact the fae who claimed it during the warlock invasion. A fae would know how the magic was used."

A shudder passed through me. A proper reaction to dealing with the fae. "Let's leave them out of the investigation for now but come back to that avenue if we reach a dead end."

"Maeve and Nix don't represent all fae," Jada chided, gesturing at herself. "I'm a planeswalker because I'm part fae."

Jada, our stepdad Phyr, and my stepmom Miriam might be awesome, but I firmly believed that's because they lived most of their time on Earth. It changed Phyr a lot since we all first met him. It changed every fae that lived here at least half the time. The fae were originally from here, cast out by the early mundanes to micro-universes known as faeries. It's like the fae found their ancient humanity when they spent time outside the wilds of faeries. Not to mention, how fae instantly hated me because my grandfather and father had slaughtered many fae in the Great War. I wasn't even born yet when that occurred. That didn't matter. Immortals could hold a grudge a lot longer than a lifetime or two and held it against entire bloodlines.

"I know. We already have shifters and neo-Norse pagans involved. Bringing in the fae now will just complicate things." Speaking of bloodlines, I looked up at the wolf shifter once again. If he was of Fenrir's ilk, he was related to me. Another wave of sadness that his life had been cut short for the gods or for someone's machinations hit me. "Let's get him down. I can't stand to see him like this."

"Me either," Singh agreed.

The three of us got the wolf shifter down, Singh, Jada, and I treating the victim with due reverence. I said a prayer my mother had taught me over the body, and then closed his eyes.

Jada sighed. "I'll call Magical Forensics. They'll probably be able to find his pack."

I turned to Singh. "See if there's someone selling shifter blood on the streets and talk to the lone shifters. I'll handle the local packs. They'll know me and give me more than a loner."

"Who's your pack? It might get in the way if the locals have beef with yours. I could do some talking. They like me."

"Greater Seattle." I grinned without any warmth, more of a bearing of teeth. "I'll be fine."

At the name of my pack, he gave me and Jada a once-over. A few years ago, he'd have recognized us on sight. In I.S.E.A. black suits, we'd become anonymous, unrecognizable. Also, Jada and I had changed a lot in appearance from the teenagers who had become overnight famous on the global news and viral videos. Yeah, she had lime-green hair and I had my blonde hair dyed blue with a shaved undercut in a French twist for work, but our faces and bodies had matured. Our parents had pulled from the limelight, too. Well, Miriam had pulled out and concentrated on her community school... My father still had ambitions. You just didn't step down from Archangel and pack alpha positions.

Yep. Supernatural legacies right before you, Officer Singh.

Recognition lit in his eyes. He shook his head and his finger, chuckling softly. "You're not *a* pack princess, Agent Crowfoot. You're *the* Pack Princess."

I shrugged and once again turned my gaze to the victim, praying that my pack and my status would hold enough sway with the local alphas to get justice for this shifter and stop more of my kind from this horrible fate.

CHAPTER FIVE

Jada materialized a white sheet, laying it over the victim like a shroud. "I'll get MFD."

Singh's jaw dropped as Jada vanished. "Never in my life have I seen anything like that."

We gave the body space, walking closer to the tape. Singh and I would also keep an eye out for anyone getting too close to the crime scene tape while Jada was gone. The fewer people who saw this, the fewer questions that would be raised and the better we could keep it out of the media for now. I didn't want this killer gaining any power from fame.

"Oh, yeah? Never seen magic?"

He turned to me with an earnest expression. "Here in Canada, supes just don't show their gifts. Period."

"You don't shift amongst friends?"

A grin lit his face, his cheeks dimpling above his beard. "That depends." He rolled his shoulders. "Shifters, yes. Mundanes, no. I keep that part of me private."

I grunted. I didn't blame him. I didn't even have mundane

friends outside of work colleagues. Sarah, Jada's girlfriend, was a mundane, but we weren't friends.

"When I visited India with my folks, I saw...a lot more of the supernaturals out in the open. Some things could be credited to real magic. Some were tricks of the eye." He shook his head. "I've never seen anyone just disappear like that."

"Planeswalkers are rare," I agreed.

He murmured the word "planeswalker" as if hearing the term for the first time. I knew of them even before I went to I.S.E.A. Academy. They were legends among angels and nephilim, and not the good kind of story. When I was small, my father and grandfather warned me often of the fae that could snatch me out of my bed. I had iron sprinkled around my windowsill and the pack farm used to have a wrought iron fence surrounding it.

Then, dear old Dad met a demigod named Rafael with a daughter that had a half-fae mom. Suddenly a girl with some fae blood was my best friend and someone I guided into the supe world. Fae were no longer the creatures I prayed protection from, but the iron stayed. Fae, like humans, weren't all good or all bad, but we look out for the bad.

"How do you discover you have an ability like that?"

"Our stepdad is a planeswalker. He saw it in her. It's a fae thing but other supes have the ability."

Singh cocked his head. "You're sisters and partners?"

I shrugged, giving Singh some respect for not going for the obvious "you don't look related." We weren't biological sisters, but the way people looked didn't mean squat when it came to blood relatives. "I.S.E.A. has more nepotism than any organization. Comes with the territory of having fewer supes than mundanes in the world. The witches of Magical Forensics, who are coming, are also siblings." I shrugged. "Some siblings work well together."

"I mean, my brother is also an officer for the Vancouver police, but we don't work together."

Jada rematerialized, followed by Maria and Hugo dressed in magi-hazmat coveralls.

Singh jumped about three feet high, hissing. Well, it sounded a bit like a hiss and a hushed roar.

Hugo laughed. "Usually, people get to know me before they hiss at me."

Maria rolled her eyes.

The shifter cop gained his composure and scowled at Hugo. The witch shrugged. "Get used to weird shit if you're going to work with I.S.E.A."

"The victim is over there." My voice sounded much graver than I ever spoke to Maria and Hugo. Usually, the Gonzalez siblings lifted my mood, but not today. I wanted things sober.

With Singh sticking close by me, we led the newly arrived trio to the corpse.

Her dark eyebrows furrowed, Maria removed the shroud.

Hugo took pictures with a camera that had a giant flash. "Why did you take him down?" Annoyance colored his tone. "You know that's not procedure."

I just stared. I knew the protocols for a murder scene, but I just couldn't leave the victim like that. It was unprofessional, but I was no cop. "Fuck procedure. That's why."

"He needs justice, not comfort. There's no comfort for the dead."

A low threatening growl emitted from my throat. "I said fuck procedure."

Singh drew closer to me. "There are photos from when I first came on the scene. I can have my department forward them to you."

Hugo swung his gaze toward the Vancouver cop, giving him a quick once-over. "Thanks, Officer—Constable?—but your cameras are not like ours."

Maria shot Hugo a scathing look. "Güey, you are so like mamá sometimes!" She gestured to the victim. "Taking him down and covering his body was the kind thing to do."

Her brother frowned. "I know. It looks like he suffered, but I would like to see how he was hung and what kind of knots were used. The camera could pick up if there was spellwork involved in the rope to restrain the shifter or if the ropes were just ropes."

Shit. Hugo had a point. I'd let my feelings get in the way of my duty.

"I didn't smell any enchantment. The knot is still there." I nodded to the discarded rope next to the tree. That's about all the apology he'd get from me.

"I didn't see any magic besides the small magics of mundanes," Jada added, her tone more contrite than mine. Normally, she was the rule follower of us two. The suffering on the shifter's face must have moved her as much as it had me. That, or she saw how much the death had affected me.

"Those small magics can do a lot, agents. Things are different now. Some mundanes know it." Hugo sighed and made his way over to the ropes.

While her brother took pictures, Maria addressed Singh, "Has the area been swept for hair or other remnants of the suspects who performed the sacrifice?"

"There was an initial sweep of the immediate perimeter." The officer's dark eyes swept the area as if he were remembering the actions the Vancouver police took there. "We didn't find any materials with the victim's blood on it. Anything that wasn't hard, damning evidence like a murder weapon wouldn't be admissible in court because this is a public space. We don't want to prosecute the innocent. Besides, I didn't smell anything that had an odor of the magic that was used."

Hugo patted his camera. "This should pick up what supernatural senses can't."

"A new invention by Luke?" I quirked an eyebrow.

"Yeah. He and I worked on this bad boy together. This records magical residue from spellwork, casting, biowaste—you name it." He pointed the camera at the remnants of the severed rope and the knot I'd cut and snapped a picture. The flash flared.

We gathered around the witch as he showed us the viewscreen on the back of the camera. "Bingo!"

The rope showed nothing in person, didn't smell like magic, but glowing runes appeared on the screen. Except the runes weren't the ones the ancient Norse used. If I stopped concentrating on the appearance and let my eyes relax, I could read the symbols.

My stomach roiled and my head swam. I didn't know if I would vomit or faint first and fought to not do either.

Jada placed a hand on my shoulder, bringing me back to myself. "What does it say, Roxy? Is it a binding spell?"

I shook my head, trying to shake away the fuzziness looking directly at the runes caused. "Yeah. I think so. It says Gleipnir, which means 'The deceiver.'"

Singh grunted. "Do you think it's about the dual nature of shifters? As in the suspects wanted everyone to see that he wasn't mundane."

I thought it was about a covenant that my bloodline had with the god Fenrir to gain our powers. I wasn't quite sure if I wanted to expound just yet.

Jada's fingers dug into my shoulder. "What's wrong, Roxy?"

"The runes affected me. Dulled my senses."

"They must've had the same effect on the shifter," Maria guessed. "That would be how mundanes or at least the neo-pagans with small magic were able to exsanguinate a shifter without being torn apart."

She was probably right. "The rope itself had no other magical scent and didn't vibrate with the hum of magic like other cursed objects I've come across."

"I didn't see any magic on it with my second sight."

"There were no physical warnings for me either. Can I see the screen?" Officer Singh asked Hugo. The witch obliged.

"Huh. Interesting. I can see the glowing symbols but looking at them has no effect on me."

"It must be coded to wolves somehow," Maria guessed.

I swallowed hard. Fenrir's wolves. I didn't say the thought out loud, not yet.

Hugo nodded at the rope. "Maybe it's blood magic? Blood is powerful."

Cautiously, I picked up the dark rope and sniffed. "Yes. There's blood here. It's mundane though." I offered it to Singh to confirm.

He sniffed and confirmed, "A hint of small magic of mundanes that I couldn't detect before because of all the blood from the victim."

I furrowed my brow and looked to my partner. Maria and Hugo were good at research, but Jada had access to the grimoires of her mother's coven. Miriam's coven had absorbed the members of the oldest witches in the world and their grimoires. Also, her school also taught magic to mundanes. Eastside Charm School was always making new discoveries of what the supposedly unmagical could do. Sometimes they could perform spells under certain conditions.

Jada bit her lip and looked to Maria and Hugo. Then she spoke. "It doesn't matter if they were mundane. Our family's story is written in our blood: every life and death, every sorrow and joy. The magic in blood was so powerful even a mundane with small magic could wield it in a powerful way."

The five of us stood silently for a moment, processing that there were mundanes out there murdering shifters, but to what purpose?

The witches bagged the rope into evidence bags that had wards on them, nulling the magic's effectiveness without breaking the spell. They then moved onto the corpse. "We'll run some tests in the lab, try to get a DNA match with known Norse neopagans, and check the database," Maria said and then looked at me as she added, "Be careful, Roxanne."

Hugo, bent over the corpse with a body bag, lifted his bespectacled gaze in my direction. "Shit. Yeah. They're going for your kind."

A shudder ran through me, but I said, "I think I've got a little advantage this guy doesn't." I only hoped being part angel made it true.

Singh cleared his throat.

I almost lost it on him until I saw the card in his outstretched hand.

"So we can keep in touch. Also—this might be a bad time, but if I.S.E.A. has some openings, maybe you all can put in a word for me?"

Jada took the card from his outstretched hand. "Sure."

CHAPTER SIX

Over the next few days, Jada and I traveled to the cities where the other murders took place. Every wolf had been exsanguinated in their half form. No traces of the blood were found. We interviewed the local packs. Each one didn't know the wolf shifter victim personally but knew of them as a lone wolf. Jada and I were in our shared office, each at our desk, pouring over the details and writing up notes.

She spun her chair away from her desk to sidle next to me. "Do you think they're drinking the blood?"

I scowled in her direction. "I'm going to assume you mean the cult who is killing shifters. Do you think this is a death cult...or vampirism?" I shuddered. A horde of vampires attacked my father once. He could have smitten them all, but a smiting would've taken out half the block in the wake. That's the problem with being overpowered with ethics. If it weren't for Jada's mom luring them into her home's wards and picking the rest off with a crossbow, he'd have died rather than destroy the neighborhood and everyone in it to protect himself.

Jada held up a finger. Her dark eyes gleamed with excitement.

"Close! In Christianity, they have something called the Communion."

"Yeah. I'm aware." Most, but not all, shifters used to be servants of the Angelic Anocracy—enforcers called Guardians. Some went to church; most had their own congregations separate from the mundanes. We'd stopped going a long time ago when my parents split, but I remembered the sacraments. "What does Communion have to do with these neopagans?"

"Theophagy!" She made jazz hands and looked at me expectantly, as if this single word was all the information that I'd need to connect the dots.

Instead of congratulating Jada on her brilliance, I blinked. "God eating?"

The smile flattened and she lowered her hands. "Something like that."

Her meaning hit. A wave of nausea crashed through me as the implications also hit. Most people didn't murder, but if our blood gave these psychopaths some power or—"Do you think this cult is drinking the blood to become wolf shifters?"

"Or to beseech Fenrir for something."

I rubbed my temples, fighting off throbbing that could turn into a migraine. Shifters rarely got sick. Our bodies were magical and immune to a lot of mundane dI.S.E.A.se, but we could get headaches and throw up.

A warm hand squeezed my shoulder. "What is the deal that your family made with him?"

"I don't know exactly. All I know is that one of us is supposed to be a tithe to keep him from starting Ragnarök."

An alarm went off. Jada looked at her watch. She grimaced. "Time to report to the Director."

NOT MUCH LATER IN Director Tan's office, she adjusted a new picture of Lady Di, Everest, and Bonnie Prince Charlie. The three cats wore bunny ears and white fuzzy suits—which made no sense because they were cats. Easter baskets laden with cat treats and toys sat before them. I had no idea if Tan was married or single, but my bet was she was single or had a dual income, no kids household.

I glanced at Jada. She had a cat named P.C. He was getting up there in years and becoming more willing to put up with things he wouldn't when we were kids. I grinned and nodded at the picture, silently suggesting we could dress him up and do a cute photo shoot.

Jada narrowed her dark eyes and gave me a curt shake of the head with a don't you dare touch my cat look.

I held up my hands, giving up. It was hard enough on the domestic feline to live in a house filled with people who could turn into frightening predators. I would leave the ears and outfits to Tan.

Jada placed a card on Tan's desk. "This is the officer we're working with in Vancouver. He'd like a chance at being an agent of I.S.E.A." There, we did our favor. Singh could out himself as what kind of supe he was and how that qualified him.

The Director ignored the card. "Explain why you didn't go directly to the pack alpha."

We'd gone to several alphas, so I didn't understand the question. "Excuse me? Which alpha? There are many."

"Vancouver. She's raising a stink and says we have her wolf and doesn't appreciate that she had to learn of the death from a loner." Tan emphasized the last word.

"We have all the wolves. There's an open investigation," Jada replied.

I was confused. "She—who? Did you get a name?"

Tan turned from her picture, perplexed. "You don't know who the alpha of Vancouver is?"

My father had been archangel for the Pacific Northwest and was still alpha for the greater Seattle area. Since he ran for state senate and won, alpha duties were relegated to Princess, my aunt. Sometimes they fell to me—she didn't want full alpha status and neither did I. My dad needed it in case he got injured, but that was not the point of this conversation. Something fell through the cracks in reporting.

"Last I knew, the greater Vancouver and Victoria packs were run by a married couple. My dad and aunt have failed to mention there was a new alpha in Vancouver, if this person is an actual alpha."

The Director crossed her arms over her chest and frowned. Then she sat at her desk and pulled something up. "This isn't just a breach on your pack's end. Packs are supposed to report to the Supernatural Council of the Americas when there's been a shift in power. All organized supes do. I have no deaths in Vancouver and no announcement. Could this be a new pack?"

I almost said no, but I realized my father was more concerned about looking out for the rights of supes in Washington State than minding the packs and the lone shifters a couple hours' drive away in another country.

"Check in with your aunt and then check out what's going on up there."

BACK IN OUR OFFICE, I made a video call to Princess. She picked up on the third ring. Fortunately for me, she wasn't teaching today at the Eastside Charm School. The school existed partly in downtown Redmond, Washington. The rest was in Miriam's faerie. A harpy named Luke, who also worked for I.S.E.A., set up a way for calls to work, but magic and tech weren't always reliable partners.

A brunette in her late forties with a pretty but hard face stared back at me on my phone screen. Princess used to wear a perpetual disapproving frown when she looked at me. I resembled my mother and my mother had caused no small amount of trouble for the pack or my aunt. Now, she grinned. "Hey, kid."

I was closer to thirty than twenty, but I would be "kid" to her. At least she didn't call me "Box o' Rox" like my father. Instead of pleasantries, I went straight into my reason for calling.

"Have you heard of a power shift in Vancouver?"

Dark eyebrows slashed downward. The old frown appeared. It wasn't disapproving though. "I haven't spoken to Rodrigo or Aaron for a few months, but that's typical to go at least a year without speaking to one pack or another. Also, I haven't heard anything through the whisper network. Why?"

I explained what was happening. Princess's face grew cold. She put her honey badger claws into her tone as she scolded, "This is something you needed to report to me or your father."

Just like that, my aunt made me feel like a rebellious teenager again. Besides, my father would want to go up to Vancouver with wings and fangs out because he'd assume this was Fenrir's doing. No, thank you. I tried my best to sound professional in my explanation. "It's an ongoing investigation. I.S.E.A. protocol dictates—"

"To Hell with I.S.E.A. protocol, Roxanne. There are shifters dying and something funky is happening with the Vancouver pack. Your first loyalty is to us. You saw firsthand what operating outside our protocols did to your pack."

Old shame twisted my gut and made my eyes sting. A lump formed in my throat as I opened my mouth to speak. I swallowed it. I would not bark back with tear-filled outrage. She might outrank me in pack and might be my elder, but I was an adult with a responsibility beyond her tiny scope. All supes were my responsibility. A shifter, even one with a non-shifter wife, wouldn't see it. She was still steeped in pack politics and had brought Aurora into the pack house.

"Yes, Princess. I sure did. Even now, when I'm working to protect shifters, not to mention the wolves of our pack, at my own risk, I might add, I'm accused of disloyalty."

The hard edges to her features softened. "Roxy, your mother made herself vulnerable. Not only did the pack suffer, but your mother did too."

Well, that's the first time she'd admitted my mother might have had feelings worth noting. "I know. Mom, really—"

"Kirsten made her bed." She waved a dismissive hand as if to shoo away the very notion of my mother like she was a pest. "And I couldn't care less about the consequences she suffered. You, on the other hand, are my niece." Her face showed some affection that was also in her tone, but I didn't get that from her the way her boys did when I was young. It means very little to me now—or so I tell myself. "You always want to go it alone. You can't do it this time. You need to bring this to the pack and have backup when you go north to investigate. They need to know you have more than the supe cops behind you."

I thought about her offer. If I went up there as a pack princess with my elders at my back, I wouldn't be there as an agent of I.S.E.A. "I understand your concern, but I.S.E.A. is neutral. The Greater Seattle pack is not. We don't want this to turn into a territory war. Besides, I won't be going alone." I glanced at Jada, who stood next to me but out of the video chat. "I'll have my partner as backup."

"I can't stop you or order you. I'm not your alpha, but I'm going to say this is a bad idea. You don't know those wolves, and you're not protected there. Jada is as green as you are and doesn't know customs." She sighed. "However, I know you too well to think I'm doing anything but wasting my breath. I'll low-key let the wolves know someone is murdering their kind. It's on you to warn your mother, kid." She muttered, "Not that she'll listen either."

Digging my fingernails into the palm of my free hand, I replied, "I got this."

"Uh huh. Going to learn the hard way it doesn't pay to be a lone wolf. Call me when you learn your lesson." With that, Princess ended the video chat.

Stuffing my cell phone into a pocket, I growled my frustration. "Why did I bother calling her?"

Jada placed a hand on my shoulder. "Like it or not, your dad has stepped away from the traditional role of alpha and has gone on to a bigger role in the supe community at large. Princess is your leader now. She knows what's up with shifters in this area better than anyone. If she doesn't know, something suspicious is going down."

"All of this is getting under my skin." I blew out my breath.

Setting aside my personal drama with Princess, I thought about what Jada had said. My aunt didn't hear anything, but her tactic was for the pack to go in wings and fangs at the ready just like my dad would. I wanted to do things differently. My way. The call was out of the norm, indeed, but not necessarily a reason to assume the pack had any involvement in the murders. Which meant we had to go up and let the real alphas know.

"Someone is pretending to be the alpha. I know Rodrigo and Aaron. We need to warn them."

Jada grabbed the fob to our agency-assigned car off my desk. "Let's drive up. We need to plan what we'll say."

Planeswalking would be faster, but she was right. Me being the pack princess for the Seattle area pack, we had to present this right.

CHAPTER SEVEN

Two and a half hours later, we pulled up to a neighborhood in Surrey—a suburb just south of Vancouver. Four- and five-bedroom houses with brick facades and neatly trimmed lawns lined the street. My father owned a sprawling house on acreage that included farm and forest. Therefore, our pack house was where a lot of the Greater Seattle area pack lived. They didn't have to. Some owned their own homes, but many liked the communal style living. Other packs either chose to live like us or separately. The Vancouver pack was mainly in houses spread out in Surrey and Coquitlam, living in single-family homes. From what I remembered overhearing my father say, the Vancouver pack gathered more often at the alphas' house than most mundanes did with their blood relatives. Today was no exception.

An assortment of vehicles ranging from high-priced electric cars, sports cars, and SUVs to inexpensive compact cars were parked in the driveway and littering the street. As we exited our I.S.E.A.-issued black sedan, the musk and deep forest scent of shifters hit me as soon as I stepped onto the sidewalk. "There are a *lot* of shifters here."

Jada nodded. "We don't need to fight. Stay close. If trouble starts,

I'll pull us to the car or home before they can even think of touching us."

The door swung open and a girl of about seven or eight skipped outside. Her brown ponytail swung to the rhythm of her steps. She stopped dead in her tracks when she saw me and Jada, or rather scented us. Her eyes had been gleefully locked on a massive piece of beef jerky in her hand that she had been about to take a bite out of before she became aware of us.

Her scent hit me, too. Wolf shifter. Fenrir's line. My stomach churned at the thought of this cute innocent pup in the hands of whoever killed the shifter found in the park. I gathered my composure before she scented my worry and misunderstood.

"We're here to see the alpha and his mate." It was a courtesy to mention the mate, but I also wanted to say "his" to see her reaction.

The girl eyed me a moment then backed up a few steps. Not taking her gaze away from me and Jada, she called over her shoulder, "Dads! There's a wolf and someone who smells funny to see you!"

I glanced at Jada, fighting a smirk. She bit her lip to keep from laughing, but mirth twinkled in her eyes.

Two men with the broad builds and jawlines of shifter men in their forties exited the house. With preternatural speed, the duo formed a wall in front of the girl. Several other pack members assembled on the front steps. A woman in her thirties slipped from the others, snatched the girl, and disappeared into the house. Despite the less than cordial welcome, a modicum of relief lifted a weight from my chest. There was no power shift. Rodrigo and Aaron were still the alpha and mate-beta.

Rodrigo wore an apron that read "Kiss the Chef" and a cartoon picture of a fork and meat cleaver over jeans and a plain black T-shirt. Aaron wore gray slacks and a red plaid button-down. They both looked as if they could model for the men's section of a department store. If it weren't for the larger-than-average bulging muscles and the threatening looks.

At the same time that I opened my mouth to speak, Aaron sniffed the air. Recognition lit his face and the alpha's mouth spread in a smile that reached his gray eyes. "Roxanne! Look at you!"

Rodrigo's jaw slackened. "Roxy...All grown up?"

Before I could utter a word, I was in Aaron's big arms. Nothing like a massive shifter hug to squeeze all the professionalism out of you. Rodrigo laughed and grabbed me from him, hugging me so hard I could barely breathe.

The alpha and his mate soon welcomed me into their home. Their daughter was the youngest and I hadn't been to this house since before my parents split, so I hadn't met her or a couple of their other younger children. My father stopped attending many intra-pack functions in the area until he married Miriam and Phyr and ran for state senate. Then he began making the rounds with the Washington packs. I declined going. One, I was not looking for a mate and if I went, they'd assume that's why I went along. Two, many didn't support my father's decision to abjure rather than challenge my mother for cheating. Looking a lot like my mother Kirsten, I was a reminder of that decision—infidelity was no laughing matter among shifters. Especially when your mate is the alpha and pack secrets could leak out. Dad only asked me once and never again. I didn't blame him. He'd moved on to a new thing, and I got Miriam and Phyr out of it.

Coming here, I was expecting the cold shoulder most outsider packs and even some insiders of my own pack used to give me. I wasn't expected to be brought in and introduced to everyone who either didn't recognize me or hadn't met me before. Then the alphas announced they were having an early dinner and invited me to the pack table. Jada was also treated like family as soon as it was established that she was the stepdaughter of the alpha. Pack princess life wasn't always good for me—speaking of pack princesses, my aunt could eat it with her suggestion to come with backup. I felt no small amount of smugness about my decision not to do so.

We accepted the food offered despite being on duty. To not do so would be a great insult. We couldn't discuss business right away.

First, we had to trade talk of weddings, births, who was old enough for initiation, and the sad business of deaths in the packs. Then we got into intra-pack gossip, who was stirring the pot, who had an affair and got challenged. What kids were being a problem for their parents. Then finally it came time to discuss our purpose.

"I'm afraid I have to talk about something going on in the packs of a more serious nature," I said, gaze flicking to the table of mixed ages.

"I'm sure you do. Pack kids—all grown up. You're I.S.E.A. agents now," Aaron stated without any hint of question in his tone. His gray eyes dipped to my suit and then Jada's tie.

"Yes, we are. That's actually why we're here." I glanced at the kids at the pack table again and grimaced before turning my gaze back to Aaron and Rodrigo. "It's been fun catching up, but I would like to seek an audience with the alpha and his mate in an official capacity."

Rodrigo needed only to give a look. The children scattered, a stampede down a hall and upstairs. The older shifters said formal goodbyes to me.

Finally, Jada, the two alphas, the shifter woman who'd scooped up the girl earlier, and I were left. The woman's scent told me she was a fox shifter, which I knew without inhaling. I'd figured out she was Iseul, Rodrigo and Aaron's oldest. We'd met when we were both kids and had played together at bigger functions. Young me had had a crush on Iseul. Older me couldn't help but notice she was even more gorgeous than I remembered and had smiled at me a lot at dinner and complimented me twice in front of the pack. This was a dance I knew well in the shifter community. Genuine interest in a mate was different than mundane dating. Normally, I'd flirt back or shut her down. Shifters in our pack positions did not play at dating each other.

Iseul was so obvious that Jada had kicked my foot twice. I couldn't possibly get in a serious relationship right now. Not with a case like this afoot. However, I had heavy news to bring and *that* would shut things down on its own.

"We think we know why you're here," Rodrigo began, glancing at his husband and his daughter. "It's the usurper's attempts, right?"

Jada got out a notebook. "We did have a woman call I.S.E.A., claiming to be alpha of the Vancouver pack." She looked to me.

"She was claiming a shifter's body Vancouver police discovered murdered in a ritualistic fashion." I got my phone out and pulled up a picture of the Stanley Park victim. Then I placed it in the center of the table. "Warning. What I'm about to show you is beyond gruesome."

The shifters knew if I, a wolf shifter who hunted game in my animal form, said something was gruesome, it was extraordinarily so. My warning did not prevent the horror on the family's faces as they each looked at my phone. Rodrigo's eyes teared up and he buried his face in his husband's shoulder. Iseul covered her mouth, her skin paled visibly, and her hand shook as she handed the phone back to me.

Aaron wiped a hand over his chiseled face. His eyes were red and glistening, and his voice shook with grief as he spoke. "That's Gerald. He used to be a part of our pack up until six or seven months ago. He was a good guy. Kind of quirky." He grinned a little as if remembering the victim. It lasted a moment before he heaved a sigh and nodded at the phone. "He—he didn't deserve that."

Jada wrote everything down, but she looked at me for a split second. I nodded. *Yeah. I know.* The first wolf shifter murders started not long before that.

"Gerald is one victim of many—a part of a chain of murders happening across the United States' packs. All wolf shifters. Specifically, wolf shifters of Fenrir's line." I watched their faces. The alphas were wolves.

Rodrigo lifted his head. Aaron faced him. Fear etched their features. Iseul bit her lip, looking at her fathers with a similar expression as the one they wore.

"Are you saying that we and Ariana are in danger?" Rodrigo asked, his voice quavering. "Is that why you're here?"

Fear danced in a frisson like freezing water dripping down my back. I could make assurances, but this was not the time to lie. I nodded. "I'd always keep a detail on her and any other wolves. It's only been Fenrir's line so far, but any wolf could be of mixed shifter lines." I didn't add *like me.* My safety wasn't their concern.

The fathers looked to Iseul. She sat up straighter. I knew the posture. I assumed it when my father was about to dole out important orders.

Rodrigo spoke first. "Contact the wolves of the pack for an emergency meeting. We need a security detail for those who can't stay here."

"Your sister is *your* priority," Aaron added.

Iseul nodded and rose. "On it, fathers." Just like that, she was out of the room. Her fathers watched her go with the kind of pride that made my chest ache.

"Tell us more about this usurper," Jada prompted.

The alpha and his mate shifted in their seats. The skin on their faces rippled. Predators lurked behind their eyes, waiting to be set free. If they were fighting their animal form, to say the subject of the usurper was a sore one would be an understatement. However, they'd brought it up.

Rodrigo inhaled audibly and exhaled through his nose. "A year ago, an unknown came into our territory. She didn't present herself to us or anyone else. We're not even sure if she's a shifter who broke custom, or an outsider somehow forming a pack."

I furrowed my brow, confused. "If not a shifter, then what is she?"

He shook his head and looked at his husband.

"Don't know. There's this cloud of mystery surrounding her. Some say she's a goddess with the capability to shift. Some say she's a wolf shifter. Others say she's a sorceress, or some sort of pagan priestess with power over wolves."

I glanced at Jada on the last conjecture, but her eyes were on her notebook. Turning my attention back to the alphas, I asked, "How did she end up with a pack?"

"My security reported someone recruiting lone wolves. I didn't think much of it." Aaron spread his hands. "Hey, if they found a community that fit better than us, more power to them." When he said "us," he looked at his husband.

I got it. Like mundanes, some shifters had a problem with anyone who wasn't straight, and some even had problems with race. Usually, they were too heavily involved with mundanes because those things didn't matter as much in shifter culture as they did to the unmagical. Princess's father was an exception. The former alpha was a right jerk, and I was glad he'd lost when he challenged my dad.

"We let the rogue pack be and that was a mistake on our part. They started poaching wolves from ours."

"What is their leader's name?" Jada asked.

Aaron shrugged. "Don't know."

"That's why we call her the Usurper," Rodrigo added, spreading his hands. "No one knows her name."

"Do you know where the pack is based?" I asked.

The alphas exchanged a look. They lowered their heads, ashamed. Still, Aaron met my gaze from lowered lashes. "The wolf shifters we'd sent to infiltrate the pack—" He heaved a deep sigh. "Left us. We sent more after them. The ones who weren't wolves came back."

"That's how you realized it was wolves she was after?"

The alphas nodded.

"All we have are whispers and a smaller pack." Rodrigo shuddered, his gaze flicking to the now dark phone screen. "And now, Gerald is dead."

After wrapping up with the alpha and his mate, Jada and I headed to the agency-issued car. It was about eight in the evening, so the sun was on its way out.

"Wait!"

We turned to see Iseul jogging our way. Of course, a fox shifter ran silently. She held her hand out and then stopped. "I overheard the conversation. There's something my dads don't know."

I lifted my eyebrows, encouraging her to continue.

She glanced over her shoulder. "Gerald had a girlfriend. A weirdo witch wannabe. She should know he died...but watch her reaction when you tell her. She might have been the one to lead him to that cult."

My eyebrows lifted slightly higher, unintentionally this time. We'd suspected some sort of neopagan cult of the murder, but the alphas had indicated a rival pack, not a religious cult.

"What's her name and where does she live?" I asked.

"She was down your way now. Just moved to Seattle from Coquitlam a few weeks ago. Her name is Chelsey Briggs, but she goes by something else as a witch or druid or whatever." Iseul rolled her eyes and waved her hand dismissively.

"Do you have any idea where in Seattle she might live?"

Iseul got out her phone. "I have her number and address. Her grandma still lives in Coquitlam. I pretended to be an old friend and she gave it up. You see, I was going to pay Chelsey a visit to check up on what happened to Gerald but..." She sobbed.

I put a sympathetic hand on her shoulder. "We'll find his killer."

Jada took out her notebook. "Starting with Chelsey's address and any personal items of Gerald's or Chelsey's you might still have in the pack house."

Iseul tilted her head to the side. "Why personal items?"

"In case she's not at the address her grandmother gave you. The item would tie me to Chelsey in time and space, and from there, I can find her," Jada replied.

"Oh, yeah. I think we have some of her stuff from Gerald's old room boxed in the garage."

Jada and I smiled and said at the same time, "Perfect."

CHAPTER
EIGHT

The unfortunate side of traveling by car instead of planeswalking was getting stuck at the border queue for a few hours. Jada had been tempted to create a Nowhere door, aka a portal, to Seattle and drive the car through. Unfortunately, at the worst, we'd create an international incident. Avoiding customs when we were in line might look bad for supes in general. The fewer people who knew about planeswalkers, the better.

The next morning, we headed into the city via car. The music we were listening to stopped. Director Tan's face and name popped up on the vehicle screen. Since I was driving, I hit a button on my steering wheel to patch the call into the vehicle's sound system.

"I expected a report about the Vancouver pack this morning. What's this text about following a lead?"

I filled her in on the details about the encounter, and Jada interjected as needed. Tan remained silent as we spoke.

"If you'd come to me," she said in an admonishing tone, her Boston accent thickening with her annoyance, "I would have sent you to investigate this new pack that might be a cult, not some girlfriend who may or may not be tied."

"We thought it best to get all the information we could before jumping out of the proverbial frying pan," I replied, expecting the reprimand.

"If Chelsey is a witch, Director," Jada added, "she should have registered with the Supernatural Council of the Americas—or at the very least the Rosemary and Oleander coven. Because she didn't, Chelsey is now a person of interest, especially since she was close to the recent murder victim."

"For two agents who didn't want to be cops, you sure sound like them." There was a hint of amusement in her tone.

"Agents of I.S.E.A.," I corrected, bristling. The young woman who didn't want to be part of any mundane organization still lived in me despite making this my career. "We sound like agents. At any rate, Chelsey might be able to give us more information about the pack and their leader."

"I thought these murders might be shifter business, but if there's a preternatural sect behind these murders, we've got serious blood magic going on. Getting all the information first was the right choice. Be careful, agents."

"Yes, Director," we replied in unison.

"Also, do not hesitate to call for backup. I could dispatch the mages and witches of I.S.E.A. in moments. Phyr owes me a favor."

The last sentence made me curious why my stepdad owed her, but Director Tan wasn't one to give up secrets. Also, I didn't need the Director to ask him. Phyr would burn worlds to help Jada and me. Not backup I'd ask for lightly.

We found Chelsey's apartment building on Roosevelt in the Green Lake district of Seattle. The building was newer with restaurants, bars, and cafes all around. The building had a security system where we'd have to call her apartment and ask her to come down. I, and I presumed Jada, had assumed that we'd knock on the door of a house or an apartment. This shouldn't be a barrier, but we hadn't worked murder cases with mundanes involved before.

"Should we just ring her on the call box?" Jada asked, voicing my thoughts out loud. Doubt crept into her tone as she added, "We're not cops. At least not ones who have jurisdiction over her—she's not officially a supernatural."

A strange sensation fluttered in my gut as the realization hit that as I.S.E.A. agents, we'd only protected mundanes from supes. We had to work with the mundane authorities if it was the other way around. The time my father and Miriam took down a mundane religious cult that was kidnapping supernaturals came to mind. If my memory served me correctly, I.S.E.A. arrested the supernaturals and the F.B.I. arrested the mundane cult members. However, I.S.E.A. then was coming out from being an underground international organization to a public one. A lot of administration and jurisdiction had changed. We had defined roles as the authorities for supernaturals and that still applied to this case.

"Someone used magic to bind Gerald. All suspects and suspected accessories to the murders are under our jurisdiction whether they're a registered supernatural or not." I punched in the apartment number on the dial pad. No one answered.

I glanced at Jada. "Think you can get us in the building?"

Her face scrunched as she warred with herself over whether it was ethical to do so.

Yeah. We were going to bump heads here.

I was asking her to trespass and that was technically against the law to do without a warrant, but we weren't cops. I.S.E.A. agents didn't play by the same rules. Dammit, I was letting these murders go against my ethics.

"Wouldn't that fall under breaking and entering?"

"We aren't breaking and entering if we just walk in. The door will be intact. We're taking an open one."

"I—I don't know if that's true. There might be a new law about this." She broke out her phone. On it, she searched the I.S.E.A. guidebook app.

I sighed audibly. She was right though. These laws protected the innocent. We had no hard evidence that Chelsey had anything to do with Gerald's murder, but it stung that we couldn't just pop in.

Still, if she was part of these murders, we needed to get to Chelsey now. Out of the two of us, Jada had her mother's goody-two-shoes ethics. I wished for just once she'd be more like her grandfather or our stepdad. Phyr and Oberon never faced any moral objections that our society created because they'd come from a whole other world. Faerie realms had their own rules and their creator Danu exacted prices for lies and broken promises. Keeping their word and telling the truth, and a ridiculous amount of rules around manners and hospitality were the only playbook they followed...or skirted around. Murder, torture, stealing, and a whole host of crimes that I won't get into were fair game—as long as the fae were honest and not rude about it.

Our moral dilemma was solved when the front door swung open and a woman that stood about a few inches shorter than me, dressed in a broom skirt and peasant blouse with a light rain jacket, exited the building. A wave of a familiar scent hit me, and the image of Gerald's murdered body flashed in my mind.

"Chelsey Briggs," I barked with more force than I'd meant as I blocked her path and flashed my I.S.E.A. badge. "We'd like a moment of your time."

Chelsey paled. Her eyes darted to the left and right of Jada and me as if looking for a place to run. Jada murmured the words to a barrier spell. I readied myself to catch her before a barrier was needed.

"I left," she bleated like a goat and repeated, "I left! I didn't do any of it. I didn't hurt anyone. I wanted a place in Asgard, but I'm not ready." After that, she rambled so fast those were the only bits I could make out and what I could understand didn't make sense. Asgard wasn't a place for mortals. Valhalla was a place Norse pagans hoped to be in the afterlife.

Jada held up her hands, smiling. "Hey, Chelsey. I need you to take a deep breath and count to ten. We're not here to blame you for anything."

Familiar, silken magic brushed my skin and the warm, honeyed scent of Jada's particular blend of power filled my nostrils. She wasn't coercing Chelsey into complying, or influencing her thoughts, but rather dousing the woman with magical anti-anxiety spray. Still, I fortified the mental barriers Phyr had taught me to make against any magic that might affect my mind.

Chelsey did as Jada bid, her features softening as she breathed in and out. Her entire countenance changed by the time she said, "Ten."

"Good job," Jada soothed. "We would like a minute to discuss your friend Gerald."

"Gerald," Chelsey sighed. "I haven't seen him since I fled. He was in too deep. I couldn't let him know I was going to escape."

I exchanged a glance with Jada. She placed a comforting hand on Chelsey's shoulder. "You did your best. What were you escaping?"

She looked past us at some unseen spot. "I have a few errands to run."

"We just need a few moments of your time. It won't take long," Jada encouraged, another wave of her power following in the wake of her words.

Chelsey chewed her lip and wrung her hands, revealing Jada hadn't cooked her brain with so much magical influence that the potential witch couldn't think for herself.

Finally, she entered a code into the wall keyboard—which I memorized—and then led us through the double doors into a foyer.

A few minutes later, we were in a studio apartment with lots of plants, an altar that looked vaguely more Wiccan than Norse pagan, and a mishmash of other occult symbology. This told me that Chelsey wasn't devout to one pantheon, let alone any sort of formal practice, so she was not likely fully cooked by a cult. It would be easier to extract information from a parboiled cultist. Jada had some ethical qualms with taking a metaphorical spoon to Chelsey's noggin, but I would press her to do so. Even her mother had done it to save herself and some supernaturals once. We'd be saving lives.

Chelsey took a seat on what looked to be a secondhand chair amongst her plants, close to her altar. She gestured to a futon that likely also served as her bed. We sat and Jada took out her notebook.

"We have some bad news," Jada began. "Gerald was found dead in the rose garden of Stanley Park."

Her eyes widened, but she didn't have the sort of shocked reaction that someone who was hearing the news for the first time would have. Figuring it was an aftereffect of Jada's calming magic, I shook things up a bit. "They murdered him by ritualistic exsanguination. Do you know what that means?"

Chelsey's eyes glistened with tears. "I had no part in his murder."

That would be a yes.

I felt my hands balling into fists and my wolf paced back and forth, waiting to be released. My voice held a hint of a growl as I asked, "Do you know who did?"

She paled. Then, quite in opposition of how she'd behaved thus far, Chelsey straightened. "I would like to consult a lawyer."

"You're not an American citizen, and we're not that kind of cops," Jada replied in a neutral tone. "A murder of a supernatural is under the jurisdiction of the International Supernatural Enforcement Agency. You have practiced magic. Therefore, you are also a supernatural and associated with the victim."

"Your rights are what we say they are."

"I'm human!" Chelsey protested. "I'm not a monster like..." She clamped her mouth shut.

"Like Gerald?" I asked, my tone dangerously civil. I even smiled. Wow. Living with Phyr and Miriam had influenced me.

She swallowed hard and nodded. "I mean—yes—but I didn't mean that he acted like a monster. I mean that he was not human." She tapped her chest. "I'm human."

Jada leaned forward. Her pleasant, empathetic features hardened into a mask so regal, so arctic, that she didn't seem like the cheerful friend I'd grown up with or the gregarious agent at work, but transformed into an ancient being void of anything close to human. I rarely saw this side of her, but I had and the lack of Jada-ness when she was like this always gave me the heebie-jeebies. Even now, part of me wanted to tuck my tail between my legs, lower my head, and run.

"We're all human here. So was Gerald. You are simply less powerful and that grates on you. Doesn't it?"

Chelsey swallowed hard. "I—"

Jada didn't allow her to continue. She waved a hand. Chelsey grasped at her throat and her eyes bulged in surprise. She breathed hard, but no sound came out, only shocked wheezing.

"That is called a rhetorical question. Since you don't understand basic conversation, you won't be able to speak until I allow you." Jada made a broad gesture then shook her head as if Chelsey was a child who hadn't cleaned her room and needed reprimanding. "You litter your home with symbols that you have only the most rudimentary understanding of because you want to be powerful. You label those with more power than you as monsters, but the only monster I see is you."

She shook her head at the accusation, so I added, "Gerald was a loyal pack member and well-liked by his friends. I checked his criminal record with the Canadian authorities." Thanks, Constable Singh. "Gerald never harmed a person in his life and didn't have so much as a speeding ticket. He was an upstanding Canadian citizen and an all-around good person. You, however, have a long rap sheet. Shoplifting, bounced checks, illegal drug use in public spaces, a DUI, fraud—I can go on, but I won't. So, in our eyes, we're speaking to a possible murderer or at least someone who led him astray to be murdered. He trusted you and now Gerald is dead."

Tears slid down Chelsey's cheeks. The silent shuddering sob didn't quite carry the thunder of a wail of grief, but I felt sorry for her. Almost. Gerald's violent death marked on his face would haunt me for the rest of my life and she played a part in it.

I felt anger swell within. My wolf wanted to harm her the way Gerald was harmed, but that wouldn't stop what happened to him or prevent more wolves from succumbing to the same gruesome demise.

Thankfully, Jada took it from there. "You are going to stop speaking about why you are not guilty of his death, and you will start providing us information about those who did harm him. Can I trust that you will not burden our ears with crass remarks and give us that information?"

Chelsey's head bobbed in affirmation as she wiped her nose with her sleeve.

Jada waved her hand, and the woman slumped in relief. Just like that, my friend was back, empathy filled her erstwhile cold mask, and she pulled a tissue seemingly out of thin air. It wasn't though. She'd pulled the tissue from what the fae called a cache—a little purse pocket universe—she'd made to store stuff. Storing something as inane as tissue in a pocket universe was another casual display of her power—a reminder that she could stuff Chelsey there if she so wished.

I was absolutely glad Jada was my friend and work partner for multiple reasons. Being on the bad side of a supe with her kind of power was dumb.

"I don't know where to begin that doesn't make me seem..." Chelsey looked at her hands. "Can I explain how I got involved with the people who might have murdered Gerald?"

We both gave her our blessing.

"My mom was a witch. Not a witch as they are known now, but a Wiccan. We celebrated the seasons and nature, and I thought I had a connection to Brigid." She laughed, but it was an uncomfortable sound. "Then, when I was in high school, that video of supernaturals revealed magic was real went viral. Then I saw the Mythic Games. I wasn't really religious, but I saw the power and believed. I felt...felt the Aesir were a good fit. I chose Freya as my patron goddess and began reading up on the sagas. I felt the goddess had blessed me with a gift. I got an online certificate to do weddings. At a wedding, I met this woman. She led me to—" She blew out her breath.

"Take your time," Jada encouraged, once again taking notes. "We know this is hard but telling the truth will help you feel better."

I almost snickered. Jada might have led with that instead of bringing out her scary side.

"She led me to what I see now was a cult, not a religion. A cult." Her eyes were earnest as she lifted her gaze to meet mine. "I looked up the definition." Chelsey then counted on her fingers. "Charismatic leader, unquestioning devotion, isolation, control, extreme beliefs, psychological manipulation, apocalyptic visions, exploitation, shunning ex-members—except there's no shunning. You disappear if you go against the leader or speak out against what's going on."

"Define disappear," I demanded.

"We just never saw them again but there were rumors that they were sacrificed." Her hands trembled and tears fell. "I thought they were only rumors, but I didn't want to take the chance and fled."

"How did Gerald become part of this cult?"

Chelsey swallowed hard. "I was assigned to seduce him. They made it sound like this sacred duty. Because we wanted Ragnarök, you see, and he'd be part of it all. We—"

I cut her off. "Why would you want to bring about the end of the world?"

"Lif and Lifthrasir will hide the chosen in Hoddmimis Holt—a magical forest."

Again, I cut her off with a hand in the air, making a halting motion. "Lif and Lifthrasir are supposed to be the last man and woman. The only two human survivors of Ragnarök. You can look that up on the internet. It's not hidden knowledge."

"Lif and Lifthrasir are not literally two people," Chelsey scoffed as if she were a Norse mythology scholar, and I hadn't been raised on the tales as cautionary due to our ties to Fenrir, not to mention my I.S.E.A. education on the real supes from the legends. "Besides, how much folklore and sacred texts have been altered by the Christians and time itself?"

I sat back, conceding she had a point by waving her to continue.

"We believe—well, the leader, who goes by Lif, taught me that all those who identify as women are Lif and all those who identify as men are Lifthrasir, if they follow her teachings as the Sacred Lif and when she finds her mate, he will be the Sacred Lifthrasir."

I dug my nails into my palms. Of course, the cult leader wouldn't go by her documented name. I wanted to scream. Gerald was dead, multiple wolves were dead, because some power-hungry zealot thought she could bring on Ragnarök. Then my blood ran cold with the realization there probably wasn't just one sect of this cult, not with murders spanning across the country.

Jada stopped scribbling in her notebook and tilted her head to one side. "So how does Ragnarök play into you bringing Gerald into the cult?"

She didn't add "to be sacrificed," but Chelsey seemed to understand.

"They call themselves the Prophets of Jörmungandr. Sacred Lif thinks she can wake him from his slumber so he will devour Midgard, metaphorically speaking. You see, Ragnarök is not the end, but a time of change. We need it." Her small hands spread as if encompassing all around her. "The world is on a precipice of chaos. We need Jörmungandr to swallow it all to bring back the natural order."

"At the small price of sacrificing monsters."

She winced at my sarcastic reprimand.

I rubbed my temples. Some of what she said was from the old stories but twisted and could bring about a lot more than a metaphorical Jörmungandr. All we needed was a doomsday cult summoning a planet-eating space serpent. If I thought giant space rabbits were a pain...

A thought occurred to me. "Jörmungandr is the sibling of Fenrir and Hel. Why kill wolves of Fenrir's line?"

The question must've hit a nerve. Chelsey stammered for a moment. Then, as if remembering something told to quell her own curiosity, she said, "The sacrifices are to make Fenrir strong enough to free himself from Odin's chains so that he can wake his brother and free his sister from the realm of the dead."

That was an outright lie. Besides, the flimsy excuse made no sense. Killing Fenrir's blood-bound wolves wouldn't make him stronger. However, the belief that the sacrifices would free him just might work.

Anger simmered low within me, but it could heat to boiling. Wolf shifters, people, were dying on some false prophet's word and for what? An end to the world these people didn't have a leg up in so thought it should end for everyone. I leaned forward, eyes narrowing on her. My voice was a low growl. "Tell me again, how you are not part of Gerald's murder?"

Chelsey's hands flew up and her excuses flew out of her mouth. "I thought I was choosing him as my Lifthrasir—my mate in the new way of things after Ragnarök. It became clear that he was different and that the other new people in the cult were not hu—that they were shapeshifters. Things got weird. Gerald and the others were no longer at our worship services. He stopped answering my calls and texts. I thought he'd ghosted me for another, more powerful witch." A tear slid down her cheek as she spoke. "When it was my turn to serve the Sacred Lif—which was just cleaning her house and taking out the trash—I had this feeling that I was being insecure, and that Gerald might be there. I did some snooping and found a key to her basement. Gerald was asleep in a cage. I tried to find the key, but there was none around. Another member found me. I asked why my boyfriend was in a cage. He told me that the Sacred Lif had said the devotee was preparing themselves to be a sacrifice to free Fenrir and the cage was some sort of place to cleanse—my memory is foggy on the reasoning."

An image of the time when I was a teenager trapped in a room by a so-called Christian cult flashed in my mind. I banished the memory. Now wasn't the time. "Blóts for the ancient Norse were voluntary. The cages meant that Gerald was not volunteering."

"I—I realize that now. I pretended to understand, to agree—I was a coward—I know, but my mind kept screaming get out of there while I could."

Jada furrowed her brow. "Why didn't you go to the police?"

Her responding laugh held a bitter note. "The Sacred Lif has important friends. Businesspeople, police, politicians—the sect goes beyond our little group. I ran. I wanted no part in it. Honestly, I didn't seriously think they would kill Gerald. I thought they'd like—I don't know—draw some blood or something."

My skin itched and my blood came to a roiling boil. My wolf was always a protector, but right now, the shift threatened to happen out of anger. Not good. A shifter of a predatory nature needed to keep their animal under a tight leash when we felt like this. Luckily for Chelsey, my father was a strong alpha and my aunt the most dominant beta in the entire northwest. Not wanting me to be like my mother, they'd taught me control since I was a toddler.

Jada looked up from her notebook. She would have to speak. I couldn't continue the questioning, not feeling like this. One look at me and my friend understood. "The best thing you could do for yourself now is to tell us the address of this Sacred Lif's house."

Terror twisted Chelsey's features. Her hand flew to her chest. "I-I can't. They'll know it was me who told you."

Knowing she had seen Gerald in a cage, had seen multiple wolf shifters caged, I had little compassion for her fear. "You're complicit in Gerald's imprisonment, if not his murder."

She held out her arms as if waiting to be cuffed. "Force it out of my head and take me to jail. I'd rather serve time than face them."

"We don't take supernatural murderers to jail. I.S.E.A. sends them for rehabilitation," I informed her.

"In High King Oberon's faerie." Jada smiled, a wicked gleam in her eye so like her grandfather when he was about to do something awful. The High King wasn't someone you wanted to notice you, let alone to give you that look. "It would be much better if you told us yourself. The king would be the one to extract it from your mind, not me. I am bound by my I.S.E.A. agent status and morals. He is not."

"You don't want him in your head. Trust me." I shuddered. It wasn't for show. I was truly afraid of Oberon.

However, this cult was big and had connections. I.S.E.A.'s arms stretched further, or at least our arms did. Director Tan was right to put us on the case, and not just because this affected my mother's line of shifters.

A loud crash preceded Chelsey collapsing. Her phone forgotten as she slid from her chair onto the floor. Blood trickled from her nose and ears. Something large and dark banged against the curtained window again.

"Something broke her wards," Jada shouted as I came to the same realization. Breaking wards sometimes broke the one who made them.

We had seconds to get ready for an attack.

I sprang to my feet, ripping away my clothes to shift into wolf form. During my shift from human to animal, I found myself in a frozen valley centered among mountains. The sky was gray but daytime. Far, far ahead, a giant tree and a four-legged figure almost as big as the tree stood beside it. A jet-black wolf with glowing cobalt eyes stared back at me.

My mind summoned a name unbidden. Fenrir.

As if in affirmation, the colossal wolf blinked slowly.

I should have felt fear, but I didn't. I didn't know how I knew, but this god, the feared wolf that would bring Ragnarök by joining his sister Hel to free Jörmungandr, meant me no harm.

My form had no way to move, but I felt compelled to go to the wolf god and ask what he wanted of me. Why he'd called this part of me here.

"Go," a voice cried as if in my own head.

But I had no body, no feet to run away. Where would I go

anyway? I didn't know where I was or why my spirit had been called here instead of Heaven.

The chill wind whipping about turned into a gale, thrusting my spirit out of that realm and back into my body. I was a wolf. A disoriented wolf. Nothing seemed familiar. The scents were strange. Burnt candy like a blood ward had broken.

A window shattered. Broken glass sprayed everywhere.

Shit.

Everything came back to me.

A blue-black skinned thing possessing a humanoid, muscular form crawled inside. Wisps of scraggly white hair clung to its head. Eyes covered in a rheumy white film searched the room. Its jaw snapped as it landed on the floor and barreled forward. The fetid stench coming from the creature invaded my nostrils, reeking of death and decay.

I recoiled from the smell of rotting flesh overwhelming my senses, my thoughts. Through the haze, I witnessed Jada shove Chelsey's unconscious body somewhere unseen—the advantage of being a planeswalker and a fae. She could conjure a pocket realm in seconds.

More of the things piled in, filling the small space. Alarm and self-preservation snapped me out of my daze. I launched at the attackers, four now in total, and ripped a chunk of putrid flesh from a throat. I spat and shook my muzzle. The taste was the most foul I'd ever had in my mouth, and I'd once been a college freshman who'd accidentally swigged from a can of cigarette butts and ashes swimming in stale alcohol.

Bracing for more of the putrid flavor, I went after another godawful smelling creature and again ripped out a throat.

In my periphery, Jada summoned a fireball and launched it at one attacker. She kicked the flaming undead out of this realm—hopefully not to the same place as Chelsey.

Heat burst behind me. The damned first creature I'd bitten had risen, which meant tearing out their throats wouldn't be enough.

They weren't monsters, at least not the living breathing kind like us. They were undead.

I'd heard of zombies but hadn't ever seen one. There were so many kinds. Most could be killed for good by burning. Good on Jada for thinking of that. How could I kill these things in wolf form?

Decapitation.

The thought made me groan inwardly. Outwardly, I bore down my teeth on the creature's neck I currently had pinned down and swung my head, my strong jaw and neck ripping the thing's head completely free of its body. I spat and looked around.

Jada had handled the other undead and was standing at the window, looking out. Relief flooded her features. "All clear."

I shifted back to my human form and then looked at the remaining body of the undead. Dark inky liquid instead of blood pooled where the head had been. The head was caught mid-scream.

Jada wrinkled her nose. "Gruesome."

Slipping on my clothes, I shrugged. "Did the job."

Jada was about to say something else, but I felt a pull in the center of my gut. I turned to see a winged woman land crouched in the sill of the window. At first, I assumed a nephil like me had sensed the wrongness of the undead in their neighborhood and came to check it out, but the large wings behind her weren't angelic white like mine when I bore them, but a soft silver.

She held up a hand. "I am a Valkyrie. I mean you no harm. In fact, I've been sent to aid you. May I come in?"

I recognized her immediately. I'd seen her twice before. Once, as a stranger in a club...but that night I'd forgotten. Maybe it was the Tank or something else that dulled my memory, but I'd seen her at my father's wedding among the Valkyrie. How could I forget the pull I'd felt then? Did Tank dull it? If so, what was the feeling?

I exchanged a look with Jada. The Aesir had a treaty with the Supernatural Council of the Americas to allow the Valkyrie to claim souls.

The last time I saw her, she had worn her chestnut hair in soft waves. Now, she wore her hair in two braids, peeking from a helmet. Her deep blue eyes held the gravity of death itself and her former amused grin had turned down into a grimace. Instead of flannel and jeans, she wore leather armor with gold adornments befitting of another time period. The one thing that remained the same was the silver chain around her neck.

My fingers found my lips and pressed them. I'd kissed a Valkyrie! —a servant of Odin and Freya—and I hadn't known it. The thought made me doubt I could ever casually kiss another woman at a bar again, which would make my already boring love life utterly abysmal.

"I don't know," Jada began. "Your timing is awfully convenient."

A low chuckle accompanied a snort, all while the Valkyrie remained perched on the windowsill. "I'd say it wasn't since I'm too late to aid you. I've been tracking these draugr for a few weeks. They've been watching this building, but otherwise leaving people alone so I didn't expect that they would attack." She nudged her head at the remains of the draugr. "Decapitation isn't enough. You're going to need to burn that draugr and scatter his ashes to the four winds."

As if she'd summoned the body to rise with her words, the arms felt around, seeking, and the head hissed from the other side of the room.

Jada murmured words in Kairska. Balls of fire formed at her fingertips. She threw the fire onto the body. Looking at me, she said, "Grab it."

She opened a crack in time and space. The Valkyrie hopped inside the apartment. The two of us hefted and threw the body in. The head sputtered and snarled. Thanks to my angelic grandfather's gift of herald, I could understand the few words the head managed to speak —insults mostly. He was well and truly pissed we'd burned his body and thrown it away. He had some sort of duty to fulfill.

Like I cared.

"She is part witch. You're right about that. The rest coming from your mouth is all offal. You're just mad we won the fight," I said in a language that was close to Old Norse as I moved to grab the head for Jada to light up and toss into the abyss as well, but the Valkyrie gripped my arm. Her grasp was firm but also light enough that I could easily break her hold.

Her eyes blocked with mine. “Not yet. Let me talk to him."

"Why?”

Unlike some undead, such as vampires and zombies, draugr weren't controlled by demons or necromancers. They didn't have much brain power. They were undead sentries with as much knowledge as a guard dog—according to my I.S.E.A. training at least. I'd never even heard of them attacking for no reason, let alone seen them in North America.

"Draugr protect treasures or treasured things. I've been watching them, trying to figure out what could be in this building. The witch girl has something of importance to them, and your presence triggered their need to protect it."

I looked to Jada.

She nodded and gestured to Bryn. “Let her try.”

"Be my guest." I gestured to the severed head that was now calling us an assortment of names while comically trying to roll itself in our direction. "Be careful though. He might bite your ankles."

The Valkyrie snorted as she approached the head and crouched near it. She placed a hand gingerly on the wisps of hair that rose from the creature's scalp. The onslaught of insults ceased. The mouth sighed as if relieved. Then the head spoke with the Valkyrie.

"Have I served my purpose?" I whispered to Jada, translating. "Are you to release me from this fleshly prison?"

"You have one more task, and then I shall release you. Tell me your purpose."

"The witch summoned us to protect the bindings. The bindings cannot go to anyone but the witches." The thing pointed at me with its lips. "That wolf can't take them."

"What bindings?"

"Dwarven made like Gleipnir. Can't you feel them?"

A dark shadow crossed the Valkyrie's face, and she touched her throat, yet her voice remained neutral, almost gentle as she asked, "If the witch summoned you, why did you break her protective wards? Surely you knew that would harm her."

The rotting face twisted as if puzzled by this. Maybe the draugr weren't aware of the wards? Finally, the head said simply, "The binding, not the witch, is my duty."

"I shall release you of this ignoble duty." All life fled from the head. The Valkyrie's eyes shone with light. When they dimmed, she said in English, "You must burn it so that no other witch can recall the soul and learn what we have. Burn it somewhere else they cannot go, planeswalker. Then there won't be a drop remaining to summon."

Jada took the head and disappeared. When she reappeared, the Valkyrie said, "Did the witch live through the breaking of the wards?"

"She's in a comatose state, barely hanging on." To me, she said, "I left her with my grandfather's healers."

I nodded. In other words, we were keeping her in faerie dead or alive. Since Jada was a planeswalker and time had no meaning when you could slip in and out of it, she'd have enough time to explain to Oberon what was happening and come back as if she'd just left. I didn't want the fae involved, but Oberon's consort was a wolf shifter. He would take a personal interest now.

"By the way, she's not a witch. No witch worth her salt would have a blood ward broken by a draugr," Jada replied, arms crossed.

The Valkyrie gave Jada a pointed look. "The world your people came from isn't the only civilization to practice magic as witches. Midguardians possess a kernel of light within them to wield and that kernel can germinate and grow. We called those witches völur."

As I.S.E.A. agents, we were privy to the knowledge of the power of belief. Giant space rabbits appearing around Easter was just one example, but I.S.E.A. had done a fifty-year study on the subject that started back when the agency was nothing more than monster hunters. No one was born completely without light. The Valkyrie was correct. A small magic spark could grow to a full flame with enough belief that it was there.

"Chelsey's a liar."

Jada reared her head back, and the Valkyrie furrowed her brow.

"The witch—her name is Chelsey," I explained. "She had said she'd left the cult but if she took a binding chain, she meant to use it on someone."

"These wolf shifter killings have been happening across the country," Jada agreed, her mouth twisting as she paused before adding, "Vancouver might be one sect of a larger cult with each sect having a leader. This Sacred Lif could be the ultimate leader or a title."

The Valkyrie nodded. "This is why I have been sent by Freyja. If these witch priestesses have enough magic to make deals with dwarves and summon draugr, killing wolf shifters of Fenrir's ilk would be more about her power—or that of the leaders of each sect of the cult—than bringing about Ragnarök."

"That's why the Vancouver priestess wanted her wolf back," Jada agreed. "Why leave the body behind and then want it back?"

We three stood, each in our own heads. Then it occurred to me. "She doesn't want it back. She wants the ropes I cut. I think they're the bindings or ones like them. You know—"

The Valkyrie interrupted, "You cut gleipnir-like bindings?"

I shrugged. "Yeah."

Admiration filled her eyes. They were the color of deep water like the lakes in the mountains. "You are a powerful wolf indeed."

"I don't know. I'm also a nephilim," I said, shrugging.

"That doesn't take away but adds." She gave me a once-over. "You are more than what one can see on the surface."

Traitorous heat crept to my cheeks. I did not usually blush. I just wasn't a blushing kind of gal. It was the remembered kiss, the heat between us before.

"We should look for the bindings in this apartment or go find them on Chelsey—what's your name? Or should we call you Valkyrie?" Jada asked, thankfully reminding me of her presence and of other important things. "Because this is the second time that we've seen you, and you've not introduced yourself."

"I'd meant to, but I'm afraid I'd forgotten all sense of duty, captivated by beauty. You may call me Bryn."

"Cool, Bryn." Jada bared her teeth in warning, but done in such a pretty manner that a person who'd never been exposed to the fae would think she smiled. "Nice to meet you. We have a slew of murders to solve to prevent more wolf shifters from dying. We should get on with that."

Bryn straightened and gave Jada a solemn nod. "Understood. I am as committed as you are to finding their killers. The binding is not here though. I would sense it."

I groaned inwardly as Jada announced what I'd feared we must do. "Then we'll go to faerie and find it on Chelsey."

CHAPTER NINE

Faerie was freaking weird, and this was coming from a person who sprouted wings at will and turned into a wolf now and then.

During the scuffle with the draugr, Jada had taken Chelsey to Oberon's castle. The witch was in a chamber, being attended to by a fae healer. We, however, were taken to court. Jada and I could've just appeared in that room, but we had Bryn with us, which meant introductions had to be made.

Fae courtiers danced with mundanes brought from Earth. Unlike in the past, they were there willingly, not spirited off in the night away from their families. The fae were actively producing offspring to repopulate their decimated numbers. Thanks to the depiction of fae in popular media, abysmal dating app prospects, and growing inflation on our world, mundanes of all races and genders agreed to be spouses. Some stayed on Earth, but many wanted to live in faerie—a choice I could understand, but in my opinion, they were trading financial freedom for a gilded cage.

The children from these unions sprinted around. Their laughter could be innocent, or they might have just picked the wings off a sprite nanny or stolen the cap off a redcap soldier, who would've murdered a child and their entire family for that offense in centuries past. Fae children were now such a blessing after centuries of none that they were allowed to do as they pleased. Which meant, they might be cute and had a parent from my world, but they'd been raised in this feral yet highly socially structured place. They weren't allowed to lie, they had to be always polite to high fae and couldn't kill another fae regardless of whether they were high or low—but they could torture someone if they said they were sorry afterward.

I wasn't fae. The little murderous rascals could eat me and get away with it. Jada would say I was being ridiculous. That Oberon would never allow it because I was Miriam's stepdaughter, therefore his granddaughter according to fae law, but I'd seen Miriam's siblings torture my dad to near death *after* she'd already named him consort.

Jada and I ignored the trays, teapots, and pitchers floating around. We were used to much more frivolous things here, but Bryn eyed everything as if it would attack. Part of me wanted to reach out and squeeze her hand and tell her everything would be okay.

Truth be told, unless the Valkyrie wanted to make a fae baby, she was completely expendable here.

On a dais, the High King sat upon a throne dressed like he was going to a comic con or ren faire—I was no historian, but his pink silk coat, white cravat, hose, and shoes came closer to a painting of Louis XIV of France, or someone approximating him, than any Celtic ruler. Instead of a powdered wig from that time, Oberon possessed long, naturally pink hair and white antlers like his daughter, Miriam, and preternaturally pearlescent skin. Glass bottle green eyes gleamed in recognition as we entered.

Seated next to him in a lesser chair, Carmen, a wolf shifter sentenced to live in faerie for multiple homicides, chewed meat off the bone of what looked like a human femur—which not only made my blood boil that she got away with yet another murder and *ate* this victim, but the cannibalism would be against treaty.

I subtly sniffed the air, seeking the telltale scent of mundane blood. However, the scent contained the wild magic of faerie, making the kill some sort of fae animal. I exhaled with relief.

Carmen barked a laugh. "Hungry, little wolf?"

Recognizing the challenge in the diminutive, I flashed my teeth, widened my stance, and lifted my chin. Body language was everything among shifters. I didn't care who she was consort to. Carmen had no pack and was not my alpha. "Your eyesight must be failing, old wolf. I'm not so little anymore."

"Sassy as when you were a girl." She laughed, and then paused mid-laughter at her own joke to sniff. "Oh, god. What is that stink? You're ruining my appetite." She threw the bone into the fray of dancing fae. The children who had been sprinting and flying around all descended on the meat still on the bone. All cuteness fading as all humanity left their erstwhile sweet faces.

Some of their mundane parents betrayed a note of fear on their faces. *That's right. You left paying rent and bills, and hookup culture for a fae that would love you for life—your life, not theirs.*

Jada and I curtsied, pretending not to notice. Following suit, Bryn made a sweeping bow.

"We've brought a representative of the Aesir to check on the welfare of their Midgardian priestess, Your Majesty," Jada announced, her voice more regal in the Unseelie tongue.

Oberon inclined his head, replying in the same language, "Very well, granddaughter. You and your guests may stay long enough to acknowledge her condition and then you must leave, as per terms of my agreement with your agency. Chelsey is my prisoner and cannot have guests longer than a cursory stay until her health improves."

Jada curtsied again. Then she opened a path between time and space to the chamber where Chelsey lay upon a four-poster bed, attended by three fae. Bryn and I passed through first. Jada blew her grandfather a kiss and joined us.

"Grandfather is in a pissy mood," she whispered to me in Kairska so fae ears couldn't hear. "Carmen is still begging for kids between them, but he still thinks she'll commit a coup as soon as she gives birth."

Carmen wouldn't stage a coup. She loved Oberon too much and a wolf's loyalty ran deep, but if something happened to Oberon and Miriam took the throne, the wolf shifter had killed before to protect her children from a religious cult. But then she killed authorities trying to help her, which earned her the prison sentence that made her kids orphans. My aunt Princess and her wife Aurora had adopted Carmen's pups so that they could remain with a safe pack instead of going to faerie. My cousins were great people and had become wonderful contributions to our pack despite their tragic beginning.

I looked at her. "He's being paranoid, but she is unstable as heck."

Jada shrugged.

On the bed, Chelsey remained unconscious. Ignoring Bryn and me, one of the three fae approached Jada and told her in the Unseelie tongue, "The sorceress will live, but it will be a long time until she wakes."

I scowled at the word "sorceress" because the draugr had referred to Chelsey as a witch. Then again, Oberon's court weren't too keen on witches. Jada's witch grandmother had made a fool of Oberon a long time ago before we were born, but over forty years ago was an hour ago to the fae.

"Understood." Jada raised her voice to address all the fae in the room. "You may leave us."

Upon her command, the fae healer and assistants scurried out of the room. Jada let out a breath, but her shoulders remained stiff. I understood. She had to be someone a little harder here than was her nature and Oberon's faerie was a place you never let your guard down. Even now, we were being watched.

I turned to Bryn. "Do you sense the binding?"

She pointed to Chelsey's folded clothes and other personal items upon the bureau across from the bed. "There. In that small satchel."

She paused, imploring, "Jada, you must retrieve it. Roxy cannot touch the bindings, not until we know if it will influence her."

Jada shot Bryn a pointed look. "Yeah. I'm not touching that thing either." To me, she said, "I'll get Magical Forensics to come bag it." With that, Jada left. Seconds later, she returned with Maria. The latter donned a magical hazmat suit. The witch's intelligent gaze swept the room, pausing on Chelsey and Bryn.

In turn, the Valkyrie eyed the witch with suspicion as she used what looked like tongs to bag the small satchel in a neutralizing bag. I noticed her shoulders sag with relief once the binding was neutralized and couldn't help but be touched that she'd worried about it affecting me.

"We'd better report back to Director Tan," Jada announced, "and check in with Maria to see if she can see how that binding works."

"I, too, must report to my superiors what I've learned. However, if I may, it would be easier if you two took the binding to a dwarf or brought one in for a consult," Bryn suggested. "Gleipnir wasn't made in Midgard. Neither were these bindings. That is how I could sense them."

Jada tilted her head to the side. "How did you sense them?"

"Valkyrie can see in ways you cannot." With a cryptic grin, she walked away, disappearing as easily as a planeswalker.

"I don't trust her," Jada said, surprising me.

"Why?" It was usually me who didn't like or trust people who weren't pack, but I'd not felt any stranger danger instincts with Bryn.

She looked around as if trying to sense if anyone was listening. "Bryn didn't identify herself as a Valkyrie at the bar. She showed up too late to help. Seems suspicious to me."

I chuckled. "Valkyrie aren't fae. They don't have court intrigues and spies."

Jada touched my arm. "Be careful, Rox. Sometimes romantic feelings for someone can blind you to people's faults."

She was saying that now that I'd made out with Bryn, I would trust her more easily. It wasn't true, but I didn't see why I shouldn't trust her. It wasn't Bryn's job to stop the draugr from attacking us. It was her job to take souls to Valhalla and see what was happening to the wolves.

"When have I ever caught feelings?"

Jada backed off. "I don't know why I was worried you'd get smitten and not see there's something wrong here. You're always the one with the least amount of girlfriend drama."

"That's because I keep it casual. I don't have time for one. All I do is work, and I'm not shitting where I eat." The words came out before I thought about her situation at work. "Not that I'm judging."

Pulling a face, she said, "I'm hoping things get less awkward with me and Maria."

"Maybe we should shower before we go to headquarters to report? The draugr stink probably doesn't help with the awkwardness."

She smiled and everything was good between us again. That's what I loved about our relationship. We gave advice but also backed off and minded our business when we needed to.

CHAPTER TEN

After our ordeal, we went to the Ballard I.S.E.A. location, showered and changed in the International Supernatural Enforcement Agency's headquarters. Because the job sometimes got messy, all agents had a locker and access to individual dressing rooms fitted with a shower.

In my locker, I kept a backup agency-issued suit, fresh gym clothes, street clothes, shoes for work and outside, and toiletries. Showered, changed into street clothes, hair secured in a bun at the top of my head that showed off my freshly trimmed undercut, and makeup applied, I grabbed the bag with my soiled suit. My intimates would go home to be laundered, but I had to drop the bag labeled with my I.S.E.A. identification number into a bin for my suit to be dry-cleaned by mages and witches, who would also eliminate any magical residue.

Jada was outside the locker room, looking at her phone, frowning.

"Are you good?"

"Yeah...no." She put away her phone and rubbed her forehead.

Her shoulders sank. "Sarah wants to go to The Veil tonight. I just don't know if that's a good idea. What do you think?" Her luminous brown eyes implored me to say it would be okay.

The Veil was a supernatural underground club established before mundanes knew we, and magic, existed. It wasn't even on Earth, and a mundane wouldn't be unwelcome there, but it wouldn't necessarily be safe for Sarah to go there. "How does Sarah even know about The Veil?"

Jada pinched the bridge of her nose and exhaled out her nose in a loud whoosh. "Lady Sif took a mundane man and his influencer girlfriend there. The influencer had a hidden camera on her and took a video. It's gone viral."

Ugh. Lady Sif made it worse. She was the representative of the Aesir on the Supernatural Council of the Americas. Like her husband Thor, she was also a pretty moron. Sif was the only goddess with a social media presence and one of the biggest fashion icons of the year. She loved mundane expensive clothes, cars, jewelry, and everything that had the words luxury and exclusive in it. If Sif loved it, the elite of the world loved it.

This was a PR nightmare.

"Did you report the video to Communications?"

Communications was the part of I.S.E.A. that controlled media and social media and the general populace's perception of supernaturals and worlds outside of ours. I didn't like it, but mundanes got bright ideas all the time, like going to a supernatural club in a pocket universe—a daring escapade that could cost them their lives.

She shot me a pointed look that said of course she did. "It. Went. Viral."

"Then we'll have to have faith that mundanes aren't stupid enough to believe social media content." I sighed. "It's a horrible idea to take Sarah to The Veil. However, if things are going to get serious with your girlfriend, she needs to know that our world is not all cool magic spells and pack compounds. Sarah needs to see the real world of supes for herself—"

Jada grimaced.

I put my hand on her shoulder. "With *our* full protection."

A ghost of a smile touched her lips. "Thanks, sis. I'll let her know you're coming, too."

Despite being stepsisters, we rarely called each other that. Maybe because we'd been close friends longer than we'd been sisters. Maybe because we were work partners. I'd fight anyone for Jada, but being lovey dove wasn't my thing. However, when we did say it, it was our way of saying, "I love you" without getting all saccharine about it.

Not long after, we stood in Director Tan's office, giving her a full report of the day's events. Her thin eyebrows furrowed in concentration as she knitted a cat-sized, pink sweater as we spoke.

"Bryn isn't listed as a Valkyrie with a visa to Earth. I'll leave it up to you to bring it up with the Midgard representative of the Supernatural Council to get the paperwork in."

Jada and I exchanged a look. Lady Sif seemed to be the topic of conversation today. Talking to that goddess was like talking to a toddler at best or a parrot at worst. I wanted to roll my eyes and groan. However, being the professional that I am, I said, "Lady Sif isn't exactly...the paperwork type of goddess."

"Sif' is already involved in that nightclub incident and is difficult to work with," Jada reminded the Director.

We were grown professionals, but we both had just said the equivalent of "Do we *have* to?"

Tan lifted her dark eyes from her knitting. If I didn't know better, I'd say that a smirk touched the corner of the Director's mouth. It could've been a trick of the light, but she had no mirth in her tone when she replied, "No, Lady Sif will be unlikely to fill out the proper paperwork, but the goddess loves to name-drop and gossip. She'll have the tea, as you kids put it, on Bryn. Talking to her is not a priority though. Rooting out the cult while R&D works on the spell work behind the binding ropes is." She sighed heavily. "There haven't been any wolf shifter killings in Washington. Let's hope finding

Chelsey gives you time to stop it. In the meantime, you'll need to work with the Supernatural Council of the Americas and your pack connections to warn the wolf shifters of Fenrir's line of this cult."

"Council Member Princess is working on letting wolf shifters know," I replied, knowing my aunt wouldn't have kept the secret and neither would my father.

"Alright. I'd like you two to track down Sif then. You are dismissed, Agent Diaz. Agent Crowfoot, I'd like for you to stay a few minutes more." She smiled. "Please."

Okay. This was weird. The Director had something she thought she needed to say that didn't involve Jada. My gut churned with unease as my mind raced to figure out how I fucked up and needed a private reprimand as I watched Jada leave, and then returned my gaze to Director Tan.

She resumed her knitting. "I don't presume to know your personal life, so can I ask you something personal?"

My chest wound tight. There was no way she knew that I'd kissed Bryn, yet I braced myself for the inevitable question about my *personal* tie to her. Director Tan wouldn't ask anything out of idle curiosity. "Yes."

"Are you estranged from your biological mother?"

I blew out my breath, half in relief and half in frustration. "My relationship with Kirsten is complicated."

It hadn't been. At one time, Kirsten had told me stories, gave me plush wolves to sleep with, taught me to hunt alongside my father deep in the forests of the North Cascades. We were a family once. A happy one to my young eyes. All the while, she was sleeping with an incubus, betraying the pack...and me.

"She's a wolf shifter of Fenrir's line. As a lone wolf, she must be lonely. Especially now that your father has remarried, and his new wife is accepted into the pack. To put it frankly, Kirsten is a prime target for a cult. She'd also be a gateway to the cult for those who aren't so happy that a witch and fae are treated like alphas."

Shit. The Director was onto something. I should warn my mother, but there had been a lot of bad blood between us to say the least. She'd forbidden me from going to my father's wedding to Miriam and Phyr. I, of course, was an adult and disobeyed. She cut me off financially and wouldn't speak to me. I didn't know what her deal was. She and Dad had severed their bond years ago. She was free like she wanted. The thought of me contacting her first felt like a knife to the gut. I was always the one offering the olive branch. This one time, she had to see I'd done nothing wrong and still loved her. Mostly.

"My mother made her choices. Looks like she's going to live with them."

Tan stopped knitting and looked at the picture of her cats. "I know what it's like to have a mother who dominates everything, causes chaos, and then can't figure out why no one speaks to her. That's why normally I don't get into family business, but you might want to at least warn her."

This was the most Director Tan had ever spoken anything about her personal life that didn't have to do with her cats. She was offering the rare gift of personal connection with her. If I refused to listen, I would damage the tenuous string of bonding. I very much wanted to connect with Emily Tan the person. She was one of the few mundanes I respected and admired.

"I'll try. Kirsten won't make it easy. I don't know if she'll even listen."

Tan nodded and sighed wearily, as if she understood exactly what I meant. "She probably won't." Emotion saturated the simple statement. Tan looked much younger for a moment, less of the self-assured director, more like someone my age and level of angst when it came to parents. Suddenly, she seemed to remember herself and straightened. "You can't control how she responds, but your conscience will be clear."

After I left the Director's office, I found Jada in the cafeteria.

When I joined her, she grimaced at her phone. “I don’t think I can convince Sarah to go to The Veil another night.”

"Tonight?" I was bone tired, and the thought of going out didn’t appeal at all. However... “We do have to talk to Sif."

"Yeah, but we need time to do that. There's a wait list for the place after Sif made it popular. You gotta know the right people now."

We both looked away. As I.S.E.A. agents, we were, whether we liked it or not, unpopular with some groups of off-world supernaturals.

She blew out her breath. "Sarah's going to think I'm full of shit. There's no way we can get in tonight."

"Excuse me. Were you two talking about The Veil?"

We both jumped at Maria's question. I had to be really invested in the conversation because witches weren't as stealthy as shifters. I *should* have heard her coming. Maria was just finishing work, too, or at least I assumed she was since she was wearing a crop top covered in pins, a miniskirt, fishnets, and boots with lots of buckles and dangling charms—not exactly her work attire.

"Yeah—Um. We're going there tonight—um with—uh—Sarah." Jada lowered her voice and gaze when she said her girlfriend's name. "Well, at least we want to. I hear it's hard to get in."

Maria's cheeks flushed. "Oh, right. Of course. I'm going with my brother—Hugo—my other brothers are too young for our folks' rules."

"Parents are—uh—like that," Jada replied, suddenly fascinated by her shoes.

Someone please pull me anywhere but here. I would even take Oberon's faerie court over this awkward conversation.

"Well, the rumors are true, it is a lot harder to get in. The whole Lady Sif incident and all. You can meet Hugo and me at Linda's Tavern. The person I'm seeing has an in. She agreed to let us bring friends."

"Oh...that's great." Jada's reply had as much pep as a limp dishrag.

With the awkward tension in the air, I would disappear into another realm right now if I could. Instead, I smiled at her broadly. "Thanks, friend. See you at Linda's!"

Her small eyes widened. Friend wasn't something I'd ever called the witch before. She shook her head and backed away. "Okay. Yeah. See you there around 9?"

"Works for us."

I chuckled to myself as Maria darted out of the cafeteria.

Jada chewed her lip as she watched Maria go. "I'd planned on going through the reopened Nowhere door in Fremont."

I shuddered, daring to ask a subject I rarely liked to think about. "Your mom's siblings reopened the door to Bizarre Bazaar?"

She shook her head. "Nope. That's forever closed to Earth. There's a new Nowhere door that opens directly to The Veil. "

"Oh." Very painful memories of the faerie market that the door used to lead to surfaced. I smashed them down and changed the trajectory of the conversation to happier topics. "Jørgen must be happy to get visitors again." Jørgen was a bridge troll who lived in a liminal space between this world and others. There was a statue of him in Fremont, but it only slightly resembled the actual troll under the bridge.

A grin crept up Jada's erstwhile worried face. "He is so happy. We should visit him sometime."

"Yeah." I forced a smile and nodded, but I didn't mean it. It had been a long time since I'd been to Bizarre Bazaar, but I wanted no chance of ending up in the place where my father had almost died.

"Alright. I'll text Sarah that we'll go tonight."

I rose. "I need to grab something first."

Five minutes later, I had Igni strapped to my back.

Jada's gaze widened at the sight of the sword. "I don't know if you should bring that. They might not let you in with a weapon."

"I'm nephil-shifter. *I* am a weapon."

"Fair...but..."

"Can you make a glamour or do a 'don't notice me' spell?"

She grimaced. "Okay. I can't guarantee that it will work for everyone. Some supes can see through glamours."

"As long as it works on the supes letting us in, that's all that matters."

CHAPTER ELEVEN

Anticipatory electricity lit my nerves as Jada, her girlfriend Sarah, and I walked into Linda's Tavern—my history with supernatural nightclubs in pocket universes made me prefer bars like this one. Established by Linda Derchang, the queen of Capitol Hill bars and restaurants, the tavern had quirky décor with animal heads mounted on the walls, a photobooth, and paintings depicting Old West landscapes. Seattle rumor had it that grunge legend Kurt Cobain, the front man of my father's favorite band Nirvana, had his last meal here before his life ended tragically in 1994. Unfortunately, although locally historic and quirky as Linda's might be, the tavern would not be our final destination and that was why my instincts had to be on high alert.

Our trio weren't the only queers in the place, nor were Jada and I the only two supes: I scented a couple of young non-wolf shifters from my pack before I saw them. They gave me a brief nod but returned to whatever they were doing. Jada waved at two witches with white-blonde hair and gorgeous Slavic features: high cheek-bones, almond-shaped eyes, and full mouths. Recognizing the duo from the former Baba Yaga coven seated at the bar, I waved, too. The witches were now in the same coven as Jada, Rosemary and Oleander, and they taught at Miriam's Eastside Charm School. If anyone deserved a night out, it was them.

When I wasn't in such an involved case as the wolf shifter murders, I volunteered at the school sometimes. The mix of magical and mundane kids were fun, but so much work. The witches and shifters must be waiting for the same back entrance to the Veil as we were because they all looked like they were fighting to fit in.

We stepped up to the second floor and grabbed a booth. I faced the door and window and Jada and Sarah sat opposite me. Jada's girlfriend glanced around, disappointment weighing heavy in her usually jovial expression. Turning her Mariners cap backward, she leaned in and said in a low tone, "Don't get me wrong, I'm happy to be out with you two, but this isn't the place we'd said we'd go."

Jada looked over her shoulder as if checking for the Gonzalez siblings. "We're meeting some people here first."

I supposed she didn't want to get into details of who they were. This fragile olive branch from Maria was a beginning to repairing their friendship and making their work relationship less awkward. So, *I* wasn't going to be the one adding any information that might stir up trouble.

Hugo came in first. I almost didn't recognize the witch. He wore his long, curly hair down and had a local underground punk group T-shirt under a jean jacket covered in pins and oversized black cargo pants. A few protective symbols in the witch language Kairska stood out among his mundane punk pins. Gaze fixed on one of the witches at the bar, he missed my wave.

Maria waved in our direction, and then beckoned someone in the doorway.

A supe I didn't recognize entered. Her curling brown hair bounced with her walk and her olive skin shimmered like sunlight dancing on dark water. Almond-shaped, midnight eyes that seemed to have no sclera took everything in. Regal is the word I'd use to describe her features and the way she carried herself. But not some mundane monarch with greed and a god complex. It was the self-assured walk of someone who had the responsibility of many and the courage to protect what was hers. A silver dress flowed from her waist in gauzy layers of strips. The strips twisted and turned, not with her movements but as if of their own volition, as if the material were living appendages. The scent of the ocean that accompanied her entrance was so overpowering that, at first, I thought even the mundanes without shifter senses could smell it, but no one around her seemed to notice. Except the other shifters—they perked up at the scent and got up from their table near the bar to approach her.

Only water fae had that strong of a scent, but none of the fae wild magic accompanied the scent. It was as if she were the sea in corporeal form.

It would be rude to ask her, but I couldn't help wondering what kind of supernatural she was. Since my father had been the archangel, when archangels had ruled the supe world, and the Greater Seattle area pack, I knew most supes by sight, if not by name. Protective instincts let a low growl rumble in my throat—not a threat, but a warning that this was my turf. A thought that I should text my father or Aunt Princess occurred. A powerhouse of this magnitude shouldn't be in our territory without someone on the council knowing.

She'd heard the growl and her gaze locked with mine. She grinned, revealing a mouth filled with shark-like teeth. The stranger then nodded her head the way Jada would in fae court when she wanted to convey recognizing a peer. Interesting.

Maria took the newcomer's hand and motioned for us to come, too. I caught Jada's face falling and then perking up when Sarah glanced at her. I winced internally for my friend but was damned glad I wasn't involved with anyone on top of this case. An image of Bryn's lips on mine, that taste of her and the way she felt as we danced in the bar that night came unbidden. I stomped the memory into a corner of my mind marked Dangerous Things. A lot of feelings were stored there and I locked that corner like a steel vault. Jada was right. We couldn't trust Bryn.

"That's our ride," Jada remarked, rising.

I shook my head as if snapping out of a trance and muttered, "This should be interesting."

Maria and Hugo made introductions outside, saving the newcomer supe for last. "This is Harvi. She will get us into The Veil."

"Pleased to meet all of you." Harvi's dark gaze swept the group, settling on me. "Do any of you have a weapon?"

I crossed my arms over my chest. "I am a weapon."

The shifters gathered sniggered and murmured similar remarks. I was glad. It took off the pressure to confess I had not only a weapon, but Igni had killed many powerful fae gods.

"Oh, good. You should have several. All of you. The Veil is a place of pleasure, but it is not a safe place." She bared her sharp teeth in a facsimile of a smile, but as a predator myself, I recognized it as the warning she meant it to be. "Danger lurks in the shadows and dances openly in the light there." She then turned her attention to Sarah. "Are you sure that you want to leave the safety of this world?"

Sarah's eyes widened and her throat expanded with an audible swallow. Conversely, Jada's eyes narrowed. She stepped around her girlfriend. "She's with me. I'll protect her."

It was all I could do to not say, "Me, too." This had to be Jada's thing. She was marking Sarah as hers. If I said something, that would make Jada look weak and Sarah up for grabs. Besides, my friend could handle herself and knew that I had her back without me voicing it. Instead, I merely glowered as much as possible to display my support.

Also sensing the tension, the witches held still, but the shifters subtly moved closer to me. I couldn't say I wasn't disappointed that the witches, especially Maria, didn't take a stance nearer to Jada. These were our people. Guide or no, the stranger was as much an outsider as Sarah. As someone who grew up in a pack, witch behavior sometimes baffled me as much as the behavior of mundanes.

Harvi displayed nails curved like claws at the tips of her long fingers as she spread her hands. "Very well. You are all consenting adults. Forgive me if I came across as harsh. I merely felt a sense of responsibility to warn those who are new to...our way of life."

"Thank you. That was thoughtful," Maria said, linking an arm with her date. Harvi placed a hand on Maria and that's when I realized that they weren't claw-like nails but claws, which, again, brought up the question of what kind of supe was Harvi. She wore a glamour but wasn't a fae.

"Jada, is it true that you are a planeswalker?" Harvi asked.

How did she hear that?

Jada and I exchanged a look that conveyed she wondered the same thing. Her ability to cross time and space, and create Nowhere doors was no secret, but she didn't announce it either. Sharing about supernatural gifts others possessed wasn't illegal or against any rule, but it wasn't done. Especially something like planeswalking. Being a planeswalker made her at once a person to covet as an ally and a target as an enemy.

Maria blushed crimson as she cast an apologetic look in Jada's direction.

Well, that settled the source. At least I thought it did. Hugo cleared his throat. "I shared since Harvi had doubts about how many she could get in. You're a highborn fae with a rare gift. That'll get us to the head of the line."

The witch who had cozied up to Hugo put a little distance between them. Many witches had two gifts: one everyone knew about and the other something held between family and close friends. Jada's planeswalking gift might not be a secret, but the witch wouldn't trust Hugo with hers.

"It's public knowledge," Hugo responded in his defense. "You were on video in the Mythic Games. Everyone saw when Jada took Maria and the witches there to save Hermes."

Jada waved her hand dismissively. "It's fine. I can handle myself."

We had to talk to Lady Sif and Jada must really want to take Sarah there, or she would have called it off. Still, every protective instinct told me to keep my friend on this world—not to mention my own self-preservation instinct. I just didn't know if the instincts were real or that I'd seen my father nailed to a ceiling and left to die at a supernatural nightclub when I was just a teenager.

Harvi clasped her hands in front of her. "Good. There's one more thing. The Veil owners need to be impressed upon our arrival. Can you prove you're a planeswalker by taking us there?"

Jada looked at Maria and so did I. This Harvi was supposed to get us in, not use Jada to get in the club. The witch gave a helpless shrug and mouthed "sorry". If Jada just accepted the half-assed apology, Maria and I would have words about her date later. She shouldn't have ever put us in this position.

"If you can't, it doesn't matter to me. I will get in regardless," Harvi purred, looking at her claws. "This is only helping you out."

"Fine." Jada uncrossed her arms.

I didn't know how planeswalking worked exactly, but there were laws and ways about it that Jada had to adhere to. She'd told me she had to have been to a place before or have contact with an object or person that had been there to get to a place.

"Can you get it that exact, to show up at the front door?" I asked in the dialect of High Fae that the Unseelie speak, grinning in a way that seemed like I was making a casual remark.

"I can't go directly there, but through another route," Jada said, not hiding her uncertainty. To the others, she announced, "We'll have to cross the Null."

"The Bifrost," Maria explained to Harvi.

Different supernatural groups had different names for what was between the universes and pocket universes of the multiverse. Most of us born in North America called it the Null as a shortcut. So, Harvi was not from the Nine Realms, or she'd know what we called it. Interesting.

The Nine Realms meant one thing to Norse pagans, and they had it close, but the worlds Asgard, Midgard, Vanaheim, Jotunheim, Alfheim, Svartalfheim, Niflheim, Muspelheim, and Helheim were in pocket universes like Oberon and Miriam's faeries.

Usually when we planeswalked through Jada's doors, it was only a moment or two of disorientation, but this time we had to go through the Null. We walked into an alley between buildings. There, Jada threw her hands dramatically in front of her and acted like she was parting a curtain as the fabric of reality spread open to reveal a dark space. Well, not completely dark. There were bright colors of magic like threads or superhighways connecting everything. I *hated* crossing the Null.

Sarah's eyes and mouth gaped. "Whoa! Babe!"

"I'll protect you," Jada assured. With her girlfriend's nod of agreement, she then gestured to the opening. "Let's go."

Harvi entered first, arms locked with Maria. The witches and Hugo were next. Then the shifters. Before I stepped through, I looked back.

Jada wrapped an arm around Sarah. Suddenly the wild forest scent of fae magic permeated the Seattle night air. A barrier formed around the mundane to keep her safe—an extra layer on top of what Jada had built to protect us from the Null. There was a reason why planeswalkers were rare. It took a lot of magic to build what was essentially a wormhole from one world to another, and that worried me. I steeled myself. Jada would protect Sarah, but I'd protect my best friend, my sister, my pack.

The Null was not for living things.

All scents and sounds died. My body fought the inevitable rise of bile from the vertigo of not having an up or down. Gravity didn't exist, yet I wasn't floating. The journey felt like seconds and ten years at once. I grew older and younger, and I think I might have seen my own wolf running beside me. I was with the group, and I was also alone.

With an arm around Sarah, Jada forged ahead but was also right next to me. She opened a way into a cityscape out of a dream with personal aircraft buzzing about and sky trains weaving between impossibly tall skyscrapers. Foot traffic paused around us, staring. There was a line wrapped around the block. They all gaped, too. At the entrance to The Veil, two troll bouncers in black robes regarded us from behind sunglasses.

Impression thoroughly made, Jada closed the portal to the Null and our bridge home. Planeswalkers were rare in every world.

The shifters shook their heads but seemed no worse for wear. One of the witches was pale, but she seemed fine. Hugo held the hair of the other witch as she vomited. He produced a tissue from his pocket and handed it to the witch.

"Don't be embarrassed. First time in the Null is hard for everyone."

Sarah's face had paled, and her eyes had widened hauntingly large. Jada whispered something to her that seemed to have a calming effect. It was likely a bit of soothing magic in her voice, but not serious influence...at least I hoped.

Even Harvi seemed to need a minute. Maria, like me, had planeswalked with Jada before and we'd known what to expect. We got our collective shit together.

"That will do. My mother should be impressed...if she saw it." Harvi murmured only loud enough for those with sensitive preternatural hearing. With Maria on her arm, she led the way to the bouncers.

My gaze locked with Jada's. Her eyes mirrored the same white-hot rage burning in my chest. If Harvi's mother owned the Veil, this was just to make her look impressive, not to impress the owner.

Maria glanced back with an apologetic look but that wouldn't cut it, not for me, and judging by Jada's hard stare, not for my friend, either. That was a wasteful use of magic.

I took a deep breath, letting the rage out with the exhale. We'd get in. We'd interview Sif. Jada would impress Sarah. We'd have *fun*. I needed fun after fighting the undead. A brief playback of Bryn talking to the draugr's head bubbled in my mind. I wondered how Freya would respond to the news about the cult and what they were doing.

One of the trolls unhitched a rope partitioning the entrance to the club. He bowed to Harvi and nodded to Jada in acknowledgment. The rest of us he let pass without recognition or comment, fine by me. It was bad enough those in line gaped as we passed. An explosion of conversation erupted behind us outside. None of this was good optics for three I.S.E.A. agents. I hoped no one had a cell phone or whatever one would use as this pocket universe's equivalent of a recording device.

The pulsing rhythm pounded in my chest and thrummed in my ears like a second heartbeat. A spiral staircase climbed the side of the club leading to other floors on the left. An elevator that would take us to other rooms with different music just as packed with dancers crowded the first floor, no doubt. Tables bordered the edges. Musicians played live in a floating, clear sphere that bounced up and down and side to side in the club like a wayward bubble. The movement didn't seem to affect the group within. A few more of these spheres had singles and couples dancing.

The VIP section had its entrance through another partition. I'd never been to the VIP section of the Veil, but I'd only come enough times to explore and forget who I was for a few hours in college. The remnants of memories from the other club in the Bizarre Bazaar haunted me more closely then.

Now, my fingers twitched to hold a sword that I'd barely touched. I wasn't certain if that was an effect of Igni's magic or my own hypervigilance.

Once in the club, the party dispersed. We all had our reasons to be here and none of them were the same. Jada and Sarah headed for the bar. I'd meant to follow, but Harvi tapped me on the shoulder.

"My mother would like to have a word with you."

Harvi's skin was no longer brown, but a shade of gray-blue that reminded me of the sea. Her hair was green like curled kelp and her skirt wasn't a writhing skirt, but thin tentacles. It was then that I realized Harvi couldn't be a fae. Krakens were their own thing.

Great.

Krakens were not exactly on the right side of much when it came to the multiverse. They held a lot of sway over the Nine Realms. They weren't as powerful supes as the Aesir or even the elves, and only reigned over their own oceanic world, but Krakens could have humanoid forms like Harvi but were able to grow to the giant sea creatures of Norse legend when they were pissed...and in salt water. That one owned this club and had discovered Jada was a planeswalker wasn't good. Like Miriam's faerie, these pocket universes contained laws of their own.

"I need to use the restroom for a sec first, babe," Maria said, and then turning to me, added, "Roxy, do you have a tampon?"

I stared blankly. Firstly, Maria and I weren't that kind of friends. We weren't friends at all, actually. Secondly, witches knew their menstruation cycle better than any mundane or supe I'd ever met and were prepared for it. Being a research witch, Maria was normally ready for anything.

Something was up.

"Yeah. I need to change mine, too, so I'll come with you." I hadn't meant to snarl when I said it but what the actual heck. None of this was good.

Harvi gave Maria a kiss on the cheek and fluttered away to the VIP. I death-glared at the back of Maria's dark bob the whole way to the washroom. Inside, there were overstuffed couches where supernaturals of every flavor from every world primped and preened. We walked past them to stalls with floor-to-ceiling doors. Maria beckoned for me to join her in a stall.

"I know that I should have told you—" she began in Kairska, the language of witches.

"A lot of things." I counted on my fingers. "First, that a freaking Kraken owns the Veil now. Second, that you're dating a highly suspicious person." I threw up my hands. "Kraken are dangerous. They're worse than fae."

Maria scowled and reared her head back. "Whoa. Prejudice much?"

"You know what I mean. We're in an exclusive nightclub. You know what happens in these pocket worlds isn't regulated. Your girlfriend's mom might be a mob boss."

"Only a minority of Krakens are in organized crime and not all fae are wicked. You of all people should know that."

I wiped a hand over my face. She was right. I was letting what happened to my father by Miriam's shady fae siblings paint my judgment in ugly colors. The wound had cut so deep, it manifested into a generalizing belief. Generalizing a group for the actions of a few could fester and spoil the mind. What was worse was that I was in a position of authority and that was worse than being a regular bigot. "Sorry. Why didn't you tell us Harvi's mom was who we had to impress?"

"Jada can't lie without pain, and she wanted you to act natural."

"*She*? Harvi?"

Maria mouthed, "Director Tan."

Silenced by the mention of the Director's name, I let it sink in. "You're with the kraken just for the case?"

The witch bit her lip and played with her hands, and then glanced over her shoulder. "I like Harvi, but it's...casual. The Director wanted me to use the connection."

I nodded, letting it all sink in. She exposed Jada so we could have a bargaining chip for information. I had so many questions. The most pressing was how Director Tan knew about Maria's dating life. It made me wonder how much she knew about my connection to Bryn. However, we didn't have much time.

Back in the chaos of the nightclub, we had an escort waiting. The bouncer stood at about seven feet tall and change. A lot of change—possibly eight feet altogether. He possessed the shoulders and the upper body of a linebacker until about his hips. I'd mistake him for a bigfoot like my Aunt Aurora, but short white fur with a blue tinge covered wherever he wasn't wearing a black suit.

A freaking frost giant...

Awesome.

This information better be good.

When we reached the VIP lounge that consisted of overstuffed sofas, floating glass tables, servers of every variety of supernatural, I had expected a kraken queen, her daughter, and an entourage. I had not expected the guests to include Sif and her mother-in-law Freya, queen of the Aesir. Sif's platinum blonde hair didn't have its usual party-goddess voluminous style. She wore it in two braids from her temples. Bits of gold and leather intertwined the braids. A thin gold circlet crowned her head. Instead of designer brands, she wore a yellow linen tunic that was belted at the waist. Embroidery trimmed the neckline and sleeves of the dress. A gold medallion sat on her chest. Fur-lined boots covered her feet. Freya wore a leather bodice over a blue tunic with red embroidery. Her dark hair fell in loose waves. A gold crown topped her head. Her arms and neck were covered in gold jewelry. I saw how much of the medieval Norse clothing was inspired by these pieces. At the same time, their garments didn't feel like any Earth era at all.

Twenty Valkyrie lined the walls. Bryn stood behind Freya. Our gazes met and I felt a jolt of excitement at the sight of her. Suspicion quickly replaced the thrill. What had she told the goddess that provoked this meeting with only *me* instead of Freya going to the Supernatural Council or I.S.E.A.?

Harvi and her mother, who looked like her older, silver-haired twin, rose at the same time. Harvi linked arms with Maria. "You're not invited to the party, darling."

Maria bade me a questioning glance. I waved her off. One didn't deny an audience with a goddess of Freya's importance, and you did it on her terms. Besides, the witch might be powerful, but she'd be safer with her kraken girlfriend than in the company of Aesir and armed Valkyrie. They left the room as did all the staff until all who remained were the goddesses, their warriors, and little old me.

My hackles raised. Like any wolf, I didn't like being trapped. Out of all the threats, I couldn't keep my gaze off Bryn. She stared back with no sign of emotion let alone familiarity on her face. The betrayal stung, but she was a stranger who helped me *once*...who kissed me once.

"Did you come by way of the Bifrost or do the kraken lie?" Lady Sif asked. The babyish vocal fry voice she was famous for on social media didn't match the enunciated words and elegant manner of speech. It must be tiring to constantly be playing a role that mundanes cast you in, and Sif had a long reputation of being dense and beautiful.

"Bifrost." Which is what I assumed the Aesir referred to the Null as.

Sif looked to Freya and then back to me. "Good. We trust kraken as far as our gold will spend and no further. You may sit."

Not liking that all of this had been a setup by the Aesir goddesses before me, I took a seat in a chair directly opposite of the goddesses. Also, I noticed the sofa on which mother and daughter-in-law sat was slightly higher to accommodate their size.

"Your Valkyrie guardian tells me that völur have summoned draugr and have used bindings of Dwarven make to murder wolves of Fenrir's line." Freya angled her head to indicate Bryn as the guardian in question.

Völvur, or völva, were a specific type of witches among Norse pagans who practiced seidr—where we got the modern word seer. Völvur were usually women but some men, including the god Odin, practiced the magic of divination. However, I believed that she meant to delineate from the witches like Maria and Jada—or, maybe, that was what I hoped. As a new agent, I'd been part of the case that had dealt with the Oracle and Apollo's plot to replace the Moirai. Their counterpart the Norns: Urd, Verdandi, and Skuld, were similar yet different. The Norns took care of Yggdrasil, the tree which held the very fabric of the Nine Realms together.

A cold chill ran through me. In the case of the Oracle and Apollo, we'd barely avoided a war among the gods on Earth. If the Norns were involved, the stakes could be the multiverse.

"That is correct." The question was rhetorical, yet I felt a need to respond. "They are led by a woman calling herself The Sacred Lif."

The goddess bristled at that but didn't comment on the name. "Do you have any theories as regards to why they are specifically killing wolves of Fenrir's line?"

I had several but I'd share one with the goddess. "Theophagy: they are symbolically eating Fenrir to gain power from it."

Bryn's face darkened and her posture stiffened. Freya and Sif exchanged a glance. I didn't know if the goddesses had telepathy like fae, but they could be speaking or they could know each other well enough that a look could be its own form of communication.

Sif asked, "Power for what purpose?"

"I can only speculate it's for the typical reasons: wealth, control, prestige, and possibly sex. As to how high their ambitions reach beyond that—" I shrugged one shoulder. "Only they know."

It was the truth, but a larger conspiracy nagged at the corners of my mind. My theory seemed to appease the goddesses, though. Freya gestured to Bryn. "I give you the use of my Valkyrie. You may call on Bryn to help you discover the truth and as your protector. The necessary arrangements will be made with the council and I.S.E.A. for her to stay extendedly on Earth."

I bristled at the need for any help at all. We had this case. Unfortunately, it would be undiplomatic of me to deny the aid of Asgard when their queen was offering.

I exhaled.

Meeting apparently over, Bryn guided me out of the VIP lounge. I spun on her. "Your goddess rules Asgard, not Earth. This is my case. You can't just shadow agents of I.S.E.A. We have protocols."

An amused smirk spread on Bryn's rosy lips. "Agreed."

I jabbed a thumb toward the center of my chest. "When *I* ask for it."

"I will only help when and where I am needed." Bryn cut the distance between us. I was tall but she was taller. I was full of attitude and snarls. She was like a statue: cold and immovable. "If you're in trouble and cannot ask for my help, I will be there. It is my sacred duty."

The binding magic of the vow married a tug in my gut. There was an inexplicable link between Bryn and me. Everything in me rebelled against it. I wanted to fling myself into the Null and run to the far corners of the multiverse. My biological parents had been a bonded pair, and that mate bond had driven them to jealousy and petty acts.

Guess who had been stuck right in the middle of all their drama. Yeah. I wouldn't romanticize this unspoken tether between us at all. However, I was curious about it. Especially the part about why I felt it for a Valkyrie.

Shifters had a magical bond for their kind even if they were part shifter. So did the fae. However, my father didn't bond that way with Miriam and Phyr because he was not even a little bit fae. Their magics were from different sources.

"Fine." I didn't hide the growl of frustration in my voice.

Bryn nodded to the dance floor where Sarah, Jada, Maria, and Harvi all danced in a circle with Hugo and the witches. One of the witches was dancing with a shifter who'd come with us. The other shifter had found a being that I couldn't name. They were having a good time. I wasn't the least bit put off that I had endured an interrogation while they danced the night away. No. I wasn't growling. I was delighted.

"We could join them," Bryn said, her breath hot on my ear. The ice queen was gone. Back was the smirking chestnut-haired girl I'd met at the bar.

"I have what I came here for. I need to get up early to work on leads."

Bryn laughed openly. It was a bright, musical sound that stirred the same sensation as frolicking in my wolf form in a spring meadow.

I cocked my head and lifted my chin. "What's so funny?"

Eyes dancing, she slid her hand down my arm leaving electric tingles in the wake of her fingertips until her fingers locked with mine. "Time is irrelevant here, so the night is always young."

Not so begrudgingly, I allowed Bryn to lead me onto the dance floor. Among my friends and with my so-called protector, I let the weight of the case lift and found my rhythm. Bryn moved with me. There was no denying we danced well together. Her lips were so pink. Her freckles so cute on her pert nose. Her scent gave me more of a heady rush than any bottle of Tank could ever give.

Bryn snaked an arm around my waist and pulled me to her as she pushed her leg between mine. The rhythm of the music contrasted the rapid pounding of my heart, yet I kept the beat as our hips moved in counterpoints. Heat built steadily where her thigh rubbed.

Her lips were so pink...

It was a bad idea. No. A terrible idea. I didn't care. I curled my fingers around her braids and pulled her head to mine.

"This changes nothing," I warned.

She grinned before our lips met. The fiery kiss led to us making our way off the dance floor to a secluded alcove. No matter the world, there were always such places in a club like this. I'd had my share of discreet encounters in them to know. There was a red suede chaise in the center of the alcove with white and red pillows. The muffled sounds of other couples, or more than two, broke through the music pumped throughout the club.

The first thing to go was our weapons. After placing Igni in its sheath close but not so close to be obvious I wanted the still invisible sword in arm's reach, I helped her out of her Valkyrie armor, placing kisses on her heated skin. The dusting of freckles on her shoulders was a shade lighter than the ones on her nose and cheeks. I kissed them twice.

With the pillows thrown to the floor, the chaise was wide

enough to fit our naked bodies. Her wings folded against her back hung over the edge. We kissed and let our fingers explore each other's curves and sinews.

Bryn hooked a finger under my chin. "I wanted the first intimacy between us to be better than this. More special."

I'd heard the line before but from Bryn the words rang true. It wasn't just her tone. Magic laced the words and pricked my skin the same way an oath from a fae or a god would. I shook my head. "I'm not asking for anything serious."

I couldn't handle serious. Not with her. Not with anyone.

Bryn opened her mouth to protest, or maybe agree? I wouldn't ever know. I'd shut her up by taking a pink nipple into my mouth. At the same time, I placed a hand between her thighs. Under a soft nest of chestnut curls, I found the sweet bud of her clit. After some experimenting, I found she liked circular motion and dipping inside of her. All the while, I licked, sucked, and teased her nipples with my lips, tongue, and teeth.

Her orgasm came with wild thrashing and a howl.

I did it for her again.

"Enough," she cried after her second orgasm.

This was the part where I'd get up and leave. Yes. I liked getting off, too, but I'd do it at home in my room, thinking about this. Alone. Trust issues or attachment issues. Whatever. It's who I was.

Bryn, however, pinned my arms over my head with one hand and pinched my nipple with another. "I do not ask for forever or even more than this night. I never ask for what isn't freely offered, but you will not leave until you howl for me. Agreed?"

I could say no and tell her to get off me, but again her words were a promise with the weight of a binding oath. No "but I thought you loved me," or "this didn't mean anything to you" later. I could be a free wolf. Right?

Doubt surfaced. Not in Bryn's intentions but mine. This was another world, but this was also highly unprofessional. Would she distract me from this case? Should I even be here with the murderers on the loose? Could I be kicked out of the agency? Would this cause an incident between Earth and Asgard?

Bryn's hand tightened on my wrists painfully enough to get me out of my self-doubt spiral. "What happens here stays between us, but I need your permission."

Fuck it.

"Make me howl, Bryn," I challenged.

Her pink lips twisted in a mischievous grin. "Gladly."

That pretty mouth of hers branded a trail of kisses both tender and passionate down my neck, along my shoulder, between the small mounds of my breasts. Her cerulean gaze met mine as she continued down. She'd let go of my arms but rolled my nipple between her fingers. The motion brought me to the edge even before she spread my lips below and lapped at me with her tongue. The pleasure was exquisite. I thought it was enough to push me over, but she would pause right before I got there.

Then right when I was about to beg her to bring me, she added her long fingers one by one until I was so full, I thought I'd burst. Then I did. My orgasm thundered through me. I howled and writhed as my center pulsed around her fingers.

I thought it was over, but she spread my legs further. Stood and then straddled me so that our vulvas were against each other.

"Move like you did on my thigh," she commanded.

"This will be the only time I'll take orders from you," I replied, but did as she said.

The friction and wet heat brought us both. She collapsed on top of me. I kissed her brow. She tasted of salt when she kissed me on the mouth. We lay like that for what seemed like an eternity, but time was irrelevant here. What we shared tonight between us would complicate things later, no doubt, but none of it mattered now.

CHAPTER TWELVE

"So, all they wanted was to ask you why the shifters were being murdered?"

Jada's office chair creaked as she yawned and stretched behind me.

We were both beat but would perk up before the end of the day, I hoped.

"That and to officially say that Bryn is our guard dog on this case." Which won't be awkward after last night, I didn't add. My chair suddenly spun toward Jada so fast that my head spun with it. "Hey!"

Jada's amber eyes held an intensity that I'd only seen when she was really pissed. "What do you mean she's our guard dog?"

I pointed to the email from Director Tan on my computer screen. "You haven't caught up?"

She squinted at the screen and at the same time waved my question away. "I was looking for leads. Shit. The Supernatural Council issued a formal request this morning for Bryn to be an official liaison from Asgard and it was granted by Director Tan this morning. Well, at least we know Bryn is legit." Jada sighed. "Weird that our parents didn't mention the request at breakfast."

I didn't find it odd at all. My father rarely consulted me about anything. Miriam used to hide everything from Jada, but once she came clean, the two of them shared everything. That gave me a theory. "I'm thinking it happened post-breakfast with an emergency council meeting. If it happened in faerie, time wouldn't matter."

Jada seemed to think about it for a moment, and then replied, "Yeah. They could've spent days negotiating with Freya or Sif there. So how do you feel about the Valkyrie you made out with half the night being our liaison now?"

We were not going to go there. I snorted and scrolled on my phone, checking both the mundane and the supernatural socials for any leads on a possible cult in the city. Jada spun back to her desk. Having been friends most of our lives, we both knew when a conversation was done.

Finding something that stood out proved difficult. The thing about the Pacific Northwest, mundanes had a lot of occult, spiritual, neo-pagan, and Wiccan groups. Because my father didn't abide by a lot of the angels' rules, we were "woo woo" out west before the real deal supes presented themselves. It wasn't that none of these practitioners didn't have a spark of power or what we called latents—those with supernatural heritage but didn't have enough light to become whatever flavor of magical monster they were—but that there was an absurdly large number of them on the west coast. Since supernaturals came out of the closet, more and more mundanes wanted power.

Something stood out from the online garbage: a simple, static graphic inviting magical lone wolves to a spring equinox event at Gas Works Park. The name of the account was The Sacred Lif Society.

"I got a lead."

Jada leaned over my shoulder and grabbed my phone. She grimaced as she handed my phone back to me. "The event is in a week. Is there anything on the account that would lead us to where the cult is in Seattle now?"

"There's an email in the bio. I could send a sob story of a lone wolf shifter drawn to the Norse pantheon and see if they'll admit me to their membership or something. Then we dig out who their leader is to get to the one in Vancouver. I have a hunch that all these other sects are branches of a tree, and she's the root." I'd shared the thought with the goddesses last night, but not in such detail with Jada.

"No. You shouldn't do that. We don't know if they possess more dwarven-forged bindings."

Bristling at the rejection of my plan, I asked, "Then what do you suggest?"

"Let's get Luke on this. He'll follow the digital trail to whoever is behind this cult."

It was a good suggestion, but a deep desire to go after these murderers myself, to seek blood and vengeance for the horrible way Gerald and the twelve other wolf shifters had died, pounded with every beat of my heart like a battle drum. I didn't know if it was the angelic part of me or the wolf shifter loyalty to pack part that drove this urge.

Maybe it was part of who I was that I'd yet to discover, but the word protector had never accompanied my name on anyone's lips. Pack princess, the brat, the emo kid...all these descriptors that I'd lived up to fully in my youth but didn't feel right now. Would I keep these names? I'd never cared before. I still didn't care what people thought of me, but I didn't want to be that kid anymore. The one who was perpetually sad and angry that her parents split so she acted out.

The perception of me might not change for others. I had no control over that, but I wanted to think differently of myself. I wanted to be different. I would avenge these wolf shifters, and I would stop these fakes trying to grab a piece of the magic I was born into by taking it from my kin. They could make their own pact. Their own magic.

"We can use Luke to figure out who's behind it all, but we need to root out the local sect ourselves. No wolf shifter is dying in my territory."

She placed a hand over mine. "We will find them. You've got to trust our colleagues though."

Maria had proved useful in getting me an audience with Freya and Sif that led to learning the Aesir didn't have anything to do with this and that they wanted it stopped as much as I did. Who I perceived as pack had to extend, I knew that, but it was hard to teach a wolf shifter new tricks.

Luke Kourakos-Morales's office had a high, domed ceiling and wasn't really an office but a full-sized tech laboratory. Screens littered the walls. Scattered around the office, marble-topped tables loaded with electronic parts and wires, and devices I couldn't name.

"Hey there. I'll be with you in a sec," Luke greeted us from where he hovered above. His wings flapped as he stared at one of the screens.

Luke was a harpy. The only male harpy in existence that I'd heard of, and that point was always a topic of controversy. I knew why, but I never contributed to conversations speculating about him. Besides, outing anyone from either of my communities—supe or queer—wasn't something I'd do. I usually nipped any talk in the bud, stating that we don't have to know why someone existed but just accept that they did. Besides, Luke's gender was the least interesting thing about him.

He had a mind that could solve complex tech problems, and not only come up with the solution, but integrate magic into it. Hephaestus himself sought Luke's counsel on gadgets and gizmos. He'd been a software engineer working with cutting-edge tech when he gained his harpy status and then he'd come to work for I.S.E.A. a few years later when I was also recruited.

Although he was older, we were recruited at the same time, so Jada and I had gone through the training academy with Luke.

The harpy landed. He stood a little taller than me and twice as broad. He hit the gymnasium for harpies in Milagro Bay and it showed even under his white dress shirt and slacks. His I.S.E.A.-issued suit jacket hung on the back of a stool. Director Tan would have an aneurysm if it were one of her department's agents, but Research and Development did their own thing.

He flashed a dazzling smile. His dark eyes lit with excitement. "Did you like my camera?"

I cocked my head to the side, trying to puzzle out what he meant. Jada, however, understood. She clapped her hands together.

"Like it? The camera was instrumental in figuring out how they'd bound the victim. We've since learned that the bindings were made by one of the dwarves of Nidavellir."

Luke ran his hand over his curls and blew out his breath. "Those poor wolf shifters. They were up against some powerful stuff." After a brief pause to acknowledge the dead, his mood shifted, and his eyes lit with excitement. "So, you mean to tell me that you didn't see the light and you couldn't smell the binding spell, but my camera picked it up?"

Both Jada and I winced at the blow to our supernatural egos. She managed a grin for Luke's win. "It did."

"Congrats. You made a great tool." I slow-clapped. The other two gave me baleful looks. Jada gave me the "I thought we talked about this" face.

Yes, I was going to grow and be nice to someone who helped, but that would take time.

Sighing, I lowered my hands and my head. "Sorry. Force of habit to be sarcastic. Self-defense mechanisms die hard. Anyway, I really do appreciate your camera. It came in handy."

Through my lashes, I could see Luke's stunned expression. "Um...

No worries. Glad it worked." He swallowed and scratched his head. "What can I help you with?"

Relieved we'd moved on from the awkwardness of my apology, Jada and I filled him in about the cult, the social media, and the email. At first, he wore an expression that matched the gravity of the situation. Oddly, he began to grin. That grin spread to a smile that was almost manic.

"Okay, why the Cheshire cat face?" I finally asked.

Luke chuckled as he got behind a screen and started typing. "They might as well call themselves the Ariadne Society."

In my mythos courses, I'd learned about the myth of Ariadne giving a thread to Theseus to navigate the labyrinth back to her after he killed the minotaur, so I got the joke. "Let's stick to one pantheon. This group is giving us enough trouble."

The harpy swiveled from his screen, eyes narrowing. "I thought you said they were mundanes? Do we have the gods involved?"

I wiggled my hand. "The Aesir are concerned but they're not suspects. Dwarves made the bindings. The Dwarves, or at least what I know of them through books, don't really deal with Midgard—what they call Earth, or our whole universe, really. However, they made an exception for this cult that the Aesir believe are Völur. Whoever or whatever they are now doesn't matter. What matters is that they want more power."

Gaze still locked on a bunch of numbers and letters on a holographic screen, Luke blew out his breath. "They really don't care about that study on belief, do they?"

I shrugged. "It's impossible to not believe in something you've seen. The belief of the masses is shaped by what they've witnessed. The Mythic Games showed them too much. There's no going back. No time when the mundanes could say there's no monster under the bed."

"We were there even when they said it," Luke said, voice hard. "They can delude themselves there was a time that we didn't exist, but we always have."

We exchanged a look. He was talking about a lot more than the existence of supernaturals, and I knew exactly what he meant.

Jada chewed her bottom lip. Her eyes had a faraway look. "What if the Dwarves are in on it? Doesn't seem like these mundanes would have anything the Dwarves wanted except perhaps a bargain they couldn't refuse."

"There's a thought," I said. Dwarves had their part in the stories, but as a child and a student of I.S.E.A., I focused on the power players of Odin's family tree, not what I'd considered the side characters. The part I'd missed, the most crucial element of this case, is that all the players have motivations, and these were not just myths, but a history. "Now, we just have to figure out why the dwarves would make the bindings."

"Gotcha!" Luke whooped, launched into the air, and spun in an aerial circle before landing. He grinned sheepishly. "This cult left a tangled web, but we have two main locations. One in Ballard. One in East Vancouver, BC."

Sharing his joy, Jada hugged Luke. "Thank you so much!"

I stood back, not sure of how to convey my gratitude. A hug wasn't happening. Luke was a colleague and I liked him enough, but he wasn't pack. "Thanks," I muttered. "Drop the locations on our phones...please."

The two exchanged a look and Jada broke away to pat me on the shoulder. "A whole thanks. You're growing."

I rolled my eyes at the duo, who were chuckling at my expense.

Sobering, Luke said, "Already done."

I checked my phone. Two location pins shared from Agent Kourakos showed up. Blowing out my breath, I did the right thing. "Thanks again for your help."

"You're welcome." Wings folded behind his back, Luke bowed, adding as we left, "Be careful out there. Don't be too proud to ask for backup on this."

. . .

Calling for backup was exactly what we did. Jada and I deduced that if we descended upon one of the two cult hideouts whose locations we knew, that would sound an alarm to the rest. The hope was that we got the leaders of the larger organization. After receiving the go-ahead from Director Tan, we contacted our connections in the Vancouver area.

"Are you going to call for Bryn?"

I chuckled. "I didn't get a phone number for her."

"Then how are you supposed to call when you need help on the case?" Jada frowned. "Seriously. I thought you two talked more about this."

My face felt flushed. There was the connection between us. I also had told her not to stalk me. Did I pray? "I don't know. Maybe she'll just sense it or something."

"Full access to Earth. No way to call her?" Jada sucked her teeth and then pulled up her email. "Here it is. Says we're supposed to just call her name."

"There you go. Not the weirdest magic we've experienced."

Her brow furrowed. "Gods should be the only ones to hear a call."

I shrugged. "Your mom didn't say Lucifer's name for a reason. Angels can hear prayers and what are prayers but calls for someone to act?"

"I guess so." She blew out her breath. "Well, we're going to have to use our phones for everyone else."

While Jada called Officer Singh, I called Aaron and Rodrigo's pack house number. We filled them in on the Lif and Lifthrasir cult and then got everyone on a video chat to coordinate the pack and Singh's lone shifters to apprehend the Vancouver sect—if it still existed.

"I'll get Officer Aune to help, too. She knows more about this kind of magic better than anyone else local," Singh offered. To Rodrigo and Aaron, who bristled at the idea of a mundane cop becoming involved, the shifter officer explained she was a Norse pagan familiar with the use of futhark runes, the legends, and other practices and would be invaluable to their capture.

As he spoke to the alpha and his mate, I recalled Helena. I'd spoken to her so briefly while digesting Gerald's gruesome murder that I'd written off the mundane as inconsequential to the case, but if Singh thought her knowledge might come in handy to protect everyone involved— Something paralleled about her and Chelsey. Neither had smelled of potent magic, but Chelsey had commanded draugr. I also hadn't smelled magic and Jada hadn't seen the aural light magic gave off on the bindings.

"How much do you trust Helena Aune?" I asked, deliberately leaving out her title. Did he know his colleague enough to trust her or did he trust her because she was a cop? It mattered.

Singh reared his head back, offense clear on his features. "I've known Helena since academy. She's one of the few mundanes who really care about supernaturals' rights."

I still wasn't convinced. "Whoever is pulling this off has been planning it for years. You just don't go up to a Dwarf and ask for a bunch of magical bindings and get them in hours or even days." I wasn't speaking from experience with a Dwarf, but my stepmother was a witch. Spellwork this complex took time. The negotiations would go on for a while, too. Any deal with immortals took time. They played a long game, and there was no rushing them into a decision this big.

"Officer Aune wants these people locked up as much as you do. It's personal to Helena, too. They've desecrated what is holy in her eyes. That matters to someone like her. She's good people," Singh guaranteed.

I glanced at Jada. We had to trust Singh. He knew the officer and I trusted his instincts. Even if he couldn't sniff out something hiding her magic, big cat shifters had the same sort of people sense as any cat. They sensed the bad ones. "Alright, I will leave that up to your judgment."

"Do you think you should go to the Dwarves first before we raid these sect lairs?" Aaron asked.

Without an ounce of reservation, I shook my head. "The Dwarves decided to take a side, and it certainly wasn't with the wolves of Fenrir's line. They won't give me anything."

The alpha and his mate exchanged a glance, communicating silently. Aaron leaned forward and made a small gesture that would only be understood by an alpha, or an alpha's kid, who had seen it before. It was a sign of recognizing the other's authority and alpha-to-alpha respect. A rare honor to give someone who wasn't an alpha.

Rodrigo winked. "Good thinking, Agent."

Returning his gesture, I nodded, too afraid to speak and give away the knot of emotion forming in my throat. How did such a simple act and a few words mean so much? I would need the encouragement. The next call didn't go as well.

My mother answered on the fourth ring. Irritation laced her voice as Kirsten answered, "Three months and no phone call. What? Did your father cut you off when your ambition crossed his, little pack princess?" She slurred her words toward the end, which meant she was swimming deep in her bottles of Tank. I knew Mom and my stepfather Dave had been going through a rough patch, so I'd been avoiding her. Time to pay for that, I supposed.

Jada winced. My phone was on speaker, so she'd heard.

On the other hand, I hadn't even flinched. I had been so over my mother's dramatics for years that her antics didn't even faze me anymore. Kirsten assumed my entire life revolved around pack politics and didn't recognize what I was doing with I.S.E.A. as a real job but rather something to strengthen Gabriel's power base.

"Mom," I began, hoping the honorific would placate her enough to listen for once. "You're in danger."

"Oh, pup. I'm always in danger," Kirsten drawled. Even drunk, my mother's voice was sultry. Everything about her was so damned pretty. Except for her attitude. She rarely spared a kind word before my father severed the mate bond. For a bit, she was better. She even gave me my first non-pack vehicle. Now that she and Dave were on the outs, she had to make someone pay for her own fuckups and that someone was always me. "Lone wolves don't live long."

I could voice the argument that even though she'd been abjured from the Seattle pack, she would be welcome to join any other, but it wasn't true in her case. What she had done to my father had been worse than cheating. She'd involved herself with an incubus who'd raised all kinds of Hell, pun intended, in the supe community. People had been hurt. The pack had wanted blood. Especially my aunt Princess, who had to deal with the succubus. The whole mess Kirsten had made would stain her reputation among shifters for years to come.

"No, Mom. This is an immediate threat. A cult is murdering wolf shifters. Pack and lone wolves. Not just any wolf shifters. Fenrir's line. Don't make any new friends or join any religions, and you'll be good. Also? Watch your back. The Dwarves have given them means to keep a shifter in a mid-shift state. That's when the suspects murder them in a ritual."

"Shit. Would that leave your spirit wherever it goes during a shift?"

Dread heavy and dense pressed on my chest. The thought of Gerald and the others lost somewhere, no Valhalla, no afterlife where they reached peace or battle awaited, that they were in their spirit form, drifting forever, was too much for my mind to bear.

Jada lifted her eyebrows, silently asking if it was true.

I answered Jada and my mother at once, "I don't know."

"Roxy, they're gaining a lot of power from this kind of sacrifice on a mass scale. I'm talking cataclysmic power. Is it...Ragnarök they seek?"

"The thought had crossed my mind." I hadn't shared it with the goddesses, but Freya didn't hand out her Valkyries to help just anyone.

"Shit."

"Yes. Shit."

She blew out her breath audibly. "I—I'll put down the bottle and watch my back. If anyone is going to ruin my life, it's me. Not some assholes trying to be gods of the new world."

"What do you mean? I didn't say they were trying to be gods."

"Ragnarök isn't the end. Destroy the old and bring in the new. They want to kill the gods—or kill them by proxy with an end-times war and be the new ones. The Dwarves went in on it because they likely got sick of the Aesir bowing to the angels and now your dad's council. At least, that's my guess."

It was a damned good one. The stakes for stopping this cult just raised by so damned much.

I pinched the bridge of my nose. "No pressure."

"If anyone can stop them, it's you, Roxanne."

A sarcastic comeback perched at the tip of my tongue ready to leap into the world, because platitudes wouldn't do me any good right now. However, I replied, "Thanks for the vote of confidence, Mom."

"Oh, baby girl. Our line has all been tangled in Ragnarök since our ancestor landed herself with a bargain with Fenrir. We are Lif, my dear, not these imposters. We were chosen to survive this end and live on. Someone misinterpreted it all. I'd been meaning to tell you, but..."

"What do you mean?"

A deep voice called my mother's name in the background. It wasn't Dave. I knew my stepfather's voice. This was deeper. Husky with need. Gross.

"Gotta go," she whispered. "Love you, Roxy."

"Mom, this is important! What do you mean we're tangled in Ragnarök?"

Too late. Kirsten hung up. When I tried to call back, the call cut straight to voicemail. I clenched the phone and balled my fist. My chest burned with futile anger. I texted in all caps to call me back. The message was left on delivered. Of course it was. Not even the end of the world could stop my mother from her hookups.

Misinterpreting the angry tears brimming in my eyes for hurt, Jada placed a hand on my shoulder. "Should we check on her?"

I snorted, shaking my head. "No. She's either teaching Dave a lesson or landing her next husband. She hates when I get in the way of that." Despite being an agent of I.S.E.A., I couldn't find my mother even if I wanted to. When Kirsten wanted to disappear, she stayed gone until she popped up again. It wasn't like we shared each other's location on our phones. We were never that kind of family. "Besides, I have no idea where to start looking for her."

"I'm sorry." Jada slid her arm around my shoulders and embraced me. "You liked Dave. He was mediocre. Such a step up from the others."

"Yeah. It hurts. Dave was the okayest of my mother's thralls." I chuckled softly and hugged her back, then patted her arm to release me. Swallowing back the tears, I said, "Seriously though. He tried, but I know better than to get attached to her men. Anyway, we have a case to work. Kirsten's shitty life is not our concern. I warned her. What she does with that information is her problem."

Jada pulled a face but made no comment.

Yeah. I knew we needed more information from her as well, but we both knew we wouldn't get it from Kirsten until she wanted to give it. If she remembered through her Tank-induced drunken haze.

"Well, we have the team for the Vancouver raid assembled. Time to get the Seattle team together."

There was a knock on the door. Promptly followed by Maria and Hugo Gonzalez walking in. Then to my surprise their younger brothers Darius and Derek, the twins, and Jaime, the youngest, newest I.S.E.A. recruit, followed. All the Gonzalez siblings at once. With so many witches in the small space—including Jada who was part witch—my nostrils filled with the aroma of witchcraft: herbs, wax, tinctures, floral notes, and rich incense. It wasn't unpleasant, and I was used to witches now, but when I was first exposed to practicing witches, the scent overwhelmed my shifter senses.

Maria cleared her throat. "The magic is dwarven, but there is the gods' magic you recognized on it, too. Fresh gods' magic."

"Fresh?" Jada cocked her head, confused.

Hugo pushed his clear-framed glasses up onto the bridge of his nose. "We suspect that someone or more than one person is becoming a deity."

I swore under my breath. My mother's theory was too damned accurate. Going against mundanes, latents, or Völva—witches of a different ilk than the ones in the room—was one thing, but to go against a god or multiple gods wasn't something the cops and the pack in Vancouver would be a match against.

"I'll go with the Vancouver team," Jada announced. "I can get directly to Singh and his team the fastest, trap the cult in Oberon's faerie, and then come back to help you." Her eyes met mine.

I nodded. I could assemble a team and go without her. It just felt...wrong. My gut said no. Also, I didn't want Jada going to Vancouver without me, and I didn't want to raid without her. Maybe because Jada and I always faced trouble together.

"I'll come with you," Hugo offered Jada.

Maria cut him a glare. "I have field experience and have worked with Agent Diaz."

While they argued, I continued my internal debate. I'd been peeved when she was originally partnered with Maria. Was it strategic that we stuck together or was it insecurity driving this feeling? It didn't matter.

Hugo threw up his hands. "Okay. I'll go with Agent Crowfoot."

The rest of the Gonzalez family debated who was going with whom. I whistled, ending the growing din of sibling debate that matched the internal one. "I'm thinking, splitting up is a bad idea—at least it never works for Scooby's gang."

Everyone chuckled. Good. I didn't want to plead my case when it was only my gut telling me not to split up.

Jada sobered first. "So, what's the plan?"

All the Gonzalez siblings leaned in, waiting to hear what I had to say. It was kind of creepy.

"We can use the same team for both raids—We'll do Vancouver first and then travel back in time to Seattle before they are the wiser. If you're up for transporting us all?"

Jada scratched her temple and looked off into the distance the way she used to while doing math in her head. She probably was. Planeswalking looked easy, but there was a lot involved besides unimaginable amounts of magic pouring into it.

"Yeah. It's doable. I will have to work some time travel to stick to the plan of raiding both places at once. That'll take a lot out of me, but we must be all in for this. Right?"

"You sure?" Maria asked, her dark eyebrows furrowed with concern.

Guilt knotted in my gut. Was I being selfish asking Jada to do so much? Part of me wanted to ask if we should call on Phyr for backup but calling one of our parents for a fight meant our parents taking over. Our parents' involvement usually went viral and I.S.E.A. was having a hard time keeping this out of the media as it was. Also, Phyr was not officially a Supernatural Council of the Americas member or a recognized leader like the Vancouver alpha. Additionally, on the "that's a terrible idea" list, the fae had a lot of restrictions on this world because they had a well-earned reputation. I didn't have the clearance and for once, this rule-breaker agreed with the rule.

Jada straightened in her chair and lifted her chin. "I'm sure."

CHAPTER
THIRTEEN

Under the cover of darkness, I stood a few blocks north of the house we would raid. Unlike our stepdad Phyr, Jada didn't like to use magic that involved two things: hair, blood, spit, bones, or fingernails without their consent or breaking the law enacted forbidding any supernatural to use bodily fluids or tissue without someone's written consent. Therefore, we had to reach the location by car once we'd met up with Singh and the Vancouver pack. It took some coordination with Singh and the alphas from there, but this would be a raid and rescue. All parties agreed the prisoners of the cult would go to the pack for healing and the cult members would go to faerie for detention. We'd shed as little blood as possible, and the element of surprise would be on our side.

Luke had armed us all with magical walkie-talkies. Magical meaning, the devices didn't operate on any mundane path of communication that could be intercepted. The witches concealed all of us with a spell that would make us unnoticeable and gave those without I.S.E.A. suits protection amulets. If the Lif and Lifthrasir cult resisted, which I put my money on that they would— With gods potentially involved, this could be a fight of a magical scale. Every bit counted.

First looking at Jada to be sure she was ready and getting a nod, I gave the signal to move in over the walkie-talkie. From there, Jada and I ran. Since we ran with preternatural speed that the witches didn't have, the Gonzalez siblings flew low and fast on their brooms.

Reaching the property, we came upon the first obstacle. The seemingly perfectly maintained front yard erupted, spewing draugr. I counted twelve total as I leapt backwards and up out of the reach of an ax-swinging arm. The retreat bought me time to let my angelic wings release from my back. Gold and red-trimmed white feathers spread in my peripheral as I shot up into the air. Amber light poured from my eyes, illuminating the scene below.

Jada pulled Phyr's sword Angel's Bane, beheading a draugr. She threw a ball of flame, incinerating the draugr. A lion, the size of a small car, with a golden mane and dark fur swathing his forebody like a cloak beheaded another draugr with the swipe of a paw with claws like scimitars. There were no Asiatic lion shifters in the Vancouver pack. It had to be Officer Singh. I would've rolled my eyes at how on the nose his last name was, but I had to get back into the battle.

Last time we fought draugr, I had to resort to my wolf form, but I didn't want to spend a second out of my body. Not now that I knew the cult had a way to trap me there, I was using something my father had wanted me to use against Fenrir. From a sheath on my side, I drew Igni. The ruby shone with a bright red light and then dimmed as the blade ignited. Determined to win, I entered the fray.

When I hit the ground, I lopped off a draugr's head with one swing and then incinerated the corpse. Between Jada, Singh, and me, we cleared the draugr in no time. I called in the rest of the shifters, witches, and Officer Aune. We were about to charge—

"Stay back! There's a blood ward around the house," Officer Aune called out. Maria and her siblings surrounded the pagan, consulting on how to break it.

Annoyed, I growled at the house, "Little pig, little pig, let me come in."

Singh, still a lion, snuffed and shook his furry head. The other shifters paced.

"You're in your angel form," Jada said, pointing to the house with her lips. "They might not get the reference."

"Helpful."

"As helpful as taunting with fairytale lines."

"Says the faerie princess."

Covered in draugr blood, we grinned at each other.

Tired of the witches talking, I lifted my sword. "Wonder if this might be a skeleton key?"

"Or you might get blown back to the Stone Age. Let them cook."

"Hopefully, it's minute rice."

The witches approached. Maria nodded at me. "Stick your sword in it. The fire will break the conduit between the ward and the caster."

I raised my eyebrows at Jada to say, "See? Igni IS a skeleton key." She shook her head and gestured for me to go.

"Brace yourself for a kickback," Officer Aune warned.

Jada cocked her head to one side, crossed her arms, and grinned, gloating she'd also been right.

With extreme emotional maturity, I used my free hand to give her a one-finger salute.

"This ought to be good!" Hugo hooted. The twins and Jaime giggled with a demented sort of glee.

Oh boy. I was in for it.

"Stop guffawing and get started on a deflection spell to protect the area," Maria chided. To me, she added, "You won't be able to hear us once we have a shielding in place. That'll be your signal that we're done."

"Got it."

The witches chanted behind me. The magic laced into the words pricked against my skin and the scent of herbs, wax, and incense filled my nostrils.

While I waited for their voices to dim, I let my wings expand and fold around me with just enough room to see and hold out Igni. The wings appeared delicate and fluffy, but they were angelic wings—i.e., magical. If there was backlash from breaking the ward, they would serve as a shield.

I murmured Igni's name, invoking the sword's power. The ruby flashed bright crimson. Red and gold flames licked the blade, thirsty to consume the power behind the ward. *Thirsty for the blood of non-believers,* a niggling voice that was not my own whispered in the angelic tongue in my head.

What. The. Fuck.

Gabriel could have mentioned that the sword had my grandfather, the archangel Gabriel's sense of One God to Rule Them All. Or maybe, he could have said, "Hey, Box-O-Rox, Igni is sentient and loves polytheist blood."

I didn't speak to the son of my maker. He was merely his father's tool. You, you have rage against injustice that burns within you bright and hot as a star. You seek righteous vengeance. You deserve my counsel.

Greaaaaaat. I had unresolved anger from my childhood, so I'm Igni's favorite.

"In for a penny," I groused, thrusting the sword into the barrier the ward had created.

My dad had a remote cabin in the northern Cascade Mountains near the Canadian border of Washington. Before my parents' divorce, we'd go there to hunt as a family. No digital gadgets were allowed. So, my room had an old, plug-in AM/FM radio. I got the bright idea to stick a safety pin inside a place I shouldn't. If I were a mundane, I might have electrocuted myself. That shock. The vibration up my arm was nothing compared to thrusting a magical sword into a blood ward.

The ground shook with the force of the ward breaking. Car alarms went off. As much as my wings protected the blowback from hitting me, the breaking of the ward was a crucible: the bones in my wings felt like they would shatter. Maybe they did and I healed. I didn't know. It took all my will to not lose consciousness as agony like I'd never known reverberated through me.

Then like a rubber band snap, the pain ended. Deafening silence followed. A short-lived reprieve.

Robed figures like Gregorian monks spewed out of the front and around the sides of the house—a sharp contrast to the suburban setting. They formed an arrow with a midsized person, face shadowed by the hood of the robe, standing at the point. The silence from behind me ended, too, as shifters in animal form, witches with their wands at the ready, a lone demigoddess, and a neo-Norse pagan flanked me.

Shaking my head, I came to my senses and took a step forward. Jada came to my side. We exchanged a look that signaled I'd take the lead. Maybe this confrontation could still be settled without bloodshed. So far, we'd only committed violence against a bunch of animated corpses and broke a ward in the name of the law. I'd at least give it a shot.

"We represent the International Supernatural Enforcement Agency. We are here for suspected kidnapping of several members of the Vancouver pack, and the murder of Gerald—" Fuck. What was Gerald's last name?

'Gerald of my kith.'

That's not really my style of speech.

That is why you need me. You speak too plainly. Gerald of my kith is an elegant and accurate replacement for a surname!

While Igni and I argued in my head about my delivery, one of the robed cultists stepped out of the arrow formation. The scent of gods' magic mingled with an odor not unlike the draugr and the small magic of persuasion accompanied their approach. This person had once been mundane.

Of course they were. They seek unholy means of power. Smite them. Smite them all.

The trouble with smiting like the angels did in Sodom and Gomorrah is I would also obliterate everyone and everything within a block or two of me. Besides, they'd done that to get rid of a bunch of Nephilim who rebelled against the angelic authority, which my father and I were absolutely guilty of. Smiting was not the answer.

"We are not kidnappers or murderers," the robed one began. "All sacrifices gave themselves to the Sacred Lif and Lifthrasir willingly. We do not recognize your authority. You have stolen what was ours and trespassed upon our home, taking our means of protection. You have committed the crimes against us. Give us back our sacred bindings, and your death in Ragnarök will be swift."

"Seriously?" I snickered.

In my peripheral, Jada gave me a *what the heck is wrong with you* look, but she stayed silent. Unlike my sword...

Yes. Laugh at her blasphemy! Armageddon will be the only reckoning! Run her through with my blade so she can feel the wrath of the one true god!

Maybe it was the breaking of the ward or maybe it was the talking sword debating which end of the world would come, but the little snicker turned into a belly laugh.

"You find the Sacred Lif's offer amusing?" The Robed One calling herself the Sacred Lif sounded genuinely confused.

She wasn't the only one. The shifters in animal form cocked their heads in confusion. The witches kept their eyes on the cult, but I got some serious side-eye from Maria and Officer Aune.

Okay, Roxanne, pull it together.

I sobered. I had a flaming sword of Heaven and a practical supernatural army around me. Time to act like an adult.

"Yes. It's hard to take you as a sacred anything with your East Van accent. You're a local who wants to be a god."

Okay. Not so adult, but it did cause a bit of the conviction of her followers to waver. I could smell it and more importantly, she could feel it. Giving her a glare befitting of an alpha of a pack, I put a bit of my angelic Grace into my voice. "By your own admittance, you have conspired with otherworldly forces to take the life of citizens of this world. You have stolen their gift given by Fenrir and siphoned belief that belongs to Aesir for your own use. You're a charlatan. Your power is nothing. You are no god. Release the wolf shifters you have in cages, and I'll make sure the Unseelie fae don't torture you for eternity."

Jada grinned a very fae grin, adding, "Much."

"Witness my power!"

The Sacred Lif raised her arms.

Magic grated against my skin. The hairs on the back of my neck stood on end. My wolf tried to escape my body. I pushed the wolf back with my angelic form, but she clawed at the edges of my mind. It wasn't rage that influenced her. She wanted out and to run away, away, away.

The shifters around me cowered and whimpered, shifting back to human form and animal, but only partially.

What the Hell?

She is using the shadow magic of the false gods to influence. Smite her! Smite them all for not submitting to the one true—

How about I run her through with you?

That is also acceptable. Be wrathful about it.

I didn't actually want to kill the Sacred Lif. Well, not all of me, but there was a teeny tiny part that wanted to eviscerate this asshole and be done with her.

"She's influencing them. Counter it!" I said it in Kairska so only Jada and the witches would understand.

Jada didn't make a dramatic gesture while she worked her influence over the shifters, but her face had that same expression she had when she was doing homework back in ninth grade. That year, she'd decided to take Calculus, Philosophy: Logic, and Statistics all in the same semester—classes usually reserved for seniors at our gifted private school. In other words, she was thinking at the shifters really hard.

They calmed and stopped shifting, but Jada was sweating. I'd seen Oberon take hold of the minds of his entire court. No small task since all high fae could control minds and block other fae out. Jada and Miriam could do the same thing, if pushed—and in a faerie. However, Jada was controlling a whole pack and fighting this abomination on Earth.

"Clever trick." I would have slow-clapped, but I had Igni ready to fight. The sword might be the only reason why the supes on the other side didn't advance. I'd not approach a weapon that could break blood magic either. "Looks like you couldn't keep it going. Ready to give up or do you have more tri—"

I wasn't able to finish my sentence. The one who called herself the Sacred Lif had been across the yard, but now she was breathing in my face. Her breath stank of iron and something salty—not unlike pork. Her teeth were filed to points like a shark. Raw meat stuck between them near the gums. Bile rose in my throat.

Oh, god.

No, no, no, no, no!

She had snacked on a shifter before coming outside.

My vision blurred as white-hot rage burned out my initial revulsion. In my mind, I fought her off with a push and then ran her through with Igni, just as I was trained to do in swordplay, but I couldn't move. Why couldn't I move?

Igni screamed in my head, but the sword's words were as unintelligible as 90s grunge lyrics. Action exploded around me, but it all seemed far away, as if I were swimming in a tank and could sense things were happening around me, but the glass and water distorted everything. Even the features of the robed woman melted and morphed into a caricature of her.

Slowly. Ever so slowly. My nerves did their job and sent a message to my brain that my stomach was on fire...and wet?

My gaze fell from the Sacred Lif's horrific visage to where a wooden stick protruded from my gut. Urgency to remove the stick trickled in from a distance. While my own thoughts seemed marooned on a distant shore, Igni screamed in my head:

Remove the poisonwood!

As if mired in molasses, my limbs became difficult to move. Flames blazed. Suddenly my arm swung with preternatural speed but not of my own muddled volition. Someone screamed, but there were so many screams, cries, growls, and grunts as a battle roared around me. One voice remained distinct.

The flames grew impossibly bright. At the same time, darkness crept in the corners of my vision. Was I dying? Could I die?

Remove the poisonwood!

Right... but something was already in my hand. It was so heavy, heavier than my leaden eyelids, but I couldn't let the thing in my hand go. It was stuck. Clinging. Speaking in my head. If the thing would shut up, I'd know peace.

Little nephil, I will not stop speaking. I will not let you go. You must remove the poisonwood. I cannot.

Poisonwood? Oh...the stick. The stick in my gut. I needed to remove the stick in my gut.

Use your left hand!

I wanted to. I really did, but I'd grown so cold. Colder than I'd ever been. The thing in my hand quieted. It was too far to reach me. Then, I was weightless, floating above a battle. A green-haired demigoddess fought. The witches fought. The shifters fought. A heap of ashes lay before a blue-haired woman with beautiful wings. She crumpled to the ground, a flaming sword still in her hand. It was me, but I felt nothing as I drifted. Darkness unfolded around me, wrapped me like a blanket, and pulled me into its depths.

I became nothing. Then, I became aware.

A frozen valley with evergreens dotting the landscape like foreboding giants. A wolf was chained to the biggest tree of all. The wolf was bigger than wild wolves or even wolf shifters. I felt a pull. A tether between me and the wolf...or rather, the god.

I was confused. I'd thought I'd go to a part of Heaven or Valhalla. An afterlife of any sort. This was the frost giant world. The world where Loki and his wife were born. Where the god before me lived. This was a realm of the living.

"Why am I here, Fenrir?"

We are bonded. When your spirit is lost, it will find me.

I knew it was true. I could sense it. It was why I hadn't let anyone satisfy me before Bryn. There was one mate for me. Then why did I also feel it with Bryn? I shoved that thought aside.

You think you know so much but there is much for you to learn. Go back to Midgard. It is not your time, little wolf.

"I'm getting so sick of the word little in front of labels for me. My name is Roxanne Crowfoot, and I don't take orders, not from you, not from anyone." Not anymore, at least. I was dead. Poisoned with mistletoe like Baldur. So Norse god tragic of me. What that meant was I was free of obligation. I finally didn't have to listen to anyone —not my parents, not my boss, not politicians, and definitely not a god.

We all take orders. Even the dead, which you are not. Even the gods. The wolf grinned. It was uncannily human, that grin. *You have killed one of the false gods trying to usurp my family. There are more. Go back. You are needed, Roxanne.*

Agony tore through my core, ripping me from one world back into the one I'd always known. Chanting filled my ears. The smell of blood, ash, burnt flesh, and magic, and a myriad of both familiar and unfamiliar scents filled my nostrils. A hand pressed against my stomach. Warmth spread from the touch. Jada. I knew her even without being able to see clearly. She was a healer like her mother Miriam.

Cold. I was still so cold. My body shivered uncontrollably. I was no longer in Jotunheim, yet the bitter cold had returned with me. Only my midsection felt warm and wet, but it was of little relief. It also burned like a bitch there. My head ached and my muscles spasmed painfully. Everything hurt. There was no way I should open my eyes, but I tried anyway. Death hovered nearby. I could feel its pull. I had to see my friend's face before it took me.

Finally, I could bear to open my eyes. There she was. My best friend in the whole world. Her eyes glowed magenta with her gods' magic, but she also smelled of wild forests with ancient knowledge. That was her fae magic, healing me.

I'm allowing the foul fae to administer their unholy power unto your flesh carriage only because I refuse to allow you to perish at the hands of the wretched demon. You had no choice in this. The purity of your soul is intact.

Ignoring Igni, who was still somehow in my right hand, I touched Jada's cheek with my left. To feel her warm skin and the staticky sensation of her magic against my fingertips gave me no small amount of joy.

Bile rose in my throat. I coughed, choking on it. Then, vomit launched from my mouth like something out of a horror movie, leaving behind the taste of pennies and something vilely bitter.

"Did I make it worse?" Jada asked someone out of my line of sight.

Bryn came into view. Her pretty face a mask of worry. "No. You're doing great. Her body expelled some of the poison." Relief and warning merged in her tone as she added, "Keep going."

I shifted my focus to the Valkyrie. "Why are you here? I didn't tell you to come."

Instead of answering, Bryn threw her head back and belted out a hearty laugh. Another wave of nausea and subsequent vomiting hit me. There would be a few more episodes as Jada poured her healing light into my wound.

A flurry of activity went on around me that I'd later learn were the witches serving in their role as I.S.E.A. agents. Also, the Vancouver shifters back in their human form had worked with Valkyries to clean up and collect whatever they could to give us leads. Local cops had come by, too. The I.S.E.A. agents and Officer Singh sent them to calm the neighbors. Apparently, the house had a lot of strange activity, so the neighbors weren't surprised that it was a cult raided.

Since I didn't know any of this until later, I asked between heaves, "Di-did we win?"

"You managed to kill the Sacred Lif with Igni," Jada explained. "Not long after, the Valkyries showed up. We got to arrest most of the rest. We managed to rescue a young lone wolf shifter...." Her voice trailed off. "The cult had recently killed the other wolves. They knew we were coming. There were casualties on both sides. Two shifters from the Vancouver pack and Officer Aune were among them. The shifters will live. Aune wasn't so lucky."

Somewhere in between the pain and nausea, I felt a pang of guilt that the pagan had died and so much more for the wolf shifters who we didn't get to on time. Part of me wondered if Aune would see Valhalla.

"She will," Bryn assured as if reading my thoughts.

"They were ready with that mistletoe," I said, my voice still weak. "They had to know we were coming."

"Since they are Völur, I assume that they had rune scryers among them," Bryn replied.

Scrying runes. That was how she knew when to show up. It had to be. Valkyrie weren't seers with visions of the future like an Oracle, but if witches could read the future with divination tools, so could other supes.

"Maria is going to analyze the mistletoe," Jada offered, beads of sweat formed on her face. Healing me was taking a lot from her. "It shouldn't have penetrated your suit."

"More Dwarven spellwork?" I hated how weak I sounded.

Bryn shook her head. "No. I interviewed the Dwarves—I'd been there when all of this started. I thought I was protecting you."

. . .

"What did you learn?" Jada asked, her voice sharp.

"They were paid by a witch to make the bindings. There is no plot on their part. They don't want some upstarts changing things and nothing to do with Midgard." She looked away. "That's all we could get out of them. Are you sure you're alright?"

Jada's brown skin had paled a sickly yellow. "She died. It takes a lot of light to fix that. I'll go into a rejuvenating sleep when she's at a point that I know she'll be alright."

They exchanged more conversation, but my body couldn't maintain consciousness.

CHAPTER
FOURTEEN

Searing heat split me in two as the spike drove through my stomach. The völur who called herself the Sacred Lif smiled as her face hovered over mine. Her teeth were needles, sharper than I remembered. Her face was longer, less human. Her nostrils flared.

My teeth were bound together by something thick and elastic like gum. It would stretch, but I couldn't open my mouth fully, let alone speak.

Igni! I thought you killed her, I screamed in my head.

The sword wasn't in my hand. I couldn't move my hands. I was on the ground, pinned by the witch. The sky was starless. The houses loomed taller, elongated. Nothing was right.

The völur let out a scream. Instead of burning up as she had before, the Sacred Lif vanished. Then there was darkness.

I bolted upright, saturated in sweat and panting. My gaze flung wildly about, taking in my surroundings. All of them were familiar. The smells of home comforted me. I was in my bed and in my room.

My stomach no longer hurt, but my chest felt like I'd had a leaden weight on it that had just lifted.

Bryn stood at the side of my bed, a smoking sword in her hand. "It's okay. You had a nightmare. It's over now."

"No kidding." I rubbed my chest.

The Valkyrie sheathed her sword. "No. I mean that a mare had entered your room and attempted to kill you in your sleep. I killed the creature. I would've killed the evil thing sooner, but they don't materialize fully until they drain a bit of your lifeforce."

"Shit. Mares—the creatures that nightmares are named after—are real?"

Bryn cocked her head to the side, a wry grin curving her pretty mouth. "Why would a woman who is a supernatural and has seen so much believe mares are a myth?"

"I hadn't ever encountered one before," I said dumbly. Perhaps being almost killed twice had an effect on my wit. "I mean, mares aren't in the International Supernatural Enforcement Agency's database."

She plopped down wearily in a chair posted near my bed, adjusting her wings. "Most don't see a mare and live. I suppose you'll have to update the database."

Knowing the protocols involved in adding a new supernatural to the database, I wrinkled my nose. "Ugh."

Bryn chuckled at the face I pulled. Sobering, she asked, "How are you feeling?"

"Considering I'd been stabbed in the gut and a creature tried to suck the life out of me, not bad." I pulled the blankets to the side and made to get up.

Bryn moved with preternatural speed, helping me out of bed. The assistance was unnecessary. Mostly. The only other time I'd felt this crappy was when the Baba Yaga coven attacked me when I was a teenager. Those witches were nearly immortal and closer to gods than someone like Maria. That took days to heal from despite having shifter healing speed. Bryn allowed me to take care of necessities alone but waited just outside the door. My bathroom was adjacent to my room and connected my room and Jada's. While I was in there, I could hear Jada's sleep sounds.

Part of me hurt that Jada wasn't here, watching over me. That no one in my family was here. I'd almost died. While I washed my hands, I recalled that Jada had used her light on me. A lot of it, I assumed. Healing wasn't planeswalking, so it was a different aspect of her magic. She was probably in a recovery sleep. That didn't explain why my father and no one else in the household weren't here.

Bryn waited outside the door. "We didn't disclose the severity of your wound to your family. Only that you were wounded."

"Why?"

"Jada felt that they would seek vengeance and make it a newsworthy event. That would only benefit these völur. Others might want to copy their theophagy to gain power."

I didn't think the average Joe would want anything to do with consuming wolf shifters or any supernatural for that matter, but there were plenty of those with a modicum of power who would like to expand it. There were enough that they could justify that we weren't human and make us some sort of sport for the rich.

I thought of how my parents thought it was a great idea to tell the world we were real. That led to the Paradise Centers, a Christian cult that wanted to pray the magic out of us. They'd also held supes captive, including me and Jada. Then there was the time that the Oracle and the council battled the giant sea monster Charybdis on the Washington coast. That led to the Mythic Games, which involved multiple worlds.

I shuddered. Jada was right. My parents should not get involved. Bryn threaded an arm through mine and led me back to the bed. I felt so damned tired.

"You made a good choice."

"I did." Bryn smiled, pulling the covers over me. She then brushed my hair out of my face. "I only hope you'll choose me as well."

I'd meant to answer, but my eyelids were too damned heavy.

CHAPTER FIFTEEN

Bryn hadn't been in my room when I woke, but she'd left a note saying she'd meet me at the I.S.E.A. Headquarters this morning. When I came downstairs for breakfast, my aunts Princess and Aurora sat at the pack table with their boys. Aurora was a willowy blonde that thought it was still awesome to dress like a nineties flower child. She had an essential oils and crystals shop. Her alter appearance without glamour was an eight foot tall Big Foot.

Princess had lost her leather jacket, flannel, tank, and jeans biker chick edge, sadly. Now she was a mom in a bun and sweats, who taught P.E.

My family and a few of the pack members said their obligatory greetings appropriate for my station in the pack, but no one voiced their concern. No one mentioned I'd been injured on duty. Guess they didn't know or didn't think it was a big deal.

Jada certainly wouldn't have told them. We'd agreed long ago that we didn't share work stories without consulting each other. This was different. I'd almost died, and she had to go into a restorative sleep from healing me. Then I realized they were hiding it from the boys. Pack kids used to know what was going on, or at least, I had to know what was going on. Things changed after Miriam moved in. She didn't care if we were shifters. Children got to keep their innocence if she had a say.

I mussed my youngest cousin's hair as I went to the counter for some food set out buffet style. His brothers giggled, but I got them too.

"Hey! I got school today," Rio groused. He looked more and more like his mother Carmen but had none of her maliciousness.

His mother hadn't been born wicked. Carmen had probably even once had the same innocence as her boys. She'd been a victim of the same religious cult that had held Jada and me. The boys had been through therapy over what happened to them, and they were young enough to bounce back—Carmen herself said that she'd never be the same. Whether they drank their blood or not, power-hungry religious leaders preyed upon innocents, feeding on it and taking everything from them that is good.

While I had been recovering, I questioned the cult leaders' motives and the practitioners' following. Why were they corrupting the original Norse pagan practice of divining to guide their community? What made them think they should be the new gods?

"Alright kids," Princess declared behind me. "Time to clean up and collect your things so you won't be late for the school bus." She gave them a look that used to make me shiver as a kid. "Again."

Instead of being afraid, the boys groaned but cleared their breakfast from the table and then took their belongings with them.

Before Aurora left the kitchen to follow them, my gentle giant aunt squeezed my shoulder. "Be safe."

I put a hand on my gentle, hippy aunt's shoulder and forced a smile and nodded.

I wasn't safe.

No wolf of Fenrir's line was safe.

The pack members took an unspoken cue from their interim alpha and made themselves scarce.

I loaded my plate, waiting for the lecture.

Instead, my aunt's scent warned me of the incoming embrace from behind before her arms wrapped around me. I didn't push her off, but she got that I didn't want a hug and backed off.

“Sorry. I should've asked, but—the thought of you dying..." Her words drowned in a loud sob.

At her sudden outpouring of emotion, I turned to face Princess. Her blue eyes, a different shade than mine, were red. Her lip quivered.

"Having kids has made you soft," I replied, my tone colder than I'd meant it to be.

I expected her to harden or lose her temper, but she only nodded and wiped her face with the back of her hands. "I deserved that."

She did. She deserved a thousand times worse. I had needed her growing up, especially after my mom had been abjured, and she'd been my biggest bully. If it weren't for Miriam's intervention when I was a teen, she'd have kept up being a jerk. Still, the little girl who had idolized her aunt tugged at my sleeve.

"I failed you a lot, Roxy. So did the pack. What your mother did was never your fault...I thought the way I was to you would keep you from being like her—from hurting me like she did. All it did is make our relationship shit. I do see that now that I have the boys. I'm sorry. I'll work on doing better."

It had never occurred to me that she’d taken my mother’s betrayal as personal. It had always been a pack and my dad matter. They had been friends once, as close as Jada and I. If Jada did to me what Kirsten had done to Princess, she would be dead to me. Any reminder of her would be a gut wound.

None of it had been my fault, but Princess had not been much older than I was now. Did I want to follow in her footsteps of bitterness and anger? Also, even now, especially now she was interim alpha, how she treated me mattered to the pack. How I, also imbued with alpha magic treated her after she offered an olive branch mattered just as much. The pack could feel our tension. I could tell her to fuck off with her sorries, let the feud between us tear everyone apart, or I could decide to forgive and heal an old wound that had festered too long. A wound that hurt more people than Princess and myself.

"I'll try not to be a sarcastic shit in pack meetings, but it'll be hard. Old dogs and new tricks and all that."

"Wolves aren't dogs, and neither are any shifters. Our animal side doesn't rule us. It's a part of who we are, but we can learn and change like any mundane."

I rolled my eyes, feigning exasperation. "Let me make a joke, Auntie."

She grinned. The way her eyes shone with love as she did so healed that wound just a little bit. "As long as I live and breathe, I'll try to teach you things I had to learn the hard way."

I put down my food and threw my arms around her, hugging her hard. She reciprocated. Things wouldn't ever be hunky dory between us, but they might just be alright. That was enough for me.

Jada, Maria, and Bryn stood alongside me in front of Director Tan's desk. We'd given a full report of what went down. We'd also reported why we hadn't called for backup or performed a second raid.

Tan didn't knit. She didn't even sigh at her cats' photos as she usually did when she was disappointed. She simply listened. She knew it all. Jada had called in what had happened the night of the incident with some details, but this was the official report.

"A former group of latents all became nearly gods in terms of magic by sacrificing wolf shifters and consuming their blood?" Tan asked, her tone devoid of emotion. She'd already had a chance to read the coroner's reports and had eyewitness accounts from the raiding party and I.S.E.A. agents involved on paper. She wanted to hear from us, her direct reports.

Jada had to sleep off bringing me back from the dead, and I had to heal from the nightmare's attack so close to when I'd died. The thought that I had died circled in my mind a lot since I felt myself again.

"They weren't registered as latents," I corrected. "I looked through the former archangel's records and the I.S.E.A. database. We might be dealing with mundanes who have gained power through a form of theophagy."

The Director rubbed the bridge of her nose. "Can you time travel to stop the Seattle group, who have now abandoned their most recent safehouse?"

My gaze fell to the floor. If I'd been prepared for anything, I wouldn't have been stabbed and nearly died. Death or near death did something to my fate.

In my peripheral, Jada looked at her hands. "I am not all powerful. I used so much of my light to heal Roxy that I couldn't time travel then, and now it's a fixed point. We can't catch them by that means."

"It was good that you assisted Officer Singh and the Vancouver pack instead of splitting the raids between two groups. They might not have survived this so-called Sacred Lif and Lifthrasir cult without you. Thank Freja for the assistance of the Valkyrie on this case, Bryn."

Bryn bowed but made no comment.

"Officer Aune did not survive." My voice quavered, but it had to be said.

Tan gentled her voice. "I've had HR send a compensation package to Constable Helena Aune's next of kin. She will have I.S.E.A. representation attend her funeral with full agent honors. I also have spoken to Constable Singh. He has accepted an offer to join I.S.E.A. We are now accepting shifters who aren't affiliated with a pack."

Interesting, considering I was most certainly affiliated with mine...not that I had any real place in the pack or pack politics. I'd once served as a junior enforcer for the Supernatural Council of the Americas, but the council had handed that work over to I.S.E.A. once supernaturals were allowed to become agents. After the Mythic

Games, mundanes felt unsafe. The general public cried for the agency, which they believed had their interests in mind, to police us monsters. The enforcers, Sean and Micah, now taught at Miriam's Eastside Charm School, and Jada and I were "legit" law enforcement.

"I don't know if they still will go through with it, but there is still a social media presence for a Sacred Lif Gas Works Park event. I checked with the parks department, and there's no official event licensed to be there. It could be a spoof to throw us off, or they could be throwing this event without permission."

Tan considered this. "What's your next move?"

"The Seattle group will still go through with their next sacrifice," I said. "We just have to make sure the park is still where they plan to make it."

"How do you plan on doing that?"

Bryn stepped forward. "These so-called Sacred Lif are völur—witches who use divination magic. That's how they knew the raid was coming. I'll scry the runes to see if they will be at this Gas Works Park. The Norns are unbiased in these matters. They will favor my ask and reveal the skein. Whether it will be good news or bad, we'll be prepared."

Tan's gaze swept from Bryn to her agents to confirm we were going to read the future for a plan.

"I'll also consult the Oracle for a cross-reference," Maria added with an apologetic look in Bryn's direction.

The Valkyrie nodded, not seeming to take offense. I supposed as a soldier, Bryn had had to deal with her superiors not wanting outside influences determining her course of action. As an I.S.E.A. policy, Tan didn't want the gods involved as little as possible, but she couldn't deny the goodwill help either. We were going up against something we hadn't ever faced before. The Sacred Lif and Lifthrasir might have started out mundane humans, but now they had god-level powers, and we weren't sure what they might be. We needed all the supernatural backup we could get.

Tan chewed on her lip and rubbed the one picture she had of

herself on her desk. In the picture, the Director was a rookie agent, probably in her mid-twenties. She stood next to Agent Roanhorse. Across from the two of them stood my grandfather, the Archangel Gabriel, in all his pompous glory. I had no idea what the meeting was about or why someone took a picture. I never asked because Director Tan was Fort Knox with her past—even if it involved my family. Especially if it involved my family.

"Alright. This is the deal. You will gather information, but not just for the Seattle Sacred Lif and Lifthrasir, but for all their sects. Meanwhile, I will put Luke on finding a digital trail, and I'm going to speak with the Supernatural Council of the Americas to enlist every supernatural willing to be part of the biggest raid coordinated in I.S.E.A. history."

I cleared my throat. "If it's alright with you, Director, I'd like to not involve the council."

Tan opened her mouth to speak, but Jada came to my defense. "We are the agents on the case. Let us handle when we'd like the council to come in. I remember distinctly that you and former Agent Roanhorse always spoke to the council, not your former superior. Were you under orders, or were you acting on your own?"

The Director considered Jada's question. "We had free reign by the time we involved the council. The former Director didn't like working with supernaturals at all. That's how I became your fearless leader."

That made sense. The International Supernatural Enforcement Agency used to be the United Nations Monster Hunting Unit. The older, mundane agents who hunted us "monsters" barely tolerated the mages and hated supernaturals. The organization took some public hits with the Supernatural Council revealing we were people's neighbors, not monsters, and then a few years later freeing supes from the I.S.E.A. prison called the Vault. I was a very new agent when that happened, but I was there when the agency went through a reorganization. Agent Tan became Director Tan, in charge of the supernatural agents of I.S.E.A. Her partner, Agent Roanhorse, retired. The former director was still a director, but of another division.

"The council was needed back then as your liaisons. Your firepower, so to speak. Let your agents be that now."

Tan chewed on that but still knitted her brow doubtfully.

Jada stepped forward, pointing at me and then herself. "Our parents were never professional agents with the kind of training to keep incidents under wraps. They were transparent and got the job done but made a lot of noise and caused a lot of destruction in their wake. We're just as powerful as them but have more skills to keep this from becoming a global incident. Let the Supernatural Council retire from vigilante enforcement. Let us agents do the work we've always done with everyone's best interest at heart."

The Director blew out her breath. "When you put it like that, I'm reminded why I recruited you two and not your parents. Alright. Scour the internet, the skein of fate, wherever you must go and put an end to these murders and whatever else this cult has planned. Use the entire agency at your discretion."

CHAPTER SIXTEEN

After the meeting with Director Tan, we dispersed. Maria left to see the Oracle in Milagro Bay. Jada said she'd talk to Luke about gathering some digital trail leads to where the other cults might be hiding. That left me and Bryn. I'd expected her to leave to report back to Freya, yet she walked with me. I had Igni strapped to my back. The sword was enough protection for now, and I bristled at the idea that Bryn thought she needed to protect me.

I agree. You have me. That is enough.

Why did I hear a note of doubt in the sword's voice? Why did *I* assign emotions to an inanimate object babbling in my head? "I'm going to go back to my office and do some more digging on my own, so..." I'd planned to scroll social media to see if there was talk about the gathering. Luke could probably search more effectively, but my method had gotten me leads before. "It really wasn't a two-person job."

"Do you want to learn to scry the runes?" the Valkyrie asked.

I chewed my lip, considering her proposal. Not that I was against scrying, but I hadn't practiced witchcraft before—at least, not without Jada and never divination.

"Doesn't even looking at the future set it as a fixed point?"

Bryn waved the notion off. "No. We're taking a peek at a potential future. There's no harm in it...but looking doesn't set the future in stone. Besides, we're only two people. That's not enough to consolidate the many threads of fate into one."

Suppressing a smirk, I arched an eyebrow. "It's a numbers game? Maria will have the Oracle looking as well. Is three too much?"

Her responding grin made my stomach flutter. "To answer your first question, yes. To answer your second, it depends on the three and their influence over others."

That answer left a lot to be desired. Mostly because the Sacred Lif were völur practicing seer magic and influencing a large group.

"Well, you can see that I have only one friend and not much influence, so I think we're good."

Bryn tilted her head so she could take me in fully. Her gaze sparked heat everywhere it landed. "You underestimate yourself. You have every gift bestowed upon your father, and he's a leader that has brought great change."

An ache burned in my chest. It wasn't the first time I was told in so many words that I had to live up to my father's legacy. I didn't want to. I saw how much he had to work. How much he had to sacrifice to stay a leader. He didn't even want to divorce my mom. His position forced him into it. I wouldn't let others rule me. "Well, he's assertive and decisive. I'm a woman, so if I act like him, I'm a bitch. No one likes a bitch. No one follows a bitch."

Bryn scoffed. "That is not true."

"My pack hates me because I look like my mother and act like my father."

"Have you considered leaving that pack and starting your own?"

I snorted. Not one bit of me wanted anything to do with filling my father's shoes.

"The Vancouver pack respects you. Singh respects you. Cats respect no one. Especially wolves. You could start a pack of your own."

I thought I.S.E.A. was big enough that it wouldn't matter what I did...it wouldn't matter if I screwed up. A niggling voice whispered, *like your mother.*

There it was. My long-held fear. That I was all the things my pack thought I would be. Words swam in my head like piranhas, ready to take a bite of my self-worth. Words like weak, traitor, disloyal, *slut..*

I swallowed hard and pushed the door open to the office I shared with Jada. I motioned for Bryn to go in first. "We're getting way far from the original topic here. Even if I could have influence, I don't right now, and I like it that way."

Bryn entered and turned around, facing me as I walked in and shut the door. She cupped my face in her calloused hands—the hands of a sword wielder. Her cobalt eyes bore into me, stripping away the layers I'd built for years.

"There are two types of leaders, Roxanne. One who chooses to take control: They want power, adoration, and glory. Then there's the other: The one who sees a need and fills it. You are the latter whether you want to be or not."

"I don't want it. I simply want to stop the bad guys from killing more people."

"Keep doing things like that. Keep acting like a leader. The lone shifters will come to you. You, not your father, not your aunt, are what they've been looking for. What will you do then?"

"Be president of the misfit shifters club then, I guess." I shrugged.

"You will know you are not a misfit. There is a place for you. That is why they seek to destroy you. Your body is young, but the magic in your blood is old and powerful. Even more so because it comes from many sources."

It was the first time someone didn't break me down into parts: angelic or wolf shifter lines. Well, not the first. Jada understood. We were family. Pack. Bryn was not pack, but she saw *me*. Unease filled me.

"Yeah. As an I.S.E.A. agent, stopping bad guys. Speaking of which...are you going to consult the runes?"

Bryn's hands dropped from my face. She straightened to her full height. A wall rose between us.

"Not here. This place is too heavily warded against any outside influence, and the Norns are very much an outside influence. Preferably somewhere wooded."

~

"Is this wooded enough?" I spread my arms, indicating all the trees and flora around me.

It had taken two hours to get to Snoqualmie Pass, and another thirty minutes to get to a secluded, off-trail spot, but it was worth it to get out of the city. First, I'd taken her to the private acreage surrounding my father's house, the pack house, but Bryn insisted that the fae living on that land and Miriam's wards on the property would interfere.

I'd argued that my stepmother's wards hadn't stopped the mare from entering my room, but Bryn had replied that wards couldn't stop them from entering a room. Nothing could. That bit of information had made me nervous about falling asleep later, but I'd kept that thought to myself.

Bryn closed her eyes and inhaled deeply, blowing out her exhale. She stretched out her arms. No familiar tingle of magic scraped my skin. No glow emanated from her.

I waited.

And waited.

She stood there...just...breathing.

Ooookaaayyy

After I'd gone gray and wrinkled, Bryn finally opened her eyes. Hyperbole withstanding, the pause may have lasted only thirty seconds, but a *long* thirty seconds.

"This will do."

"Great." I extended an arm, gesturing for her to get on with it.

Bryn smirked. Then the Valkyrie lowered herself to the ground, sat cross-legged, and motioned for me to do the same. I watched her remove a small pouch and a folded piece of dark material from a larger pouch at her waist. Her hands moved with precision, unrolling the cloth. At the center of the cloth were interwoven rings. Four stubby candles in glass holders came out of her pouch next. With a flick of a match, she lit each.

Her cobalt gaze lifted to meet mine as she lifted the small pouch. "Hold this, put your hand inside, and shuffle the runes around. When you feel them activate, ask the Norns to show you what is to come. Then you may empty the pouch onto the cloth."

I bit my lip, resisting an urge to bat the pouch away. Rune divination was something my mother had warned me against. Kirsten had always said we had more freedom if the Norns didn't notice us. She'd said a lot of things about keeping my head low when I was a kid, but she had sex with an incubus spy. So, I considered the source wasn't that great at keeping her head low. Besides, I'd met Fenrir (at least in my spirit form), had two attempts on my life, and I also had to stop some völur from potentially starting Ragnarök early.

"I can't read them."

"You can read any language, granddaughter of the Herald." Undeterred, Bryn shook the bag. "Besides, these runes are not like mortal Elder Futhark runes left to interpretation. These will *show* you the future."

I bristled at the thought of surrendering to a vision or any experience that I had no control over. It was bad enough I didn't have control over where I went when I shifted. However, I had to either do this or let the völur kill more shifters because they were willing to do what I wasn't. Scowling so hard I could feel the press of my eyebrows, I accepted the pouch, opened it, and dipped my hand inside. The smooth sensation of polished bone juxtaposed rough grooves that whispered meanings in my head.

I closed my eyes and thought at the runes: *Tell me where the völur plan to sacrifice the wolf shifters next.*

The cool runes warmed. Needle-like stabs pricked at my fingers.

Without opening my eyes, I poured the runes. Wind rushed around me as if I'd opened a door into a hurricane. I opened my eyes. The runes glowed as they swirled in the air before me. Past the divination pieces, Bryn watched transfixed. Her chestnut hair floated around her face. She didn't blink, and all that moved was her hair. The stillness reminded me of when Jada would have us walk *between* time.

On impulse or perhaps compelled, I reached out to touch one of the runes. My surroundings spun. I tried to pull my hand back, but my muscles strained against an unseen force, frozen. All the runes gravitated to the rune my hand touched, twirling and spinning around it. They fell to the ground, dully clattering against roots.

Gnarled and twisted roots extended as far as my eyes could see. At their center, a tree so broad that it might be at least a city block wide and stretched higher than a skyscraper; so high, I couldn't see past its canopy of branches and leaves. Power emanated from the tree like warmth from the sun.

Suddenly, my muscles obeyed, and I retracted my hand, almost falling backward with the force of it. A growl escaped my lips. It was lupine, yet I was still in my human form. Mostly. Wings shot out of my back and fur sprouted from my still human-shaped hands and arms. My canines painfully extended to fangs that I touched with my tongue to test their sharpness. Electric blue hair still swept over my shoulder. I wasn't fully an angel or a wolf, yet I was fully myself. What was more disturbing is that I didn't leave my body for this form.

My heart raced and I panted. *What's happening to me?*

Warmth emanated from the sheath fitted tight between my wings.

I do not know. We are no longer on Earth. The magic of false gods lives here. Draw me, and I will ensure you slaughter them.

Igni hadn't talked to me since I'd almost lost the fight with the Sacred Lif, but I'd kept the sword strapped across my back every time I left the house now.

I assume this tree is Yggdrasil where the Norns live.

Why are we here?

I asked the Norns for a peek at the future.

Indignation laced the sword's tone as it asked, *Why would you want a prophecy when you have free will?*

When my grandfather forged this sword, he obviously forgot to mention he'd aided prophets throughout time to warn people of this or that, and he influenced the book of Revelations that contained a prophecy like that of Ragnarök and other end-of-the-world stories. Gabriel learned these things through reading the threads of fate somehow, but he wouldn't ever admit it. However, I didn't want to argue with Igni.

I'm here now. I'm going to go through with this.

That's illogical. Sunken cost fallacy, for certain.

I snorted. *A sentient sword wants to talk about logic. That's rich.*

Igni sputtered and stammered its retort. Quite a feat, since it had no mouth. Words like *insolent* and *ungrateful* made it through. Apparently, I'd offended the sword's delicate sensibilities.

I'm sorry. I appreciate your guidance and presence.

After a long pause, Igni replied, *Apology accepted. I will always aid you with my holy fire, but mark my words, seeking the future will not guarantee victory.*

On that, we agree.

But I hoped seeing the future would give me a leg up. Taking in a deep, tree sap and bark scented breath, I looked around. A scent other than tree, a scent of flesh and hair, and...something familiar but not, caught my attention. I sniffed the air, testing to see if I'd imagined it. I let my gaze follow that smell. My eyesight was keener than when I was in human form, or wolf or angelic alone. It was like I'd gained a level of perception that I'd had pieces of and was now complete. This made me wonder if I could sustain this form outside of Yggdrasil's realm. My father, who taught me how to shift to animal and angelic forms, had never taken a hybrid form. We were the only two of our kind though—as far as I knew, very few Nephilim existed and none were half wolf-shifter. Perhaps it never occurred to him.

Something in the far distance swung from one of the branches. Contemplating my abilities combined, I had almost missed it. I focused. My stomach dropped like I'd swallowed a leaden ball when I realized someone had hung themselves.

Hoping I wasn't too late, I ran and sprang into flight.

The god's magic hit my nostrils before I reached the body. The light inside him was fading with the diminishing scent.

My heart raced as I fumbled with the noose. A hand shot out and grabbed my wrist. My gaze lifted to the god's face. In my panic, I hadn't recognized Odin. To be fair, I'd only seen him once over the span of my life. The patch over one eye gave him away. The other eye bulged and his face was red. Gods, unless ascended, could die. It was very hard to kill them, but they could die.

Confusion set in. Why didn't he want me to free him? Why would he kill himself? A vague memory of a story my mother told me as a child from the Poetic Edda surfaced. Odin had hung himself for knowledge before. He even sacrificed an eye. Surely that was a metaphor? Yet here he hung and didn't want me to stop him.

"Leave him be," a harsh feminine voice cried in a language akin to Old Norse.

Another voice with annoyance lacing her tone joined in. "He's at it again?"

"Every. Single. Time," a third chimed, huffing afterward in exasperation.

Three women in long loose dresses stood below. The Norns each wore crowns with branches and flowers. One had silver white hair and pearlescent skin like a fae. The other had dark curly hair and metallic-appearing bronze skin like Phyr. The third had pink skin like that of a white mouse, not a human. Her wavy hair was also pink, and her purple eyes crinkled in the corners as if she heard a good joke. They all had black paint around their eyes.

The pink one waved and smiled. There was a gruesome death

happening and she was waving and *smiling*. Perhaps when you were a goddess of Fate, you'd seen too much?

The one with silver hair cupped her hands around her mouth. She had the harsh, gravelly voice. "Odin will be fine. He'll resurrect in a couple days."

Perhaps sensing my resolve to save him softening, the god released his grip. I gave him one last look. Hating how terrible a death he chose but also respecting whatever process he felt he must go through, I left him.

My feet hit the ground smoothly, much better than my usual landings, and I already had great landings in my angelic form. This hybrid form had even better reflexes, strength, and coordination. I smiled, feeling a bit proud.

The Norns did not cheer for me—not that I expected them to, but it would be nice. They did, however, smile back at me. This was going great. Just me and three ancient entities all awkwardly smiling at each other while Odin swung from his neck above.

This wasn't the oddest scenario I'd ever been in even before I became an agent for I.S.E.A.

The pink Norn gestured at herself and then the bronze and pearlescent Norns. "I am Skuld, this is Verdandi, and Urd."

"I'm Roxanne."

Urd chuckled. "We knew before you could say your name."

I shrugged and lifted a fur-covered hand. Thick claws tipped my fingers instead of nails. *Fun.* I waved my hand in demonstration. "Why am I like this?"

"It is who you are," Verdandi replied, her gaze swinging to the trunk of the tree. "When you are here, Yggdrasil allows you to see your whole self, not a piece that is convenient to whomever is present."

"That is not why you're here," Skuld began, then turned away. "Follow us. We cannot pause our work for long."

With that settled and how I felt about it to be more thoroughly examined later, I accepted what they said and followed the Norns. We entered a door in the bark of the tree to a cozy lodge. Inside, a fire burned in a large hearth with something in the cauldron hanging over the fire. An enticing aroma of meat and stewing roots combined with that of woodsmoke filled my nostrils. It was comforting and homey. It made me miss Miriam and Phyr—not my biological parents or my pack. Funny that.

The Norns took places at three wooden chairs around the fire. A fourth appeared. None of the goddesses seemed surprised that a chair suddenly existed in their home. I'd been to faerie. Nothing phased me either. Urd nodded to the chair. "Please, have a seat."

Once I took the offered chair, a wooden bowl filled with stew and a spoon appeared in my hands.

Urd pulled a skein from a basket on a table next to her chair, but her eyes were on me. "You liked the smell. We have plenty. Go ahead. Eat."

Be wary, young one. The stew isn't stew.

I hesitated at Igni's warning. In faerie, unless it was Miriam's faerie, you did not *ever* take the food. Imbibing in ancient realms usually trapped you there, or worse, made you married to a dude. *What is it?*

I don't know.

"Um. I'm not hungry."

"It's not food you desire, but you are hungry for knowledge," Skuld waved a pair of shears as she spoke and then pointed at the food. "You must satisfy that hunger and eat."

Is it poison or bespelled?

My gaze swept to the door and then back to Skuld. Stalling for the sword's reply, I asked, "Why is Odin doing that, if all he has to do is eat this?"

The Norns exchanged glances, their eyes dancing with amusement. Urd shrugged. "Picky eater. He doesn't like stew."

All three goddesses laughed and resumed their work. I'd expected the Norns to be scarier. Perhaps they weren't as scary as my mother had said, not a trio of cheerful weavers. Well, perhaps the goddesses didn't feel a need to be terrifying when they held everyone's literal fate in their hands. Certain things were implied.

Igni?

I'd been annoyed by the sword at first, but I trusted the gift from my father, even if my angelic grandfather I was working on trusting had forged it. Igni's pause felt like a pregnant pause, not an abandonment, as if the sword were thinking—no, analyzing. I'd only run into an inanimate object with full sentience before. The Vault—or John as it liked to call itself—was a living building the size of a planet with omnipotence and omnipresence within itself.

"Why will eating this stew give me knowledge?"

Verdandi sighed. "Who cares why? You threw runes and asked us to show you. Now you want to question our method."

"Don't mind sourpuss here." Urd waved her sister off. "She doesn't know how to tell you. Honestly, I don't know how to explain it other than you absorb the knowledge like nutrients. Or you could just sacrifice yourself and Yggdrasil will show you."

"I can explain so her mind can comprehend, sisters." Skuld waved her shears again. "This tree is like a supercomputer loaded with information. The stew is a way to download it into your brain." She tapped her temple.

I stirred the contents of the bowl, still dubious. Yet...it was the better of the two choices.

The stew is as she says it is, but I don't understand it. It is...not an unholy magic meant to trick or bewitch, but it is...somewhat like Grace—and it is with great hesitance I call it as such.

Grace was Jehovah's blessing unto the angels—and some humans. The magic that made them powerful, part of what made me powerful. Was Yggdrasil a sentient god, able to imbue knowledge, or was it simply a magical tree? —not the question I wanted in my mind.

I focused on the wisdom I sought from Yggdrasil, not contemplating about *what* the tree could be. I scooped a mouthful. The blend of vegetables, meat, and herbs tasted delicious. I chewed and swallowed.

Nothing happened.

Skuld kept to her work, but commented, "You must eat all of it."

Wanting to get it over with and get back to Bryn, I wolfed down the rest and licked the bowl clean, which was not unusual for me. Shifters tended to eat fast and a lot. A small piece of me questioned where the meat and vegetables came from on a tree that was a world, but the logical part of me ate a concept my mind could comprehend.

Nothing happened.

Just as I lifted my empty bowl to show the Norns, my vision blurred. The weave the three worked on, once the same color as Yggdrasil's roots, glowed a pale yellow. When I rose, I let the bowl and spoon fall. Their purpose served; the objects disappeared before they hit the floor. My hands reached for a certain thread as if on their own volition. The Norns watched with ancient eyes as I plucked that thread from the rest.

"Careful not to remove it completely," Skuld warned.

The cabin faded away, but not completely. I could still smell the stew, the fire, the scents of the three Norns, and their magic—the ever-present Yggdrasil.

Then, the vision slapped me in the face...

The moon hung pale and full, outshining the few stars visible in the city sky. A crowd wearing hooded robes gathered on a hill at Gas Works Park. Music played. Drums and a stringed instrument. It wasn't great.

I knew this park well. As a kid, I'd flown kites on that hill many times. As a college student, I'd gone to a myriad of concerts and punk shows there. This park had a million memories linked to it, but what I saw overshadowed those good memories.

Not quite at the apex of the hill, a wolf caught in mid-shift hung. Someone had bound her wrists and ankles to a pole. Not quite in human or wolf form, I couldn't tell if she was pack or a stranger. Next to her, another pole with another victim hung from her wrists and ankles. She wore nothing but a loose sheath. It was bloody and dirty. Even in the dim light, even with a gag around her mouth, and battered and bruised from head to toe, I recognized the second person. It wasn't a wolf shifter. It was a Valkyrie.

"Bryn!" I screamed, uncaring if the Sacred Lif and Lifthrasir gathered could hear me. No one turned around. No one heard me. I reached for Igni but could not. I had no hands, no sword, and no corporeal form. I was but an apparition, witnessing the impending death of my lover and a wolf shifter.

Where was I in all of this? Future me couldn't possibly be failing them both. Where were any I.S.E.A. agents?

A robed figure in white approached the wolf. They raised a hand. The milling, murmuring crowd silenced. A person with a sack on their head was brought out. The sack was removed. Perspective didn't matter in this vision; I could see Jada's face. She looked back and forth between the two victims. Fear limned her features.

Jada faced gods and monsters all the time. Why was she afraid? Why didn't she have backup? Where was I?

The white robed figure approached her. I strained to hear what was said, but Yggdrasil did not let me have the same access as I had to the visual. Tears ran down Jada's cheeks as she lowered her head, shaking it. The wolf shifter, even in apparent agony, howled something that sounded like mangled words, but I wasn't allowed to hear that either.

Frustration sang in my blood. I wanted to howl to release it. Why was I receiving this partial information?

The figure walked away from Jada to approach the two who were awaiting sacrifice. A long dagger appeared in the hand of the robed person. I didn't want the wolf shifter to die, but as they approached Bryn, the part of me that recognized what the Valkyrie was to me when we met, when we sealed that bond by making love, knew that they were going to kill my mate.

A mere witness, I was helpless to do anything about it. Jada, my best friend in the entire world, my sister, and partner at work, somehow was helpless—or worse, intentionally chose Bryn. The betrayal stung, but what worried me more was the consequences.

I tried to look away. I didn't want to see the killing blow or the slow torture that might ensue. Yet, I saw the dagger slice into the flesh of the woman I cared for.

I screamed in my head, begging to be let out of the vision.

Suddenly, I was yet again in the Norn's cabin within Yggdrasil. The grief, the rage still burned hot within me. I howled, finally releasing it all. I fell to the floor on my hands and knees, panting.

"Why show me my mate's death?"

"You must prevent this at all costs. More than your mate will be lost," Skuld explained, snipping a piece of thread. "These völur are becoming gods through corrupted means and will corrupt the Nine Realms."

I wiped my mouth and sat on my knees. "The cult will bring on Ragnarök, then?"

"Ragnarök represents the natural shift from old to new—an event that will come of its own volition as a passing of a torch from one generation to the next. Just as the winter snow will kill a field with its frosty blanket, but waters the soil for the spring growth when it melts. If you melt that snow too fast, it will cause a flood, damaging the soil and tearing anything standing from its roots. Forcing Ragnarök will bring on an event that no one can escape. Flooded with this violence, Yggdrasil will become uprooted and will wither and rot. The realms will collapse without the tree's support."

Urd shifted in her seat and agreed with her sister. "No one will survive, not even the instigators."

Despite the fire burning in the hearth, icy dread drained all warmth from me. I wouldn't just lose my mate. I'd lose everything. "Did you show them the outcome?"

Spreading her thread-laden palms, Verdandi replied, "We cannot control what those witches see. We are but mere caretakers of Yggdrasil and weavers of the threads."

"You cannot tell anyone of what you saw or what we've told you," Skuld admonished. "Those who have tapped this thread have had many bear witness to it. It is nearly inevitable."

Faces solemn, all three Norns nodded in agreement.

"How much of a shot do I have to stop them?"

The goddesses silently conferred with looks. Skuld answered, "There is no shot, currently."

Urd held a thread. "We are caretakers, but we have seen everything change. You must believe it will and convince everyone else that it will because it must."

Verdandi nodded. "Manifest it."

A manic laugh bubbled up, escaping my lips. "That is how I save the world, possibly the multiverse, with a social media trend?"

The Norns' appearance shifted. Suddenly they didn't seem like three sisters living in a cozy cottage, but primordial beings with eons of existence behind them and close to infinite light within them. Mouths in unison, they spoke as one entity, "You know better than most that belief can make the mighty crumble and the weak a pillar of strength. You have witnessed it many times. If you do not believe this is not the end. If you do not manifest a different future, all will be lost."

CHAPTER SEVENTEEN

Bryn's scent enveloped me as I came to. We were still on the ground in the forest. My head rested on her shoulder as she cradled me in her lap. She smiled down at me, but her chestnut eyebrows were still furrowed, and worry creased the corners of her cobalt eyes.

"Welcome back."

"I was in Yggdrasil. The Norns fed me stew."

At that, Bryn chuckled. The levity was brief. "What did they show you?"

"If the cult is successful, it will not be Ragnarök. It will be the end of everything."

She nodded as if she'd already expected them to say that. "Did they provide what you must do?"

I didn't want to lie to her, so instead I simply nodded. "They'll gather at the park for the equinox as they'd planned. We will stop them."

"We will." Her tone and expression resolute. Then she gave me a plaintive look. "I must leave you for a short time to report to Freja what you've learned from the Norns but will be back by the morning."

"She might know. Odin was there," I offered.

"All the same, I am obligated." With that, Bryn leaned down and kissed me. Her lips were warm and the kiss tender.

I reciprocated gently at first, then put all my feeling into it, digging my fingers into the hair at the back of her head and thrusting my tongue into her mouth.

She lay back and I tumbled forward with her. We lay in a tangle like that, kissing and exploring with our hands. My suit and her armor came off. Piece by piece until we were naked in the forest.

The tug in my gut that had drawn me to her grew stronger.

"Do you feel that?" she asked.

I chuckled low. "Your hand? Yes. Yes, I do."

She stopped her tender ministrations and cupped my cheeks. "No. The pull between us."

My cheeks heated and my pulse drummed a rapid beat in my ears. Getting enough air became impossible, so my voice was a breathless whisper as I replied, "Yes. Every time I'm with you."

She cocked her head to the side. Her chestnut hair cascaded around my face. "We are fated to be together. We can accept it or deny it, but it is a rare thing. What would you like to do about it?"

If she'd asked me before the vision, I'd say wait and see. I was not even out of my twenties. I had my life ahead of me. All the excuses I'd used with other women to get away from feeling.

"My parents had bonded young. It was a mistake."

"They performed a ritual of magic that is not...this."

My entire adult life, I'd been running from everything that had to do with my mother to the point I'd avoided even Kirsten herself. I wanted to belong, and she'd always messed things up—with the pack, with my school friends, and even with our own relationship. I didn't think about this part of me that was through her. That I'd had magic in me that was from another world, or that my mate would be from there.

"Is it common among Valkyrie?"

Something passed in her eyes that I couldn't quite read. With a slow grin, she shook her head. "A mate bond is rare, even in Asgard, but it does happen."

I pushed some of her hair away from her face. "Okay. I say we go for it."

Bryn laughed and leaned down. "Are you sure? Once done, we cannot undo this."

Was I sure? Part of me thought not. The rest was pulled to her, to what we might be if the world didn't end. If it did, I wanted to know love. Everyone around me had it. Why not me? A million reasons popped in my head. I shoved them all down. I would be happy, even if it was for a little while.

"Yes. I'm sure."

"As am I."

Magic pricked my skin, sinking in like claws until it was coursing through my veins and pumping through my heart. Surprise widened my eyes.

"That was it? No blood drinking?"

She laughed. "No. A promise is binding for us."

"My word is my bond," I whispered, amazed.

Still laughing with her eyes, Bryn leaned all the way in and kissed me.

Later, as we dressed, we kissed and laughed as we picked pieces of leaves and grass from each other's hair. All the while, my gut hurt with the knowledge that her life was in my hands. She didn't once ask if I was holding something back or if I had more to tell her. Bryn trusted me. As she faded from this world to return to Asgard, I hoped I'd be worthy of that trust.

Eyes almost the same color as my dyed electric blue hair stared back at me in the mirror as I brushed my teeth. I never thought of them as my eyes. They were my mother's eyes. My grandmother had had them too. I'd always wanted to look like my father. That wasn't true. As a small child, I thought that my mother was the most beautiful woman in the world. My Aunt Princess came in as a close second. After my mother had slept with an incubus, thus leaving my father, and by extension the pack, vulnerable to Lucifer's spy, I'd felt that if I resembled the alpha more than the Betrayer, people would respect me more.

Strangers, people who didn't know my family's history, would tell me that I was beautiful and could be a model. Every single time I looked in the mirror, I'd felt sick. All I could see was Kirsten. I started dying my hair blue and getting an undercut. I wore dark eyeliner and black lipstick. I even tried wearing contacts that were purple. That only got me more crap from the pack and Gabriel, but instead of conforming, I put on an attitude like armor.

I dressed like the punk music that I loved, but I was a selfish little shit. The therapist I saw after seeing my father half dead and pinned to a ceiling as a teenager had said I wasn't selfish or even really that mean, but rather trying to carve out my own identity and protecting myself. Maybe.

I'd once told Kirsten that my father had replaced her with Miriam just to see if she still loved me. Because, despite all that she had done, I wanted my mother to love me like she had when I was little. I wanted that version of Kirsten back. It didn't happen, but I'd believed with all my heart. A tiny piece of me still hoped it would.

If I couldn't manifest my mother turning around and being an actual mom, how the fuck was I going to get everyone to believe these evil witches weren't going to kill Bryn and end the world?

Three taps on the door that led to Jada's room let me know my time for introspection and self-pity were over. I needed to finish up and get some sleep, somehow. I spat into the sink and rinsed my toothbrush before unlocking the door from the inside.

Jada walked in, scratching her leg just below her sleep shorts and looking as exhausted as I felt. "Do you need a few more minutes?"

We dreamed our whole lives of this exact scenario where she and I had rooms with an adjoining bathroom. She was so lonely in that house when her father ascended to full godhood and her mother was left to raise Jada alone without a clue how the mundane world worked. Now, I was used to sharing a bathroom with her but didn't really want to be around her.

Why, why would she choose to let them kill Bryn?

"Nope. Let me clear out." Not meeting her gaze, I slid my skincare items into one of my drawers and headed to the door that led to my room.

"What did you see today? Really?"

Earlier, I'd given Jada a brief rundown that we would need to coordinate a team to raid the equinox gathering. She'd told me that Luke found no online leads to where the Seattle völur hid now. Maria had reported that the Oracle in Milagro Bay had confirmed that there was going to be a big event in Gas Works Park, but she couldn't see the exact outcome.

Lydia wasn't always the Oracle. She used to be a professional grifter and lied through her teeth with no tells. She'd also called me and said, "Kid, I changed the fate of the world once by believing I could. Do what you must and believe it will work."

So, I had three Fates and an Oracle saying to wing it, and I didn't know how.

"It doesn't matter."

"Rox, I could—"

I turned around. "No. Do not try to time travel there. What you see could make it a fixed point. Besides, we're not letting a fucking tree tell us what will happen. Okay?"

She bit her lip. "What did you see? I don't think telling me will make it happen. I want to be prepared."

My mind warred over what I should do. What if telling her what happened in the vision made it more likely? What if not telling her made her make the same choice? I was missing something.

"Do you trust Bryn now that we know she's been working for Freja?"

Jada crossed her arms over her chest. "I don't know her and neither do you. Not really. We don't know if she's working both sides."

"Bryn has come to our aid more than once. She's proven herself as an ally."

She counted on her fingers. "She's shown up last minute after the real fight is over. She didn't reveal that she was watching you before that. She didn't tell you that Freja knew about the cult or that völur were behind it. We had to figure that out. What do you know about her, really?"

"Bryn is my bonded mate. I'd know if she were deceiving me." My voice was a low growl. I was growing desperate, but not desperate enough to risk the fate I saw coming true.

Dumbfounded, Jada stared at me for several moments. "Why would you bond with her? You barely knew her."

"Tell me in a hundred years when you go through fae puberty."

"So you're saying you needed to bond with her?"

Fae and shifters bonded for different reasons. For Fae, it was a ritual, so they didn't crave consuming people they had sex with. For shifters, it was...a tying of souls. She had every right to know why I'd bond with a person we just met, but some shifters were rumored to be perfect for each other from birth. We didn't talk about it outside of our community because no one believed it—not even us.

"Yes. Now I trust her implicitly."

"Gabriel trusted Kirsten." She threw up her hands in exasperation. "That worked out spectacularly."

"You don't understand. They were bonded, but they weren't meant for each other. Bryn and I are fated mates." As soon as the words fell from my lips, I heard how ridiculous it sounded. I didn't even believe in such a thing. Most shifters didn't even talk about it.

Jada, though, didn't find it so. Instead of laughing or scoffing, she tilted her head, curious. "What do you mean?"

"Bryn was among the Valkyrie at our parents' wedding. I felt this tug. When I saw her at the bar, I felt it then too. I trust her because I feel a connection with her that links us like Phyr and Miriam."

Jada swallowed hard and her eyes shone with tears.

Unlike our parents, Jada and I were not polyamorous—so this stung. Jada had a biological dad who had been married to her mom before he ascended. It was all very lovey dovey—except Rafael had hidden things from Miriam. Phyr hid nothing. He couldn't hide anything. To be honest, I didn't like that Miriam and Phyr had a bond that they didn't have with my dad, but the three had been married for a while now and seemed happy most days.

"She's not a shifter, let alone a wolf shifter."

"I can shift through the same magic that makes her a Valkyrie." It seemed like sound reasoning to me despite not fully understanding the why. I was also an angel and a wolf shifter through my father, but I clung to my theory.

"Okay. Let's say that even if fated mates, or whatever, are a real thing." She flicked her hand dismissively. Perhaps she didn't mean to be condescending. Subconscious or not, the gesture telegraphed how she felt about the concept. "What if it's something else that drew you to her?"

The thought of something nefarious linking me to Bryn made my blood run cold. "What could it be?"

She looked away, hesitant. "There are many ways to make someone your thrall."

I leaned against the bathroom counter, wanting to cross my arms but didn't. If I acted defensive, Jada would think it was because I was under some sort of bewitchment. "Let's say that you're correct. That Bryn has put a spell on me. Why? What purpose does it serve?"

Jada thought about it for a few minutes. I did too. I couldn't come up with anything.

"Your maternal ancestors bound themselves to Fenrir to become shifters. The Sacred Lif and Lifthrasir are killing wolf shifters of this line. Maybe Bryn is in cahoots with them because she no longer wants to serve Freja. Chelsea had obviously lied to us about her purpose in Seattle. I bet that völur had lured Gerald away from his pack to join the cult somehow. What if Bryn, a Valkyrie, not a wolf shifter, put a love spell on you that makes you think you are fated to be together to lure you into trusting her?"

Vision of the sacrifice still in my head, my stomach dipped. My thoughts gathered and swirled like a tornado in my head. Did Bryn have a change of heart? Why would her sacrifice bring on a twisted version of Ragnarök? Odin hung himself to gain knowledge. Was Bryn the actual leader of the cult; a double agent, pretending to serve Freja, but in fact was acting against all the gods?

Jada's warm hand on my arm brought me out of the vortex of suspicion. "Look, this is all conjecture. You've bonded with her. Fine. Just remember that you can sever that bond. There is no fate, only the reading of possible futures. We always have choice."

I licked my lips, nervous I would give away too much and spoil everything when I said, "Even if Bryn has duplicitous intentions. Let her come to justice, not harm."

My friend nodded, backing away and turning to her sink on her side of the bathroom. "Of course."

"I mean it, Jada."

She spun on her foot to face me. "Why did we agree to become I.S.E.A. agents?"

She wanted to protect people from those more powerful than they are and see that supes weren't swept away to eternal imprisonment or killed by the erstwhile monster hunters. I had wanted to protect her and a job that didn't require me working for my father or my stepfather.

"I'm unemployable, but you're mostly good. We both know you'll kill if necessary." It wasn't a lie, and it wasn't something Jada was proud of. We were in college when we warred against some warlocks, and she'd ripped through them.

Hurt in her eyes, Jada placed her hand over her heart. "I wouldn't ever hurt someone who isn't actively harming others. Even then, I'll do my best to subdue them."

"It will hurt me if you let harm come to her."

Fear replaced the injured expression. "Is the bond that strong?"

I brushed my hands through my hair, not answering. She knew what it was about. She had fae heritage. She'd seen the change in her mother and Phyr.

Jada wrapped her arms around herself. "I wish you'd talked to me about this before you did it."

Guilt twisted my gut. We'd always talked about everything before. No secrets between us, had been our pact since we were young girls because our parents had kept so many things from us, and we'd hated it. However, we were adults now.

"There will be some things we can't tell each other, even if we want to, but that doesn't mean we're not sisters."

Not knowing what else to do to make things better, I hugged her.

CHAPTER
EIGHTEEN

I woke up from a dead sleep with a start, my phone blasting the song I used for Kirsten's ringtone. Blearily, I felt around my nightstand for my cell and answered the call.

"Kirsten, it's like three in the morning."

She didn't reply, but I could hear someone breathing. Kirsten did this sometimes. There was no way she was sober, calling at this odd hour. How much Tank did she drink before she decided she'd call me and list the ways I'd failed her as a daughter?

I took a deep breath, controlling my temper.

"I can hear you breathing. If you don't say something, I'm going to block you for a week."

Usually, this would prompt the inebriated tirade, but all I got was the steady rhythm of her breathing.

Did she call me in her sleep by accident? No. Dave didn't let her have the phone in the bedroom. Something about the bedroom being a no tech, peaceful space. My stepdad rarely put his foot down, so I'd been proud of him when she had told me about it. She bitched that I should say something to him about needing her mom. I laughed in her face and that was the last time she brought that up.

Dave's rule had stopped these calls for the past few years. I'd thought she'd been doing better, but—It suddenly occurred to me that she hadn't been with Dave on the last phone call.

"Mom, are you alright? Do you need me to come for you? Say something...please." That please cost me, but I didn't care. All I needed was for her to say something belligerent, and the wave of panic that washed over me would ebb.

"It is the daughter's phone," I heard a woman say to someone—her voice sounded muffled as if the mic was far from her mouth.

My heart leapt into my throat. I reached for my second phone that I used for work on the other nightstand and texted Jada: SOS.

She immediately appeared in my room.

Planeswalking was so convenient.

I put a finger to my lips before placing the call on speaker phone so Jada could hear.

"Is this the consort of Fenrir?" A sharp masculine voice asked.

"This is Agent Roxanne Crowfoot of the International Supernatural Enforcement Agency. Who am I speaking to and why do you have my mother's phone?"

"Kirsten has dedicated herself to the Sacred Lif and Lifthrasir. All property of devotees is property of our society. We are not your enemy, Roxanne. Quite the oppo—"

I snorted in derision. "Cut the bullshit. I won't listen to another word until you let me speak to Kirsten."

A brief pause followed. Some whispers and shuffling later, a familiar voice came over the speaker.

"Hey Rox. They said you asked for me?"

It was my mother alright. Casually addressing me as if joining a doomsday cult and handing them her phone to call me was perfectly normal.

"These people are dangerous. Don't trust a word they say. I'm coming for you."

Jada nodded encouragingly. We'd assemble a raid team. It was easy enough to gather some of my mother's hair from her house and

Jada could planeswalk us right to where they had her. I couldn't feel excited that we had a route to find the cult directly. It felt almost too easy.

"I've gotten everything all wrong." She slurred her words. Did she drink Tank or was she drugged? There were very few drugs that were known to affect shifters, but they were völur, they'd have old secrets that modern supes might not be aware of. They certainly had known what effect mistletoe would have on me. "They know Fenrir. He's not bad. They'll free him, and you'll be happy."

"Mom, did they give you something?"

"Everything. They'll give you everything, too."

"Tell me where—"

"Your mother is right," the male voice interrupted. "We want the best for you. You are important to us."

"One of you stabbed me," I countered. "I don't know, but I don't happen to murder people who are important to me. Call it a cultural difference."

"That was an unfortunate occurrence. We didn't know who you were then. You bear no mark of Fenrir, and you have...other influences that made it difficult to discern your nature. Please believe me, we revere you as Fenrir's wife."

"Fine, if you revere me so much. Release my mother and stop killing wolves of Fenrir's line."

The man's exhale was audible. "No. You all made a promise in exchange for a piece of his magic. The price of your power is due."

A million retorts flashed in my mind. Most importantly, what gave him the notion that he and his cult had any right to collect that price. However, I'd dealt with zealots before. There was no derailing this crazy train.

"What do you want from me?"

A breath later, he replied, "Your willing participation in the next sacrifice. We believe you are the key to bringing what we all want."

My stomach dipped. So much for being Fenrir's respected bride, which I didn't believe one second. They had tried to kill me—twice. I hadn't forgotten about the nightmare. "And that is?"

"For Fenrir to bring on Ragnarök, of course. This world has suffered under the false, corrupt gods too long. It's time to restore order as it once was."

If I wasn't furious and fearful for my mother's life, I'd laugh at this megalomaniac and tell him that he had some serious balls to call the gods corrupt when he was the leader of a death cult. "What happens if I say no?"

"We will kill enough wolf shifters to free Fenrir. Your mother has volunteered to pay the bride price if you won't."

Of course, Kirsten volunteered to die. She never valued her life let alone anyone else's, including mine. My chest burned as if they'd rubbed salt in an old wound. She picked men, the bottle, and now a cult over me. I'd warned her and she'd acted like she didn't know a damned thing all the while, she was agreeing to let them string her up.

Still, she was my mother.

Was this the path to saving Bryn and stopping a world-collapsing calamity?

I blew my breath out.

Jada shook her head adamantly, but I ignored her.

"No need. What do you want me to do?"

"You must show up alone at an address we shall provide at a time that we designate. If you bring anyone, we will retaliate against your entire pack, starting with your cousins."

As he spoke, a photo message came from my mother. I clicked on it. There were Princess's adopted sons. The boys were at a skate park a few blocks from the Earthbound side of Eastside Charm School.

Protective fury rose in me, and I bit out the words, "Coercion isn't freely choosing. Are you sure my sacrifice will mean anything?"

"That's why I hadn't mentioned your pack before. I merely want to ensure that you don't bring the Valkyrie, any of the agents from your organization, or the Supernatural Council. No one. Not even that friend of yours that's listening."

Jada stiffened and then dashed to the window preternaturally fast, closing the blinds.

"We see the future, Roxanne. Even the Norns themselves can no longer hide our destiny."

I rubbed my temple. "No one will come with me."

Jada glared, and when a fae demigod glares at you, the pressure is immense. It didn't matter though. I would do as they asked.

"Good. I believe you," the man said, smiling. "You have thirty minutes to be at Bellevue Park. Be alone. No phone. No weapons. You will find instructions under a bench near the waterfall. We will know if others follow you."

The line cut at that point. The nameless Lifthrasir decided he'd messed with my head enough to do as he wanted.

Jada swooped in. Her face close to mine as she gripped my shoulders. "We can go there right now. It won't take long for me to get Phyr, Mom, and whoever else we need. This is family."

"There are over sixty members of the pack, who do not live on this property. That's including children and family. My cousins go to school and hang out with their mundane friends. We can't lock everyone down."

"This is suicide."

It was. I was hoping to find a way out of it. "I think that they saw the same thing I saw and are offering me an alternative. I just need to come up with a plan to turn things around on them."

Jada loosened her grip and sat on the bed. "What did you see?"

I couldn't tell her about Bryn, but maybe I could tell her about the other part. "There was a wolf shifter being sacrificed like Gerald, like the others. She was a female—that's all I could tell. It could've been my mom, but it also could've been me. I must figure out a way for it to be neither of us."

"I'm fully recovered from the raid, so this is what we're going to do," Jada began. She then laid out a plan where she would open a portal for me to Bellevue Park a few minutes from now—at least from the völur's perspective. We would be traveling back in time from ours. First: we would check in with our director and assemble a raid team. I'd then show up, follow their breadcrumbs. Once I was with the cult, Jada would open a portal and unleash the raid.

It was a solid plan. I wouldn't have broken a promise.

"Okay. Let's do this."

She took a few strands of my hair between her fingers, wrapped it around them, and yanked, pulling the strands out.

"Ow!"

"Don't be a baby. I need this to find you."

"You could've used some from my brush!"

She grinned. "I could've, but I'm your sister and that means I need to be a little shit sometimes."

I WALKED from my bedroom to the highly lit art installation at the northeastern end of the park instead of the waterfall feature on the pond. I could sense rather than see the portal close behind me. I couldn't look back. My heart couldn't take one more second of the worry on Jada's face. Not with the future I'd seen at stake. I had to follow the Norns' and the Oracle's advice to believe that our plan would work, and we'd stop this insidious cult before they even had a chance to fulfill the vision.

You are not alone.

Even late at night, Bellevue Park had people in it, so I wasn't surprised. However, Igni wouldn't speak unless it was needed advice—thankfully. I couldn't take a talking sword in my head twenty-four seven.

I am glad you appreciate my discretion, but you must stay alert. This is a trap.

Igni, I'm willfully going to them. I'm laying the trap.

The sword didn't respond.

I left the bright lights of the pillars of the cloudlike canopy installation into the dimmer lights of the fountain feature not far to the west. The area sat on a knoll that overlooked the rest of the park. There was a vantage point so close to the street, I could scan my surroundings. Igni wasn't the only one that sensed a presence that wasn't just mundanes on a stroll.

The hackles at the back of my neck stood on end. Someone or something was watching me from the shadows of the park below.

Unsheathe me.

No. I told them I'd come willingly. You come in later.

Yes. So that you may ambush them. I know. However, what if the threat is not these witches?

It's not worth the risk of letting them know that I plan to ambush them.

They've tried to kill you twice. Why would they need you now when they have your mother?

That was a good question. What made me so special? My connection to Fenrir? I didn't know how I was tied to him any more than my mother. I was missing something. It didn't matter now. I had to move forward for the plan to work.

The sound of the fountain behind me faded and the rush of the waterfall grew louder. Bellevue, despite its high rises, quieted this late on a weekday. The squirrels, ducks and crows had all nested for the night. Every small noise got my head to swivel.

I knew better than to act like this; I'd hunted as soon as I could walk. Even in this small piece of manicured nature, I knew how to behave. Still, this cult had my mother and had threatened harm to my little cousins—to my pack.

As I descended the stairs next to the waterfall, something sloshed in the pond below. It had the rounded hump of a seal's back as it rose from water. Seals were common on the Puget Sound and my dad used to take me to watch them in the Ballard Locks or near the ferry terminals, but Bellevue was on the eastside. The entirety of Seattle and Lake Washington sat between those shores and this park. Even the smaller river otters and beavers that frequented the lakes and rivers of the area didn't go to this chlorinated water. It was too big to be one of those or a bird, and the hump only grew bigger... and bigger...

Despite being a shifter with angelic heritage, despite all my experiences of wrangling giant space bunnies, despite battling griffins and other monsters, my mind couldn't grasp what emerged from the shallow pond.

By the time I reached the bottom step, a head emerged. Scales shimmering like onyx gemstone covered the immense, serpentine body. Wings expanded from the back of the monster, spanning wide, knocking into the trees lining the perimeter of the park.

I'd seen dragons before in faerie. Nothing of this scale. Also, this creature's eyes with golden irises and elliptical pupils gazed at me with a preternatural intellect. The head must have been the size of an SUV, if not larger—and was not that of a snake. Nostrils bigger than my head flared as I realized what this must be. It—and I say it because I refused to name who I believed it to be—snorted.

"You're supposed to be dead," I muttered, stupidly. I knew legends, myths, and folktales tended to be wrong or contained partial truths to relay a lesson, but some monsters were so terrible because they'd once been a horrible person.

The rumbling laugh telegraphed that the creature enjoyed my confusion, my panic, and most of all my understanding of who I faced. Instinctual fear colder than the water sliding off the serpentine monster flooded my nerves.

Fáfnir would relish in killing me.

Unsheathe me now!

The words boomed like thunder after a lightning strike. Released from a stupefied trance, I shook my head. With preternatural speed, I unsheathed Igni. Immediately, the sword blazed with angel fire. At the same time, my wings extended.

"I agreed to come alone." My voice echoed with the wrath of an avenging angel and the resonance of a Herald's judgment. For the first time in my life, I allowed my Grace to burst forth, illuminating my body with a soft glow. "I did not agree to let this maggot eat me."

For the briefest of moments, something I wouldn't have expected flashed in the dragon's eyes. Surprise or fear, maybe both, I'll never know. I evoked an emotion. That meant I stood a chance to kill it and it knew. A small part of me took glee that I would slay a monster bent on aiding the end of the world.

Fáfnir's maw opened wide, revealing teeth like that of a crocodile. A noxious odor like the fumes of a diesel engine smacked my nostrils.

Take flight.

Putting all my power into it, I rocketed into the air. Superheated air blasted me from below as I escaped a steady stream of fire. The trees behind me erupted in flames and the structures of the playground beyond melted, enraging me. I'd played there as a child after preschool.

I dove, brandishing Igni, driving my flaming sword into the neck of the dragon. I might as well have hit cold iron. The shock of hitting its scale reverberated through my whole body. Fáfnir twisted and snapped, almost catching me with its sharp teeth. But I'd been too quick to recover and barreled out of harm's way.

Go for the belly while it's exposed!

I dove again. However, Fáfnir knew its weak point and rolled away, causing me to miss and curse. We went on like that. The dragon spewing fire and me trying to find an opening.

Feign an injury and let yourself fall.

What? No way. It'll flambé me before I hit the ground.

I will protect you.

I know you're flame resistant, but I am certainly not.

Trust me.

Igni had kept my father alive against incredible odds in the Fae/Angelic Wars and my grandfather alive when he kicked Lucifer and the Fallen out of Heaven. The dragon even feared my sword. I could sense that it had not expected to fight me with such a weapon and witnessed flashes of doubt in its eyes, but I also saw its resolve. Unlike the Fae and the Fallen, who had both surrendered to the Angelic forces, Fáfnir would kill me or die trying.

The tip of one of the wings grazed me. I used the opportunity to overplay how hard I'd been hit, tumbling in the air and then went limp, dropping to the ground. Landing on my side, my body shook with the impact. For a second, I saw stars. Everything hurt. However, I didn't lose grip of Igni.

Keep your eyes closed. Feign slumber.

Sure. The dragon is going to believe I'm taking a nap.

When I say now, burst to your feet and lift me above your head.

Rancid breath blew in my face as Fáfnir sniffed me.

Gross.

Stay still.

The dragon laughed, a deep rumbling sound. I got the impression that it believed the victory had been too easy. I'd never been able to read thoughts or get these impressions. It's almost as if the thing had a form of telepathic communication like Igni, but more primitive. Victory and images of the völur freeing it from its dragon form the former dwarf had been stuck in for millennia flashed in my mind.

Noxious fumes billowed from the dragon's nostrils.

Now!

I burst to my feet and thrust Igni in the air like I was She-Ra and had the power of Greyskull. I screamed with just as much rage. Something built inside of me. A force that could render cities to ash. A niggling voice bubbled up that I would smite Bellevue, maybe the entire Seattle area if I let any more rage out.

Pour your Grace into me!

Flames showered down but they were parted by an unseen force. I pushed my Grace into the enchanted sword. Light burst from Igni like a beacon, illuminating the interior of the dragon's mouth. Not just illuminating...I blasted a hole through flesh, bone, brain matter, and scales that had been impenetrable by Igni's flame alone.

Fáfnir projected a brief thought of never being whole again. Whether it came from its mind or the soul leaving the body, I didn't know. I didn't care. It had tried to kill me to be whole and that made it as bad as the Sacred Lif and Lifthrasir cult. However, my rage died and so did the beam of light.

Move!

I sprinted to the side faster than I'd ever moved as the dragon's remains crashed to the ground.

From out of nowhere, something flew fast and furious in my direction. I recognized Bryn before she landed.

I pointed at the dragon with Igni before sheathing it. Igni grumbled about not being a pointer stick but then silenced. I cocked an eyebrow and grinned at her. "This is the third time you've missed the action. You're a real shitty protector. You know that, right?"

Bryn didn't laugh at the joke. Her expression was grim, and she was dressed for battle. Dressed as she had been in my vision.

The smile dropped from my lips. "What happened?"

"I scried what will happen."

My heart dropped and the ground tilted. "You know, then?"

She gave me a rueful smile. "Yes. I know this was a distraction so they could sacrifice your mother before you could enact a plan to save her."

Forgetting all about the prophecy I saw, I looked left and right, not knowing which way to run to reach Kirsten in time. Bryn grabbed me by the arms.

"Look at me. Make use of their erstwhile trap and eat Fáfnir's heart. You'll need the strength."

If you do, you will not remain who you are now.

Will I be strong enough to fight nascent gods?

Igni's lack of answer was all the answer I needed. I removed the sword and my clothes, shifting into my wolf form. Normally, I'd thank Mother Earth and the Creator for my kill, as my father had taught me, but this being wasn't from Earth. The kill was mine.

I tore through the soft underbelly of the dragon, pushing bones aside, and ripping fascia to reach the heart. The muscle still had hot blood in the chambers. The potency of the creature's magic, a heady wine coursing through me.

When I finished, I could sense the ducks and geese sleeping at a far distance and the incoming crows ready to feast on the carrion from the battle. I didn't begrudge them their meal. I couldn't and didn't need to eat the whole thing. There were other differences, but I would tally them later. Right now, the urgency to rescue my mother overwhelmed any need to consider what I'd just done. I shifted back with greater ease than ever before. I'd always been considered a gifted shifter, rarely tiring from the change.

Hurriedly, I dressed. After strapping Igni once again to my back, I sprouted wings. "Okay. Let's go."

Bryn, who had watched me devour a monster's heart as disinterestedly as if I'd been sipping boba and eating a cookie, nodded. We launched, flying in the direction of Gas Works Park. I could only hope that we were not flying to my mother's or Bryn's death and that Jada and the team we'd assembled before I'd left would meet me there.

CHAPTER NINETEEN

The lights of Seattle twinkled below as Bryn and I flew over the city together. It would be romantic, if my mother's life weren't at stake.

I'd made a crucial error in interpreting the vision by assuming that the events would occur on the equinox. I made another when I'd assumed the cult who had tried to kill me twice hadn't been trying to kill me again.

"It was no distraction. They wanted me dead," I shouted to Bryn.

The Valkyrie flew closer. "They see the future, but they don't know everything. I assumed they wanted to distract everyone from pursuing them before they drank the blood of a powerful shifter like your mother."

My stomach knotted at the irony of what Bryn had said. She didn't know everything. I needed to warn her somehow without setting her death as the only possibility. "Wouldn't we be more effective if you went for reinforcements?"

"The Valkyrie will come when they are needed."

Well, wasn't that cryptic. I'd hoped to try another tactic, but we came to our destination: the gathering on the hill at Gas Works Park.

There were at least a hundred torches. Since there were concerts and festivals held there all the time, no one would guess that it was a cult performing a ritual sacrifice. Also, the völur likely used spellwork to camouflage their other sacrifices, even if local authorities came by to check on licenses or do some crowd control. Mundane minds were easily tricked by witchcraft and glamours.

They've set wards around the ritual, Igni warned. *Use me.*

I was glad the sword had broken its silence. I would need it. I drew Igni. The sword didn't ignite right away, but I knew it would when the time came. "I'm going to break their wards."

Bryn gave me a thumbs up. Her face was a grim mask.

I believed everything would work out. I believed that she would not die tonight. I'd defeated the dragon the völur sent to stop me, she'd killed the mare, and Jada had brought me back from their mistletoe spear. The Sacred Lif and Lifthrasir would not become gods, or if they already were, gods were hard to kill, but they bled. The old adage was true: if something bled, that thing could be killed —and I'd seen gods bleed and die in the Mythic Games.

Holding Igni pointing down, I dove headfirst at the barrier created by the wards. The sword ignited, blazing bright. The impact reverberated up my arms, but Fáfnir's magic made it much more tolerable than the last ward I broke.

Hope sparked in my chest that this would work, but it soon died when I landed among the völur dancing and celebrating with drums and stringed instruments. At the center of the crowd, a pole held a female in mid-shift. I couldn't recognize my own mother, but I caught the scent of her, her fear, even among the crowd—another new gift.

Next to Kirsten's pole, there was another pole, waiting for a victim. Just like in my vision—I shook my head. No. I wouldn't think of that.

Fury that these cultists would kill my mother, try to kill me, my lover, and all my kind for power, set my blood on fire. I swung Igni, lopping off a völva's head and turned and stabbed another. Bryn landed and went to work. The völur chanted spells and some had weapons imbued with magic, but my reflexes were faster, my defenses against their spells stronger.

And Bryn? The Valkyrie moved like an avenging goddess, double my speed and strength.

Hope kindled anew. We'd save Kirsten, and we'd defeat the Sacred Lif and Lifthrasir once Jada brought the team here. I fought my way from the circle. A woman and a man in white robes stood below my mother. The woman held a chalice, and the man held a dagger.

"Stop!" I threw all the power of the Herald into my voice, hoping the dragon's heart and blood would amplify the persuasive part of the magic.

The woman with the chalice froze, but the man with the dagger slowly turned, resisting my magic. Recognition sparked in his eyes when his gaze landed on me. What he didn't express was a single drop of fear with that recognition. He smiled as if he was happy a pissed-off supernatural wanted his head. He casually lifted his hand.

An iron grip seized my wrists. Crushing pain caused me to lose my grasp on Igni, and the sword flew out of my hands.

No matter. I ran at full speed, which was much faster than before. I was going to knock that dagger out of his hand with brute force if I must. He would not taste a drop of my mother's blood. He would not kill my lover.

The cultist murmured something indistinguishable. I froze in my tracks. Paralyzed. Helpless against whatever telekinetic magic was holding me in place. I let out a frustrated howl. At least I could still do that.

"Just in time," his voice was exactly like on the phone call. "But you're not alone. I can't keep up my end of the bargain and must kill your mother."

"You're making a mistake. This will not free Fenrir. You'll destroy everything. All the realms. Even yourselves."

He chuckled like a cartoonish caricature of a villain.

My god, I wanted to smack that mirth off his face.

"Not the gods' realm. Two powerful wolves, a Valkyrie, and so many more supernaturals will be enough to make us Ascended."

In my peripheral, I saw Bryn overwhelmed by the remaining völur. Icy tendrils of fear gripped my heart. It was all going to come true. They never wanted Ragnarök. The cult didn't want to become like gods in a new world to rule. They wanted to become pure magic.

"Your will won't be your own." I could hear the desperation in my voice. "You'll have to answer prayers."

"No one will be around to control us. We will have ultimate power and no one to tether us to anything." As he spoke, the völur bound Bryn to the other pole.

It can't come true.

It can't.

Her gaze met mine. She seemed totally calm. Not the drugged-out kind of calm, but either she was resolved to her fate, or she'd scried something. I wished we had the kind of mate bond that was between Miriam and Phyr. They could speak telepathically. I had to hold on to hope that the rest wouldn't happen.

What I did feel was a sense of warm reassurance through our bond. I was so confused. Then it all happened like it did in my vision.

"Bring forth the demigod."

Just like in the vision. They brought her forth with a hood over her head. Unlike in the vision, I could see that two robed figures held her up and a third removed a hood from her head—she, too, was caught in some sort of holding spell. Where did they find her? Did they try to raid and come across the ward I broke? I had so many questions about where this all went wrong.

The white-robed man approached Jada. Again, I couldn't hear what he said. It was strange. I could understand all languages, but it was as if the words were blurred by spell so I couldn't understand them.

Jada refused to speak.

The man shrugged and walked away. He again brought out the dagger. I could see it better now. It was made of wood.

It was mistletoe. Even if Bryn could survive a dagger, there was no way she could survive that.

"Trust the bond," Bryn shouted in the language of Asgard. Only I would understand, but what did she mean?

He didn't bother slitting her wrists like the other victims. The dagger went straight into her heart.

Unlike the wolf shifter in the vision, my mother didn't howl when he stabbed Bryn. It was me. I was howling. Not only for my love but out of pain. Through the bond, I felt the dagger just as keenly as if he'd stabbed me.

However, I wasn't hurt. I could only feel Bryn's lifeforce fading through our connection as her life's blood poured from the wound into the chalice. All hope darkened as the light in Bryn's cerulean eyes diminished. The chain around her neck she'd worn since I met her glowed bright and then fell apart, the links falling to the ground. With it crumbled my heart.

Yet...I still felt the warmth from our bond. The reassurance that everything would be fine. My mind crashed against the shores of hope and despair, not finding a place to moor.

Use your bond, you fool! Channel the gift of the dragon's heart into it as you channeled your Grace into me.

Desperate to understand what the sword meant, I asked, *What gift?*

The gift of eternal life. Immortal light existed in the dragon. That's how you changed. You're immortal as an angel now.

With no time to contemplate what I'd acquired, I concentrated where I'd felt the pull to Bryn from the first time that I saw her and poured everything I had into it. The Valkyrie gasped for air. Her eyes glowed bright magenta.

The bonds that held her shattered. She kicked the white-robed man in the face. His head flew past me. Bryn dropped to the ground. She grew bigger until she was a giant of nine or ten feet tall. Smoke-colored fur sprouted from her skin, and she morphed from a Valkyrie to the largest wolf I'd ever seen.

No. That wasn't true. I'd seen her before. Everything all added up and some things didn't. One thing was for sure. Through my bond, I could feel my mate. The mate I'd been destined for my whole life.

Fenrir howled.

The völur fell to their knees. The ones who had imbibed the blood of my kith carried with it the oath that our ancestors had made. The fools made themselves his thralls. I knew this through the bond. The rage of thousands of years of imprisonment warred with the love she/he felt when his gaze landed on me.

You did well, Little Wolf. Care to start Ragnarök with me?

No. I want you to be Bryn. I want to love you and see if we have more than this bond. But that isn't a choice, is it?

It never had been. The god had used me to break his chains and now he would destroy my world. The heartbreak of another person who I'd loved betraying my trust seared my chest and hurt much more than the dagger. Tears fell unbidden. I didn't want a pity party.

"Roxy, why are you crying?" Jada asked. "We won. This is what Lydia saw."

The wolf huffed and shook his head and shifted back to Bryn. She breached the distance between us, enveloping me in her arms. "Hey, I was joking. I haven't wanted to bring on Ragnarök since I was a teen. That's why Freya lengthened my leash and Odin let me handle this."

Odin was seeking knowledge from Yggdrasil. Shit. In everything, I didn't think of why the god would sacrifice himself again. He was seeing if his grandkid was going to end his reign.

Bryn's eyes were once again a beautiful dark blue.

I glared into them. "That was a shitty joke."

She cupped my face. "I'll spend eternity making it up to you."

With that, she lowered her head and kissed me.

CHAPTER TWENTY

Director Tan listened to Jada and me give our report in stony silence.

"The Sacred Lif and Lifthrasir cultists admitted that they'd all flown in from different locations for the event and there were no more cult members left."

Tan arched an eyebrow. "This was after Oberon's interrogation in faerie, I presume?"

I grinned. It wasn't a nice grin. "It was the consort Carmen who interrogated them."

The Director shuddered. It hadn't taken much to make Carmen want to rip the cult apart. All I had to do was show her the photo they'd sent me of my cousins from my mother's phone. Carmen was ruthless, but she'd crossed the Pacific Crest Trail pregnant and with pups to protect them from another cult. Her love for her children guaranteed we got the confessions.

"The Oracle in Milagro Bay confirmed the cult will no longer be a problem," Jada added.

Tan sighed. "I still don't like that you and Lydia chose to keep everything from your partner."

I hadn't liked it either until I understood that if I saw the vision the Oracle saw, so would the völur. That was why Bryn kept things from me, too. The cultists didn't know that she was Fenrir, but they did know that Fenrir's mate was one possibility of stopping them. They were watching my fate very closely. I couldn't know anything. I had to half believe that Bryn died, and the cultists would win and only have a half-baked plan to stop them.

Tan's dark eyes took me in. "You're different."

I nodded. I'd become a bit prettier and more well-defined. Leveled up to an immortal but not a goddess.

"What about your mother?"

Swallowing hard, I said, "Kirsten sustained no permanent wounds. They had given her a drug that they'd given all wolf shifters. She's doing better and in her husband's care." I had to lie through my teeth to my stepdad, so he'd take her back. It was the last time I'd ever do anything for my mother though. Kirsten had willingly shacked up with a völur under the guise of becoming a wolf goddess.

We were no longer on speaking terms. I had to sever the relationship. I broke it to her and my stepfather over a dinner at their house. Dave understood. My mother screamed at me. I left and didn't look back. Finally, I blocked her after she'd left me a thousand messages about how this was all my father's fault. Kirsten would be on a never-ending toxic spiral, pointing the finger at everyone else until the day she died. Until she proved otherwise, I was taking myself out of the scenario and doling forgiveness to people who deserved it.

I could forgive Aunt Princess because she wanted to be different than the way she used to be. It would take time, but we could repair our relationship. The pack would change their attitude toward me, too. They threw me a huge party for closing this case. My work impacted shifters and brought honor to my pack. I would prove more and more that I was my own person, not the woman who gave birth to me. But I wouldn't do it for them. I would do it for me.

Tan gave me a rueful smile. "Well, that's good to hear that she's doing well."

I shrugged.

The Director changed topics. "Bryn has applied for a permanent resident visa. The Supernatural Council granted it on the condition that she does not reveal her true identity. The world isn't ready for a god of her reputation to be openly walking the streets."

My heart did a little jig. "Thank you."

Tan gave me a pointed look. "Thank the council. Princess, as the interim alpha, and Miriam were her biggest advocates. Has your father returned from D.C. yet?"

Gabriel had not—not even after hearing how dire the circumstances were. I looked at a picture of Director Tan's cats. No one could cry looking at the cute little guys. Especially not a tough woman like me, who slayed a literal dragon. "No."

"State senator Crowfoot is running for federal senate, isn't he?"

I spread my hands. "Maybe? I wasn't asked to be a part of the campaign."

"The thing is we only exist in this country as a UN organization. We're not an official police force. We need him there."

"Guess we do." He had a pack and a community that needed him here. Not to mention his partners. I didn't see myself in that equation either. I said none of this. Tan was thinking of the agency not the agent.

"Alright, I consider this case officially closed," Director Tan said, her eyes on the door. That was our cue to leave.

Outside the Director's office, Jada grimaced at her phone.

"What's up?"

She shook her head slowly. "Sarah made some new friends at work. Looks like she's going out with them tonight."

I placed an arm around her shoulder. "Mom and Pops are cooking."

She blinked at me as if I'd sprouted scales. "Did you just call—"

"I'm trying something new. Don't make a big deal about it."

. . .

An hour later, I walked into the kitchen. In front of the stove, Phyr held a ladle out to Miriam. She made a face. Mom hated being his guinea pig because Pops stressed over whether she liked the air she breathed let alone how good he cooked.

Bryn sat at the table playing a game with my cousins and aunts. She lifted her cerulean gaze to meet mine and winked. I winked back. Jada plopped herself down next to Rio and asked if she could join the game. I would too, but first, I had to save the day. Again.

Using my preternatural speed, I swiped the ladle from Phyr's hand. "Thanks, Pops." I winked at Miriam. "I'll be the test subject tonight, Ma."

The fae witch's pretty face lit up with the honorific. Also, I seriously believed she felt I was her knight in shining armor at that moment. The fae prince looked peeved, but he watched me take a sip with nervous anticipation.

"Perfection!" I declared.

Phyr puffed his chest with triumph. "Undoubtedly. I made it."

And it was. My family, my mate, my best friend in the world were all alive and well. And the best part? I loved every single imperfect one of them because they all loved me, rough edges and all.

ALSO BY T.J. DESCHAMPS

Midlife Supernaturals

Eastside Hedge Witch (Midlife Supernaturals #1)

Eastside Witch Hunt (Midlife Supernaturals #2)

Eastside Mórrígan (Midlife Supernaturals #3)

Eastside Coven (Midlife Supernatural #4)

Eastside Rock Witch(A FREE Midlife Supernaturals Novella)

Midlife Olympians

Westside Oracle (Midlife Olympians #1)

Westside Harpy (Midlife Olympians #2)

Westside Titan (Midlife Olympians #3)

Westside Titanomachy (Midlife Olympians #4)

Supernatural Legacies

Wings and Fangs (Book 1)

Blood and Spirit (Book 2) 2026

Beakers and Brews (Book 3) 2027

Faerie Tales

The Ballad of Brave Janet

Tam Lin

Warrior Tithe

Vow Unbroken

Fomorians 2027

By T.J Deschamps and Beth Whiteman

Jills of All Trades Mystery Series

Deviously Delicious (Book 1)

Bizarre Brews (Book 2)

ACKNOWLEDGMENTS

I'd like to thank my readers, my brain, and my kids for putting up with me while I bounced ideas off them and struggled to finish this book within deadline.

A special thanks goes out to my beta readers: Amanda Gray, Ana Shaffer, and Kelley Scarrow

About the Author

T.J. Deschamps is a multi genre author living in the Pacific Northwest with her family, cats, and a tortoise. When she's not writing, she likes to hike, kayak, and lift weights. Sometimes she can be found dancing in her kitchen and singing off-key. Legend has it she may be a feral witch tamed by baked goods and promises of good stories.

www.ingramcontent.com/pod-product-compliance
Lightning Source LLC
Chambersburg PA
CBHW050343030726
47503CB00008B/2587

* 9 7 8 1 9 6 1 7 1 5 2 2 6 *